MW00576899

SHADOW OF HOPE: A CHRISTIAN ROMANTIC SUSPENSE

SHADOW LAKE SURVIVAL
BOOK 4

SUSAN SLEEMAN

Published by Edge of Your Seat Books, Inc.

Contact the publisher at contact@edgeofyourseatbooks.com

Copyright © 2024 by Susan Sleeman

Cover design by Kelly A. Martin of KAM Design

All rights reserved. Kindle Edition Printed in the United States of America or the country of purchase. Without limiting the rights under copyright reserved above, no part of this book may be reproduced in any form or by any electronic or mechanical means, including information storage and retrieval systems, without permission in writing from the publisher, except by a reviewer, who may quote brief passages in a review.

This book is a work of fiction. Characters, names, places, and incidents in this novel are either products of the imagination or are used fictitiously. Any resemblance to real people, either living or dead, to events, businesses, or locales is entirely coincidental.

1

He was at her front door, and he was going to kill her.

Ava had ignored his demands. Waited too long. She had to act fast. Move. Quickly.

Run!

Her foster care days taught her how to bolt at a moment's notice, and she could disappear in a flash.

She grabbed her backpack and raced to the back of her house. Down the stairs. Into the old-fashioned root cellar. Up the concrete steps. She flung open the doors to her backyard and dashed into the darkness.

She glanced around the yard. Into the inky night. Moon behind clouds. Drizzle spitting.

Good for cover. Not so good for the risk of falling.

Now where?

Her car? No! She couldn't risk approaching the garage and revving her engine. Alerting her would-be killer.

She would have to hoof it. Simple as that. *Yeah, right, simple.*

Heart galloping, palms sweating, she charged over her yard, spongy from months of Oregon spring rain.

She reached the fence where pickets had recently

fallen, revealing her neighbor's yard. Swing set. Slide. She slipped past their patio door. Light glowed from the dining table where the family of three was gathered for dinner. Heads bowed in prayer, they didn't notice her.

Perfect. She wouldn't have to get them involved and potentially put them in danger, too.

Thank You!

She slipped along the far side of the fence to the squeaking of Timmy's guinea pigs. Thank goodness he hadn't wanted his parents to get him a dog, or it would reveal her location.

She reached the street. Kept going. Pummeling her sneakers over the sidewalk. She risked a glance back at her house. At the car out front. Black. Sports car. Dented and rusty.

Yeah, it was Layne Boyle's vehicle all right, but no sign of Layne. At six foot tall, the thirty-something buff guy with blond hair and striking blue eyes would be impossible to miss.

She kicked it into gear. Rounded a corner. Then another. And another, then ducked into bushes near the neighborhood playground.

She gulped the humid air, sucking it in as if it were from an oxygen tank she would use for one of her patients. *Patients.* Not anymore. Her nursing career was over. Layne would see to that, and the police would be after her. Bringing her up on murder charges.

Her! Murder charges. How had her life come to that?

She didn't kill Layne's mother, Holly Boyle, last month. The police had no reason to suspect foul play, but Layne told them she had changed her will at the last minute and could've made the killer mad. The police agreed to look into it, but they did nothing, claiming high caseloads, and with the autopsy not showing any sign of foul play, they blew him off.

So he decided to investigate on his own and located circumstantial evidence that made Ava look guilty. He'd threatened to kill her unless she turned herself in within three days. She couldn't do that when she wasn't guilty—wouldn't—and she'd made plans to flee. To move to a secluded Oregon town. To learn to live off-grid. Alone.

But he'd come hunting her before the time was up.

She couldn't change that, but would still go through with her plans. Head to Shadow Lake Survival's compound and complete the deep immersion course to learn necessary skills needed to live off-grid in the small cabin her cousin had left to her.

Become Kari Curtis. She'd paid big bucks for a fake ID. She liked that name and started using it right away. Gone was Ava Weston, her real identity. She'd bought a car with cash from a private individual and filled it with personal possessions, including her bassoon, which she still played in a local community orchestra. Then she'd parked the second car in a storage facility, paying cash again.

So yeah, if she could get to a bus, she could get to her future. Run from Layne. From the law. Live a life of solitude. Not what she wanted. She'd always imagined a life with a husband and family. That was out of the question now. A lonely life in a cabin was better than a life behind bars.

She peeked out of the shrubs. Down the treelined street. Past the cars parked in front of houses with lights glowing, alluring warmth and safety. Misleading, and she couldn't let down her guard. Her house was emitting the same vibe, and there was no safety inside. Not with someone wanting to kill her.

She spotted nothing unusual.

Move. Now!

3

She eased out. Pulled up the hood on her jacket against the misty rain. Walked at a rapid pace when she wanted to bolt. But better not to draw attention to herself.

Head down, she moved on. Step after step. Her shoulders braced for an attack.

She reached the bus stop. Turned away from the street. Studied both directions.

Alone. Alone on the quiet Portland neighborhood street. Cars passing. None with a loud muffler like Layne's.

Please keep him at bay. Please.

Her future stood before her.

If she made it onto the next bus when it arrived.

If she survived the night.

Micha Nichols rarely liked the first day of their weeklong intensive survival skills training. But today? Today was different.

Thanks to the petite blonde doing her best to start the fire they needed for tonight's dinner.

Kari Curtis appeared nothing like the pictures he'd located when doing her background check. She'd had coal-black hair in those photos, but was now blonde. And thinner.

Which coloring was natural? He couldn't be sure, but her fair skin said blonde to him.

What none of it explained was this zing he got in his belly every time he looked at her. But it was there. Like now. He wanted to wrap his arms around her, take her petite hands into his, and help her start the fire she was struggling with so badly.

Totally unprofessional behavior. He shoved his hands into his pockets instead.

She was nibbling on her lower lip as she rubbed her hands on the spindle to create a hand drill fire. Basically a slim branch they'd scavenged from the woods and processed after creating a sharp edge by striking two rocks together. The Shadow Lake Survival team believed their clients needed to be prepared all the way. Not to have a single item in their possession to use in most situations. Scavenging in the place they found themselves was the only sure way to survive every situation they faced in the wilderness or off-grid living.

Her spindle jumped out of the divot on her hearth board.

"Argh!" She tossed it down to sit back, brushing her hand over the perspiration on her face from the hard work.

"You won't want that to hit the ground," he said.

She frowned and grabbed up the spindle. "Sorry. I forgot it can't get wet. Is it ruined?"

"Could be, but it wasn't on the ground long. You could be okay." He smiled, but it did nothing to change her frustration. "Only one way to find out. Try again once you're rested."

She scowled at him. "I *have* tried. How many times? Five? Six? Everyone else did it in three or less. Why can't I get this?"

"Because it's not as simple as it seems. Sure the concept of rubbing wood against wood to cause dust and friction is simple, but in reality?" He shrugged. "Not so much."

She glanced at her fellow participants. Five men, ages twenty-five to seventy-three. "Everyone else has gotten it. Even Ernie."

"Hey, now." Ernie scratched his silvery gray goatee. "Is that an old age joke?"

"Sorry, I didn't mean anything by it. You look to be in great shape, but this is surprisingly physically taxing."

"I get it, hon." Ernie smiled, the wrinkles around his eyes narrowing. "My wife, who's only a year younger than me, loves to say I'm a vintage model, and I'm proud of it."

The others laughed, and Kari joined in, but she didn't look up from her work.

"Maybe you could try using your foot to hold the hearth board." Micha dropped down beside her and took off his boot and sock, then placed the side of his foot on her hearth board. "Like this. Holds it tighter. Keeps the spindle from jumping as much."

She removed her boot and sock to reveal a delicate foot with nails painted an equally delicate pink. Okay, not the style of their typical preppers or survivalists, but utterly captivating.

He scooted back and put on his sock and boot before he did something more to help. She seemed so fragile. Not only physically, but he caught worried—maybe fearful—expressions on her face when she didn't know he was watching. Problem for her was he was always watching.

Not only watching her, but the guys, too. As a former military intelligence officer, he didn't relax around strangers. Especially ones who might lean toward the far side of society's norms, like many of the people who came to their off-grid survival training camp.

She spit on her hands to better grip the spindle, another act he couldn't imagine this very feminine, pink-toenailed woman willingly doing. Yeah, he was putting her in a box. Maybe one he wanted her in. It'd been a long time since he'd had any real interest in a woman like this. And if she fit his criteria, maybe he could consider pursuing something once she graduated this week.

If she graduated. Today didn't bode well for her.

Her hands traveled down the spindle, and she started back at the top, holding on to the spindle with one hand as

6

he'd taught her. She'd remembered all the directions to this point except dropping the spindle.

Come on, God. How about cutting her a break? Let this work.

Micha asked, but God didn't always make things easy in life. His sister Tristin and her freak accident were a perfect example, one that he had yet to reconcile. Why did she have to lose the use of her legs—be wheelchair-bound, maybe for life? Sure, he knew God grew people under pressure. Shaped them. Molded them. Micha should know. He'd been molded under pressure for far too long. Since childhood in foster care, trying to keep his sister safe. Time she caught a break, wasn't it?

The hearth board smoked.

"There you go." He put as much enthusiasm as he could muster into his tone to cheer her on. "You got it. Now put down the spindle. Use the tiny stick you cut to transfer the coal to your tinder bundle."

She shot a hand out for the large leaf holding the spark, or what they called the coal.

"Careful. Slow down. Make sure to keep it in one piece." He held his breath as she moved the very fragile object.

She slid the tiny coal onto the top of the bundle of shredded cedar bark.

"Now hold the bottom and blow gently. Very gently."

She pursed her lips that had started the day with a pale pink lipstick, and a flame emerged. Her large blue eyes widened. "I did it."

"Not quite yet. You have a flame, but you still don't have a fire. Set it down and start with your smallest sticks to form a teepee over it." He'd had the clients gather dry sticks and break them into small pieces, then lay them out in size order. That allowed them to begin with the smallest size and work their way to the larger ones.

She gradually added the larger sticks until she had a nice teepee formed and a strong fire going.

She shot up a fist to bump with him.

"Finally. I was about to die of old age waiting." Ernie chuckled.

She laughed, a sweet sound that wound through Micha like the warble of the songbirds they encountered in their wilderness hikes, freeing him from his past and making him hope for a future he didn't think he would have while his sister was paralyzed.

Why did it even have to happen? She'd already suffered so much in foster care. But then she'd finally had it all. Was happily married. Lived in a big house. Had a beautiful daughter. The ideal life. Which, after foster care, didn't often happen. And now? Now it was all gone. Poof, vanished in a flash of time that changed her life forever. Just like when their parents died.

Enough. He had work to do. No time to consider his own potential happiness at the expense of the other participants. "Now, as the last one to master fire-starting, you get to cook dinner."

"Hey, wait." Jamal Thomason uncrossed his legs and sat forward. "The website said the meals were catered."

"Some are."

"But not ours?" He cast a suspicious look at Micha through dark eyes, a look the twenty-five-year-old mechanic had worn since he'd arrived. "I paid good money to be here and not to have to cook my own food."

"You paid to be trained in survival skills in a one-week immersive course, and that includes procuring and prepping your own meals. We'll start out by providing the food, but you'll soon be hunting for your own."

His eyes brightened. "Yeah, the hunting I understood. Not so much the cooking it for our meals."

8

Micha took a breath to maintain his patience over this guy's erroneous take on the week. "Some of the longer courses *do* start with catered meals, and we take longer to get to the nitty gritty, but not this one."

Jamal crossed his arms. "Not what the website says."

"I'm not that familiar with the website, but I can mention it to one of the owners, and he'll get back with you."

"Yeah, well." He stuck out his chin. "I'd show you where I read it, but you confiscated my phone."

"We all had to turn them in," Kari said. "Something they told us to be prepared to do."

"I get it." Jamal tightened his arms. "Just don't like it."

"Why don't we move on to that dinner?" Ernie asked. "I'm getting hungry."

"Sounds good," Micha said. "But before we do, I want to mention food storage again. We do get black bears on the property. Not often, but occasionally. Means we have to prepare for them. FYI, don't let the name fool you. Their coloring can be black, sure, but they can also be blond, brown, and cinnamon."

That worry he'd found in Kari's expression intensified.

"We'll be fine as long as we practice good bear hygiene," he said. "Our KP tent will never have food left in it. We'll store all food on platforms ten feet high, and we have bear-proof garbage cans."

Kari shuddered.

Micha had to ignore her worry and go on. "When we hit the trail, we'll sleep at least a hundred yards from cooking and eating areas. Then please leave all soap, suntan lotion, candles, and any other scented items back at your cabin."

"No soap!" Kari's voice squeaked high, and she gaped at him as if he'd said they wouldn't eat for a week. "Just how are we supposed to stay clean?"

9

Wow. A strong reaction to a little bar of soap.

"We'll provide the soap and store it on the platforms," he said.

She swiped a hand over her brow. "Phew, because I could use a shower right now, and all I did was spin a little stick." She laughed.

Micha laughed with her, but it was all for show. She sure didn't seem like a survivalist, so why was she here? His gut said she was hiding something, but what? Something illegal? She'd passed their usual background check, but the review had turned up little online information for her. Maybe the secret she was concealing made her keep a low online presence.

His path was clear. Crystal. Even if his radar hadn't gone off due to his attraction to her, he would be paying her special attention to ferret out the answer to that question.

Mark his words. He would find out what she was hiding. No matter what it took.

2

Ava stepped into the tiny bedroom of the small log cabin, her mind on Micha. He'd watched her far more intently than she'd liked and far too often for her liking. She hadn't done a good job of pretending everything was A-okay in her life. Probably the opposite. She'd taken turn after turn on that spindle to start a fire. Let her worry that she wouldn't be able to get it right take over. Imagined herself running from Layne and getting stuck in the wilderness, losing her way and not possessing the skills to start a fire to keep warm. Freezing to death.

Panic had set in, her hands and movements turning clumsy. Despite her best efforts, she'd let the spindle jump the hearth board too many times.

Grr.

She'd drawn attention to herself. Not only from Micha but the other guys. Not a good thing when she was wanted by the law. But maybe Layne hadn't handed over the video to the police that made Ava look guilty of killing Holly. Ava had been hiding out for two weeks now, waiting for this week's camp to start, so she believed he would've handed it over by now. Or maybe Layne would try to track her down on his own and follow through on his threat to kill her instead. Or even a combination of the two.

She didn't know, but she had to figure it out if she was to stay alive.

She got out the burner phone she'd kept hidden from Micha. Sure, she'd given him a phone. Her everyday one, also a burner, but when she'd read in the orientation packet that all electronics had to be surrendered, she'd bought a second one.

Against the rules? Yeah, sure. More anxiety when she was a rule follower through and through. But no way she'd be here without some means to get help if needed. Or hide out here and not know what was going on with the murder investigation back home in Portland.

She grabbed the towel from her shower and slipped into the bedroom closet, the only windowless room in the cabin. She sat and pressed the towel along the bottom of the door, sealing herself in utter darkness.

Perfect. Exactly what she needed. She'd closed all of the blinds in the other rooms, but she couldn't risk the light from her phone flickering and shining through. With all electronics off limits, she didn't need Micha's amazing brown eyes fixed on her even more. Not when looking into them did funny things to her stomach, and she'd lost her focus.

She turned on the phone. Watched the light flicker over the wood walls as she inhaled the familiar scent of her coconut shampoo. The phone came to life and fully booted. She double-checked to be sure the volume was muted. Sound traveled a long distance in God's amazing yet quiet wilderness. She couldn't risk any hint of the device making it out of the closet.

A few taps of her thumbs, and she'd entered a search for updates on the death of Layne's mother.

The screen flashed several new links. *No. Oh, no.*

She bit her lip to keep from crying out over the top story.

Recent hospital death deemed suspicious. Local nurse wanted in connection.

She scanned the interview with Layne. He'd gone to the police and was quoted as saying as much. Would Micha see this?

She'd probably left enough questions in his mind about her behavior that he might decide to do a Google search. The good news was this article reported her real name. But the picture was a dead giveaway for someone with criminal investigations experience to put two and two together. If he simply browsed Portland headlines...

What could she do about it? Anything?

She leaned back against the wall.

She could come clean, but she'd only known him a day. Long enough to know he was the kind of guy who would do the right thing. The legal thing. The thing an honorable guy would do.

Turn her in.

Maybe she should flee.

No. Not a good idea. She needed the survival skills he could teach her, as she had no clue how to live off-grid. Today only further emphasized that.

Maybe she could distract him. But how? Not with her nervous behavior, that was for sure. She could flirt with him. Get romantically involved. Then maybe he would look the other way.

That might work. After all, he didn't do a very good job of hiding his attraction to her. And she reciprocated. She wouldn't even have to act with him. Her response would be real, for sure.

Her stomach knotted. Man, this was getting more and more out of control. She didn't much like the person she was becoming in order to stay out of prison for something she didn't do.

And trying to start something romantic with him? That wouldn't be fair to him. Lead him on. It would be downright low in her opinion. His, too, as she'd heard him talking to Ernie about his faith, and he wouldn't condone lying. Too bad. She was already lying, right? She'd be gone in less than a week. How much could he come to care for her in such a short time? Surely not enough to really hurt him.

"But would he give in to his attraction or pull the professional card?" Either way, she had to try.

On the one hand, eager to get started, the other dreading it, she powered down the phone, wrapped it in her sock, and placed it under the mattress. She headed to the bathroom to put on makeup and dress in the cute knit top she'd been told highlighted her fair coloring and showed off her curves.

She would take a walk and accidentally run into him. Perhaps knock on his cabin door. On the property tour first thing that morning, he'd mentioned the staff cabin painted a crisp white was his. Neat and tidy outside like all the others, but more sparse without any landscaping.

She grabbed a flashlight and key for her cabin, then stepped into the shadows, clinging to the small building. Pausing outside the door, she gave her eyes a chance to adjust to the dark and peered at the sky, littered with sparkling stars.

Oh, man, how beautiful. She could get used to seeing how God planted the stars in the sky like little lights to lead the way. Maybe walk under them and the warm moon hanging high with Micha for real.

Nah, she couldn't do that. Not with him. Not with any guy. She not only was a fugitive from the law, she was a fugitive from the life she'd always wanted for herself.

"So get your fake on, girl," she whispered. "Charm the

man and don't feel bad doing it, or you will fail. That is not an option. Not an option at all."

~

Micha had delivered his guests to their cabins for the night and settled into a chair at Shadow Lake Survival's small meeting room, located in their training facility. The other five guys on the team sat around the table and glanced at him. He was always struck by how looking at them left no question that they were a team of former law enforcement or military guys who had stayed fit to do their best for the people they served.

Reid Maddox, managing partner, ran a hand over dark hair. "Long day. Problems?

Micha leaned back in his chair. "Took a little longer on the fire starting, but everyone finally got it, and they're tucked in for the night."

"I got a look at Kari," Colin Graham, a former FBI agent who'd specialized in information technology, said. "Probably no hardship in tucking her in."

The others laughed.

"Not going to touch that," Micha said.

"Ah, then there *is* something there." Colin's brother Devan, a former Clackamas County deputy and expert in water rescue, scratched his close-cut beard.

"Yeah, maybe, but you know we don't get personally involved with clients." Micha shifted his focus back to Colin. "And I think she's hiding something. No evidence to that fact. Just a gut feeling, but my gut is rarely wrong, and I'd like you to do a deeper dive on her."

Colin took a hearty breath and let it out. "Pretty much all of our clients try to hide secrets. But we don't go digging into things unless it interferes in the training sessions."

"Or if we believe they're involved in illegal acts," Reid added.

"You thinking she's breaking the law?" Sheriff Russ Maddox, Reid's younger brother and the only active law enforcement officer of the team, asked.

Did he? Did he really? Could he even be objective? "Not sure, but do we want to take a chance?"

"No." Reid looked at Colin, his no-nonsense boss expression in place. "Do you have time to do a deeper dive?"

"Maybe." Colin frowned. "After I finish the basic background on the latest class to sign up."

"How long will that take?" Micha tried not to come across as demanding, but Colin's narrowed eyes said he'd failed.

"If all goes well, Wednesday morning."

"That's two days."

"You were always a math genius." Ryan Maddox, the youngest of the three brothers who owned the business and was a frequent joker, cocked a grin.

"You'll just have to keep an eye out for now," Reid said.

"Like I said, I doubt it's a hardship." Colin chuckled.

Micha didn't want to respond to that, so he didn't.

"What about the guys in the class?" Ryan asked. "They seem legit?"

Micha nodded. "Jamal's got some issues." He shared about the website issue.

"He's wrong," Reid said. "Each session type spells out the meals and prep or lack thereof."

"I don't think it will help to point that out," Micha said. "He copped an attitude with me and will likely claim you changed the site after I told you about it."

"Still, I'll have a word with him," Reid said. "See if we can work it out and not get a one-star review online."

Ryan shook his head. "I hate online reviews. We do our

best all the time. Do we mess up at times? Yeah. But we fix the mistakes if we can."

"Don't worry," Reid said. "I'll handle it."

Russ leaned back, his sheriff's badge pinned to his belt. "Which is why we're thankful for you."

"At least some of the time," Ryan added.

They all laughed, and the tension that had grown thick in the air fled the room.

The brothers owned the company together, but Reid was the day-to-day boss. He'd served as an FBI agent, but then his wife died of cancer, and he'd moved back home to Shadow Lake from Portland to spend more time with his daughter Jessie. He also wanted her to be closer to family.

That's when he took over the former family resort and started the business with his brothers, and Micha was glad he did. Micha had served as a Marine weapons expert with Russ before Russ left to pursue a law enforcement career. Micha hung in with the Marines, moving into special investigations, but he'd needed to get back home to care for his sister Tristin and her daughter, and an outdoor job like this one was perfect for him. At least until he figured things out in life.

Ha! Thirty-two years old and still trying to adult to the level that was needed. His parents wouldn't be proud of his waffling in life if they'd lived to see it.

"You hear me, Micha?" Reid asked.

Micha shook his head. "Sorry. Got distracted."

"I asked if there was anything you need for tomorrow on your expedition into the wilderness with the group?"

"I'm good. Nothing out of the ordinary. At least I don't think there will be."

"You think that way, then you need to plan for something to happen." Ryan laughed.

"He's right," Dev said. "Slippery slope and all of that."

They were probably right, and he should be thinking of all eventualities, but his brain was consumed with Kari and her secret.

The team moved on, hashing through the schedule for the week. They rotated through leading this basic week to keep from burning out on the mundane and then plugged in areas that fit their backgrounds.

Didn't take long to work through the schedule, and they were starting for the door. Good thing. Micha needed a shower and bed if he wanted to be fresh for the morning. Hopefully he could let go of thoughts of Kari and get some sleep.

Ryan pointed down the small dirt road. "Looks like you didn't do such a good job tucking in your class for the night."

Swinging a flashlight, Kari strolled their way.

Micha gritted his teeth. "I told them all to get some shuteye."

"Guess she doesn't listen real well." Reid frowned. "Maybe you're right, and she could turn into a problem."

Yeah, she could. A problem for Micha.

"Kari," he said when she reached them. "I thought everyone was taking it easy tonight after the hard day."

"I wasn't sleepy and figured a walk might help." She turned to the other guys and introduced herself.

After a round of sharing names, she peered at Micha. Her skin glistened in the moonlight, raising his awareness of her as a woman. *Ugh. Let it go already.* He shoved his hands into his pockets.

She gave him a sweet smile. "Is it okay if I walk down to the lake?"

"Can't see why not," Reid said. "But Micha should probably accompany you. Wouldn't want you to get lost."

"It's right at the end of the road," Micha said before this

got out of hand and he had to take a moonlight stroll with the woman he was trying to avoid.

Reid met his gaze and held it. "But it can be confusing at night, and I wouldn't want her to fall in."

Micha glanced at the other guys for help, but found only smirks. They knew what was going on and weren't about to bail him out when they were enjoying the show. "Then I guess the logical person to accompany her is Dev since he's a water rescue expert."

Dev glanced at his watch. "Logical, but no can do. I have a video call in a few minutes."

What kind of a call could he have at this time of night? Micha wanted to ask, but Dev was a straight shooter, and if he said he had a call, he had one.

"It's not that big of a deal." Kari smiled sweetly at Micha. "I can head back to my cabin and play my bassoon for a while to relax. That is, if it won't disturb. I can choose some soothing scores to play."

"No need," Micha said. "I'll take you."

"Are you sure?" She batted her long lashes that she'd coated in mascara since he'd last seen her.

In fact, now that he studied her, she'd put all the makeup on. Was she planning to flirt with whoever she ran into or did she simply like to be put together when she went out in public?

"Great," Reid said. "Let us know if there's anything we can do to make your stay with us more enjoyable and productive."

"I was most impressed with Micha's skills today." Her gaze lingered on him for a moment, then shifted slowly to Reid. "I can see what a professional operation you run and doubt I'll have any suggestions."

"Then we'll let you get to your walk." Reid stepped off and leaned close to Micha to whisper, "She's putting out serious attraction vibes. Take care and remember she's a client."

Yeah, Micha caught the vibes, and he caught Reid's warning. Problem was, he wanted to explore the vibes, but that wouldn't happen for as long as he had to care for his sister and her daughter. Besides, he had to do his job right. The job had to come first.

He made sure to take a professional stance and tone and looked at Kari. "After you."

She started off at a slow pace. "I'm sorry if this is too inconvenient. I really can go back to my cabin. I don't mind."

There were those batting lashes again. Not really in a flirty way this time, more like a habit, but he doubted that, too, as she hadn't done it during the day's training.

"No worries. It'll help me unwind for the night, too." At least if she quit coming on to him.

"How long have you worked here?" she asked.

"About a year now."

"And you said you were in the military before. What branch?"

"Marines. I was a weapons specialist and then moved into military investigations."

She nodded at his belt. "No wonder you carry a gun."

"We all do."

"I'm surprised it's necessary in a tranquil place like this unless you're really worried about animals."

"The two legged variety, yeah. I appreciate everyone who wants to learn to live off-grid or how to survive in the wilderness, but along with that can come all kinds of crazy at times." He chuckled, but eyed her. "Sometimes our guests try to keep things from us that we need to know for their protection."

She looked away. "I'm not one of those nutso preppers if

that's what you're getting at. Just a girl hoping to learn how to survive on her own."

"But why?" He stared openly now. "Don't take this the wrong way, but you're pretty soft around the edges. Makeup. Perfume. Nail polish. Lipstick. What appears to be designer jeans. We don't get a lot of that look around here."

She glanced at him, then quickly away, but he caught her cautious expression. "You're right. I'm kind of a girly girl who likes the indoors and creature comforts. But sometimes you have to challenge yourself and branch out in life."

"Understood," he said, but really didn't buy her answer.

"I mean, what good do creature comforts do if I freeze to death or can't find food and water?" Her sincere tone hit him hard. She really was worried about these things.

Question was, why?

He met and held her gaze. "You seem concerned that you might find yourself in that situation."

"You never know, right? With the way our world is going at times."

"True," he said, but doubted that was her reason for being here.

"Are you married? Engaged? Involved?"

Way to change the subject. Evasive for sure. "None of the above."

"A good-looking guy like you who seems to have a decent personality and a good job? What are the women around here thinking?" She chuckled and ducked under a low-hanging tree branch.

He followed and a cobweb caught on his face. His fear of spiders kicked his heart rate into gear. He swatted the clingy web away and jumped back, searching his clothing for the insect that had made it.

"Something wrong?" She'd stopped and was staring at him.

No way he would admit to his fear. He swallowed and moved on, chastising himself for being irrational. "What about you? Significant other."

"Same as you. No one right now."

They reached the lake, the moon shimmering off the calm surface. He took a moment to enjoy it, but knew all kinds of things were churning underneath the water. Like his gut clenching over a silly spider. Or unsettled things that seemed to lay underneath the calm and very lovely Ms. Kari Curtis's fine exterior.

And God help him, he wanted to figure her out, not only for the job, but for his own personal interest. And that scared him almost as much as the very real threat of bears in the area.

3

Rocks. Ava's backpack weighed down her shoulders on the trail the next morning as if Micha had loaded it with large rocks. Of course he hadn't. His only part in the weight of her pack for this four-day expedition into the wilderness was to give her a list of the items she needed to pack. Not that she was special in getting the list. Before arriving at the compound, they'd all been sent an email naming supplies to bring for their week of immersion.

Her makeup bag was the only extra thing she'd added beyond the listed items to her pack. She did like makeup, maybe excessively so, and might have more products than many women, but that wouldn't weigh the pack down much. Still, after an hour hike uphill over a winding, wooded, and rocky path, every ounce now pulled on her shoulders like a pound.

Micha struggling with his pack? Not so much. He led the way as if out for a leisurely morning stroll. Then Jamal followed, his step eager still, too. Even Ernie, who was next in line moved better than she did. These guys were followed by Buck, Fritz, and Garrett, who also seemed to tolerate the climb, though Buck grumbled a bit. As a nurse, she was on her feet all day and often got in more than twenty thousand steps, but clearly it hadn't prepared her for a grueling hike.

Micha looked back at them and held up his hand. He ran his gaze over her. "We'll break here. Be sure to drink some water. Don't want anyone getting dehydrated."

He didn't need to tell her twice to take a break. She shrugged out of her pack and resisted sighing as she sat on a nearby boulder. She also slipped out of her jacket and set it on her pack. The temps for April were on the chilly side, hovering around fifty degrees even with the sun beating down on them, but she'd worked up a sweat on the hike and needed to cool down.

Micha put down his pack and grabbed his canteen, then eased past the others who were also looking for places to sit. She took a long drink from her canteen, the cool liquid doing a lot to refresh her mood. He stepped near a tree and swatted his hands at something. His face contorted in the first sign she'd seen of distress in the man. Maybe there were bees and he was allergic.

"Bees?" she asked when he stood in front of her, breathing deeply.

"What?"

"You were swatting. I thought it might be bees."

"No bees. Just a spider web."

Was he afraid of spiders? Couldn't be, right? Not a guy who spent a lot of his time in the Oregon wilderness. That would be a big problem, wouldn't it?

He nodded at her canteen and settled on a fallen log next to her. "You'll want to ration that. We have another hour's hike."

She eyed him. "Did you have to pick a location so far from the compound?"

"This area is the best place to simulate off-grid living, and that's what everyone is expecting us to provide."

"Yeah, but..." She shrugged.

"But this is harder than you expected?"

She hated to admit it, but why lie just to save face? "It is. But I'll get through. I always do."

He studied her face. "I like your determination. I saw it yesterday, too, when you didn't give up on the fire. It'll serve you well out here."

She appreciated his compliment, but..."We'll see how much it helps in the next hour."

She forced a laugh she wasn't feeling, but he didn't take his assessing gaze from her face. She had to direct the subject away from her. "How did you get involved in this business anyway? Seems like a far cry from military investigations or even working with weapons."

He shifted on his log but kept watching her. "It can be hard to find civilian employment that a military background fits with. Especially if you really don't want a nine-to-five office job. Which I don't. I like being outside. A lot."

"But weren't you in an office in military investigations?"

"I was, and I hated that part of the job, which is why I didn't want to go into law enforcement when I got out. Besides which, I would've had to start as a patrol officer and would have to put in my time to get to a detective slot. A car is actually more appealing than an office, but the hassles patrol officers go through these days isn't appealing at all." He clutched his hands together. "So when Russ called about this job, I didn't hesitate. As a bonus, this location is perfect. It's near to my sister and her daughter."

He frowned.

"Why the frown?"

"Tristin is battling some health issues that I want to fix but can't."

"I'm sorry," she said and resisted asking the private

details that he would share if he wanted to. "Are you close to your sister?"

"Very. Our parents died when Tristin and I were kids, and we grew up in the foster care system. Had to look out for her, and she's relied on me for years. Grows a bond you can't imagine."

She could imagine all right. She'd had the same experience. Minus an older brother to help her navigate foster care living. She'd had to become determined. Scrappy even, or she wouldn't have made it out of the system without even more emotional issues than plagued her now.

She didn't talk about those days. Best left unsaid, and she wasn't going to tell him about her past. Not only because it would open old wounds but because the backstory she'd invented for Kari Curtis didn't include growing up in foster care. Kari had the perfect, idyllic childhood with two doting parents, living in one of those big two-story white houses with black shutters and a two-car garage. She also had a brother and sister who adored her and even a dog named Bella, who was totally devoted to her.

Yeah, she might hurl if she had to explain that, too, because it was her dream. Had been her dream. Now it was gone. Who would believe the former foster girl who'd gotten into trouble most of her life and didn't pull herself together until her twenties to go to nursing school wasn't the one who killed Holly Boyle?

Move on. Let it go. "I'm sorry for the loss of your parents, but it sounds like you have a special relationship with your sister."

He nodded, but stared off into the distance. "Like I said, we have an hour left to go on this hike. I can slow down a bit if you need, but if we're to accomplish everything today, I'll need to keep moving at a solid pace."

"No need to make an exception for me. I'll be fine." She

tried not to sound testy, but she didn't like his assumption that she couldn't hold her own. She could and would. Always had and didn't need anyone else's help. God's maybe, but not people.

He held up a hand. "Hey, I didn't mean anything by that. Just trying to help."

"Then in that case, how about not treating me like I'm fragile all the time?" she asked, turning the discussion to her physical stamina and away from the past.

"Is that what I was doing?"

"Did you ask the other guys if they needed a slower speed?"

"No, but..." He shrugged. "Yeah, I guess you're right. Probably comes from my need to protect my sister. Others. Not from any prejudice against you being able to hold your own in the world." He gave her a sweet smile. "I'm sure your determination has and will see you through."

"You got that right." She stood, hating that she was bordering on rude to shut down any questions about her past. Or maybe she was running away from what the sweet smile did to her heart rate.

Either way, she needed to be on guard around him, or she might slip up and find herself revealing too much and end up serving a life sentence for murder.

～

"Who's fished before?" Micha asked from his place near the large firepit as the others gathered around him.

Ernie shot up a hand, the tiredness in his expression flooding away. "One of my hobbies."

"Then you'll probably have the hardest time of all. We'll use a very primitive method, and I'll bet you have all the latest gear at home. Am I right?"

Ernie grinned. "You know it."

"Today we'll make our own hooks, starting with scavenging for the materials. You can make hooks from all kinds of things people leave behind, such as metal soda can tops, a safety pin, etcetera. But let's assume we can't find any of those items."

"Would be odd not to find anything to use," Jamal said. "So why not skip it?"

"Because you can probably figure out how to use those items. But I want you to know how to make a hook with only a tree and your knife." He waited for Jamal to toss out more questions, but he simply pressed his lips together behind his full black beard.

Micha shifted his stance to take in the others in the group. "We'll make what's called a gorge hook. First you'll use your knife to collect a strong branch from a sturdy tree, like a pine. Find a stick about a third of the thickness of your finger and bring it back to me at the river. You can use your knife, but bonus points if you don't have to. It would be good to try. Never know if you might find yourself stranded without a knife."

"How long of a branch?" Ernie asked.

"I'd try for around a foot, but we'll be cutting it down to pinkie size so use your judgment. You'll also want to find bait. Insects or worms will work." He waved his hands in a dismissive gesture. "Bonus points to the first one back to the river, too."

Jamal arched a dark eyebrow. "What do these bonus points get us?"

"Nothing but bragging rights."

"Not worth it then."

"It is for me." Kari shot to her feet and shouldered her pack.

"You can leave that here," Micha said, hoping to lighten her load.

"Not a chance." Her vehement tone shattered the quiet, sending birds flapping from trees above. "First rule of survival for me is never leave my belongings behind."

Oh, really. Micha had a similar philosophy. Probably the same for a lot of kids who lived most of their life moving from foster home to foster home before aging out of the system. Could she be a former foster kid? He'd seen things stolen and discarded often enough—his things included—and he'd learned to keep his stuff packed and ready for moves, plus his sentimental items close at hand.

"Make sure each of you have your walkie-talkie and don't go far. I don't want to lose any of you."

"We're not babies." Jamal rolled his eyes and set off at a slow pace.

"At that rate, you won't be eating tonight," Micha said.

Jamal shrugged and didn't speed up but disappeared over a ridge.

Micha liked most of their clients. Even the zealous preppers as they had a cause that they believed in. But guys like Jamal, who seemed to think the world owed them something, didn't sit well with Micha.

And speaking of sitting, he needed to get a move on. He got out his satellite phone from his backpack and texted home base.

Arrived at camp. All is well.

He shoved the phone back into his backpack down at the bottom so no one would notice it and complain that he had a phone. And by no one, he meant Jamal.

He dug out his emergency fishing kit and headed for the river. It was up to him to find a spot where the fish were biting and haul a few in to ensure they would have a fresh-caught dinner if the others failed. It didn't happen often, but it did happen.

He knelt by a small tree, cut a branch, then notched the end of it. From his kit, he took out a fishing line with a hook already tied at the end. He didn't feel like digging for worms, so he went to a rotting tree stump and poked around with his knife until he located a few grubs and baited one on his hook. A quick toss into the gently moving water, and he plopped down to enjoy one of the few free moments he would have this week.

He loved his job, but he also loved his solitude, which he didn't get enough of these days. Not with the way the business was booming. But he was glad to help the Maddox brothers build it up. The Maddox family's success was good for everyone on the team.

He heard a rustling behind and turned to see Kari emerge from the brush. She lifted her hand. "Got the branch and the worms. Now what?"

"Sit," he said and stuck his pole in the ground to free up his hands if needed. "Start by stripping the bark from half that branch."

She sat, putting her pack behind her. She applied her knife to the branch and took nice, even slices as if she'd done this before. Her tongue peeked out the corner of her mouth, and her eyes narrowed in concentration. She used a small-bladed pocket knife with a pink handle, fitting with her feminine style.

"I was surprised about your number one survival rule," he said.

She glanced up, but only for a moment. "Keep my things with me? Why? It makes sense, right? You'll never be caught empty-handed."

"True that, but it sounded more like you spoke from experience. Like you'd learned the hard way to do that."

"Did I?" She shrugged and raised her branch for inspection. "Stripped."

Subject averted. Was she really trying to hide something from him? It wouldn't work. He would figure it out. Not if he put her on guard. Better to leave it alone for now. "Go ahead and shave a fine point on the end."

She set to work, that tongue came out again, and she looked adorable. Like her child might look someday.

She raced through her work and held it up. "Done!"

"Now cut that section off to about a third the length of your pinkie, sharpen it too, and notch all the way around the end you didn't sharpen." He continued to watch her, appreciating not having the guys back yet. Odd that not one of them had gotten here, and he should probably be wondering where they were, but he'd give them a few more minutes before investigating.

She held out the stick. "Ready."

"The next step is to affix the fishing line. In an emergency situation, I would tell you to take the hem out of your clothing or unravel your clothing and weave thread into a strong line. This isn't something I feel you need to practice, so I'll give you a length of fishing line that you need to tie in the notch you made."

He got the spool out of the pack and handed it to her. "Wrap it around the notches, then tie it vertically in place. That way when the fish swallows the bait, the gorge becomes horizontally lodged in his throat, and he can't spit it out."

She made quick work of the task and looked up with a gleam in her eye. Before he could give additional directions, she dug in her sweatshirt pocket and produced a handful of wiggling worms.

"Worm goes here. Choose a big one. Will fit better." He pointed at the end of the hook she should bait.

She didn't hesitate but selected a fat worm and shoved the others back into her pocket. Maybe he'd misjudged her, and she wasn't as much of a girly girl as he'd thought.

She dropped her line into the water and wrapped it around her leg. She made a sour face and grabbed some leaves to clean her hands, then reached for her pack. "I have sanitizer in my pack. No way I'll leave this goo on my hands."

She opened the outer pocket and squeezed a generous dollop of sanitizer onto her hands. Dropping the small bottle back into the bag, she tilted her head. "What in the world?"

Instantly alert at her tone, he sat forward. "What's wrong?"

"Someone put a piece of paper in here." She glanced at him. "Did you?"

"No."

She reached inside the pocket to pull out a folded sheet of paper. She pressed it open on her knee. Lines of large typed text with music notes above each line filled the page.

She dropped the paper and gasped. She shot a look around, fear lodged in her beautiful eyes.

"What is it?" He picked up the paper. Read.

Ode to Death
[Dm] [C] [B ♭]
In the darkness whispers fall,
[B ♭] [C] [D]
I've found you again, now heed my call,
[F] [A] [E]
Turn yourself in and don't you bail,
[Dm] [C] [B ♭]
Or in the stillness, nightmares will prevail.

. . .

He shot his gaze to hers. "Care to explain this?"

She waved a hand. "It's nothing. Just a silly prank from one of my fellow orchestra players. We do things like this all the time."

No way. "Doesn't sound like a prank. Sounds like a threat."

"No. Nothing like that."

"I'm not buying it. This is a threat, plain and simple, and it's my job to protect you while in my class. If you're in danger I need to know about it."

Jamal came around the corner. He and the others joined them.

She quickly shoved the paper into her pack.

Jamal frowned down at them. "We were waiting at the campsite."

The others trudged behind, looking tired and ready for dinner.

"He told us to meet him at the river." Kari's leg jerked. "Fish! I got a fish."

She started reeling the line in hand-over-hand. He had to let go of the threat for now, but as soon as they'd had dinner and settled down by the fire, he would take her aside and insist on knowing who was threatening her and why.

She may not realize it yet, but that note had likely been left in her pack since she'd arrived in their compound or she would've discovered it sooner. If so, that meant the person threatening her life was part of their group and could strike when she least expected it, unleashing that nightmare he spoke of in the song.

4

Ava finished KP Duty and could barely keep from squirming under Micha's scrutiny. He didn't bother hiding the fact that he was watching her. Questioning her with every look and putting pressure on her to be more forthright with him. If possible, his concern seemed to ramp up as time went on.

But so what if she was uncomfortable under his watchful eye? She had to stay vigilant. Keep quiet. She was talking about her life here. It could very well depend on keeping her secret to herself. And if not her life, her freedom from prison.

She could—must—handle this on her own.

That's the way you like your personal life, right? All alone.

Besides, she had an idea how to figure out who'd left the message. She'd given it nonstop thought, and two things seemed to be true. She'd hummed the song. It was a pretty good melody, although haunting, and the sender of the message probably possessed music knowledge. That message hadn't been in her pack last night when she'd filled it for today. The person who added it had to be in this group or one of the staff members.

And she was positive the song was connected to Holly. Holly possessed a strong music background, teaching piano as her main job and playing as a guest artist with many orchestras. Music was one of the areas Ava and Holly had bonded. It would be too coincidental if it weren't connected.

Ava ruled out the staff for now and would start with the five men who'd joined her class, but she had to keep in mind that Layne could've given the message to whoever placed it in her pack. He wasn't into music. Not at all. Holly had tried to teach him piano and encouraged getting involved in music, but he had zero interest and refused to practice piano or the trumpet, which he'd started lessons at one point.

Ava hung up the dishtowel and started for the firepit they'd built with scavenged rocks. She dropped onto a log. Time for operation *Ferret Out The Threat*.

"We don't see many females at these kinds of immersion classes." That condescending tone Jamal seemed to use often was alive and well in his voice.

"You attend a lot of them?" she asked, hoping to steer the conversation in the direction she wanted to go.

He looked down his nose at her. "Enough to keep my skills current."

"Me too," Garrett said. "Almost didn't get into this one though, due to the time it took to process my application. Other companies don't require a background check. Which is why I wanted this one. Been to enough of them where I had to deal with some nutso preppers and hoped these checks ruled them out."

"We're selective," Micha said, eyeing something on the nearby rock with fixed interest.

A bug scurried across the rough face. Maybe a spider. He lurched to his feet and went to stand on the other side of the pit. Yeah, the guy was afraid of spiders. An endearing thing that made the uber-strong man more human. More approachable.

"No kidding on being selective," Fritz said. "I had to wait weeks to find out if I was in."

"Not sure what your damage is, but I just applied on Monday." Buck cocked his head. "Got in right away."

"Me too," Ernie added. "Not Monday, but over the weekend."

"It took two weeks or so for me." Jamal stared blankly ahead as if bored.

"Same with me," she added so she didn't seem to be questioning others.

Looking darkly dangerous, Fritz lifted his chin and eyed Micha. "So what's the deal? Why'd mine take so long?"

Micha cleared his throat. "Most likely you don't have much of an online presence to get a complete picture on the background check, and we had to do more digging."

"Well, yeah, on the online stuff." Fritz crossed his arms. "That goes without saying. My life is my own to decide who gets to know about it. Not some big cheese search engine that's out to track my every move and leverage every bit of it into profits to fuel their greedy machines."

If attitude made a person in the group guilty, Fritz led the way, followed by Jamal. But one thing she'd learned. If the guys were telling the truth, she could eliminate Fritz. Garrett too. No way these men could possibly know she would be in this group when they applied. They'd sent in applications before Layne's mother died, and even Ava didn't know then that she would take the class.

That left Ernie, Buck, and Jamal as her top suspects.

Jamal topped her list. A gut feel, but she'd also heard him humming a few times. Not your usual pop song, but an obscure symphony. Told her he was into music.

"I was meaning to ask," she said. "When we get back to

our cabins, I'll want to play my bassoon at night. Would that bother anyone?"

Fritz wrinkled his forehead. "What in the world is a bassoon?"

"A woodwind instrument," Jamal said.

Fritz scoffed. "Like that makes it any clearer."

"Yeah," Garrett said. "Don't know a thing about instruments."

"It's an instrument played in a band or orchestra," she said. "Not a single reed, which is most common, but a double reed, to be exact."

"Single?" Fritz rubbed his chin. "Double? I don't get it."

And that also helped put him to the bottom of her suspect list. "It's kind of boring."

"Oh, I get it." Fritz jutted out his chin. "You think we're too dumb to get it."

She resisted sighing. "Not at all. Just trying to save you from boredom."

"I for one would like to hear it. So bore away." Ernie laughed.

"Okay, but remember you asked." She smiled. "So many woodwind instruments have a plastic or rubber mouthpiece to which a flat reed made from cane plants is affixed. This would be a single reed like for a clarinet or saxophone. But a double reed is just what it says. Two reeds strapped together. No plastic mouthpiece, but the reeds are placed on the instrument, and they vibrate against each other to form the sound. The oboe and bassoon are the most common double reed instruments."

"You're right." Fritz mimicked yawning. "Boring."

"Shut up, Fritz. She warned us." Ernie glared at him, then cast a softer gaze at Ava. "And you play the bassoon?"

She nodded. "It's the largest of the two—four and a half feet long—and plays really low, kind of haunting sounds."

"Low and haunting is right up my alley." Jamal smiled for the first time she'd seen. "I was a drummer in high school and know all about bassoons and bassoonists."

Hmm. Interesting comment. "Bassoonists?"

"Oh, come on." Jamal cocked his head. "Don't tell me you haven't heard about how musician's personalities fit the instrument they play."

"Well yeah, but—"

"But bassoonists are usually real killjoys." He smirked at her.

"Not all bassoonists." Why she felt a need to defend herself and her fellow bassoonists, she didn't know.

He flashed a cold smile. "You could be right, but I never met one yet who didn't bring the party down."

She should let it go, but she couldn't. "Is that what you think I'm doing now?"

"Well, it *is* boring. And who cares if you play your stupid bassoon as long as you know how to play it, and we don't suffer through the learning curve."

"I am pretty good, if I say so myself." She didn't brag on herself often, but she did excel in playing the bassoon. An odd skill, but one she was proud of, and she felt an irrational need for him to know that. Maybe from years of teasing about not having enough money to buy her own instrument and needing to use one belonging to the school.

"I'm not much of a music buff," Ernie said. "Don't know what a bassoon even is, but I go to bed early, so as long as you don't play after nine, I'm okay with it."

"I don't care either," Buck said. "At least I don't think I do. I like music just fine. Country's my thing, though. You can be sure once I hear the thing played, if it's gross, I'll let you know."

Ernie glanced at his watch. "Speaking of bedtime, it's about that time now. I'll say goodnight."

He got up, holding his back as he moved. This training was hard on everyone's body for sure.

"'Night, Ernie." She flashed him a smile as she'd come to like the older guy. Which meant he was probably the guilty party, as that was the way things went in life. But then, he said he didn't know much about music, and that would not put him at the top of her list.

Jamal still claimed that place due to his caustic attitude and knowledge of music. Garrett seemed in the dark on music, but Buck didn't make his skills clear, and she couldn't rule him out. Still, she'd made progress.

Question was, what did she do next?

She had to figure out if any of the men had a connection to Holly Boyle. She would have to handle that far more delicately. Something she would ponder once she was zipped into her tent alone. Then in the morning she would start questioning the men again.

She glanced around the firepit at them. Which one of them had left the song? She hadn't seen any of them near her backpack. Of course not. That would be too easy. Before they departed for the trip, she'd left the pack on the back of the utility vehicle for about five minutes while she'd taken a final bathroom break and then one time at the campsite to go to the latrine. Plenty of time to slip a note into the pocket.

She studied each face. She knew nothing about any of these men. Including Micha. Forget about someone hunting her for a moment, was she even safe in this situation? The only woman out in the wilderness with six men she didn't know. She should probably have considered that.

The company had a solid performance rating, and the staff underwent criminal background checks, including fingerprinting. Or at least that's what the website said. She had to trust that Micha was safe.

Still, she had to believe whichever of these men left the

note could also do her harm, and she would have to protect herself tonight. Her knife was in her pack in the tent, and she needed to start carrying it at all times. She had no qualms about using it if it meant saving her life. None at all.

"I'm turning in early like Ernie." She got up and stretched.

Purposefully not making eye contact with Micha, she nodded and headed for the tent. She had the zipper half open when footfalls sounded from behind. Without looking, she knew it was Micha. They'd been interrupted after she found the note, and he'd wanted to talk about it then. He came across as a tenacious guy, and she doubted he'd dropped his desire to discuss it.

"Before you go to sleep," he said, "I'd like to talk about the message you got."

Just as she'd thought. She pivoted. "It really has been a long day, and I need my sleep. Can't it wait until morning?"

Which she would put off then, too, but he didn't need to know that.

"You could be in danger, and I won't sleep until I know you're taking it seriously."

"You don't know that."

"And you don't know you're safe." He arched a dark eyebrow. "But I'm assuming you do know whoever left the note has to be in our group."

She eyed him. "Or someone who works at Shadow Lake Survival."

"You think *I* did it?" He shoved his hands into the pockets of his cargo pants. "Unbelievable."

"Could be someone else on the team."

"None of the guys would leave something like that."

"You can't be certain."

"Of course I can." He jerked his hands from his pockets

and crossed his powerful arms. "I know these men. They would never scare a helpless female, no matter what."

"I'm not helpless."

"Defenseless then."

"Not that either. I took karate for years and can hold my own."

He widened his stance. "Ever been in a real fight and put those skills to a test?"

"No, but—"

"But you don't know how you will handle yourself." He ran a hand over his head. "I don't want to get in your business. Trust me. I don't. But I have to make sure you stay safe. That's my job, and I'll do it with or without your help."

Oh, wow. He was fierce when pushed. She liked it as much as it scared her.

"Point taken. Now if you'll excuse me, I'm going to bed." She slipped into her tent before he could stop her.

"This discussion isn't over," he said before she tugged the zipper closed.

She scrambled over to her sleeping bag and crawled in, shoes and all, in case she had to flee. After grabbing her knife from the front pocket of her pack, she settled into the bag. She clutched the knife tightly in her hand and closed her eyes.

She must have dozed off as a noise coming from outside her tent woke her. The sound of someone talking at a close distance drifted through the nylon wall, so quiet she doubted it was what had broken through her sleep. She couldn't make out the words, but she was sure it was Micha's voice. She couldn't hear the other half of the conversation at all. Either he was talking to himself or the person he talked to was extremely soft-spoken. Or maybe he was on the phone.

He stopped talking. Silence reigned. Had he finished?

Moved away? Was coming for her? She really didn't believe that. She'd gotten to know him enough to believe he was a good guy, but maybe the person he'd been talking to wasn't.

She clutched her knife. She'd pitched her tent off to the side of the camp away from the men. From help if she needed it. Why had she thought segregating her tent from the others was a good idea?

The noise. The sound that must've woken her broke the silence again. A scratching, gritty sound on the fabric of her tent. On the side. She scrambled out of her bag. Moved to the back wall. Clasped her knife even tighter.

A great weapon. But it was only good if an attacker got within arm's range. Depending on the person's size and fitness, they could overpower her that close.

Footsteps moved closer. Lumbering like a man. Big hulking shadows lurked over her. Darkening her tent.

Please, Father. Please don't let him hurt me.

Micha heard it. Someone moving outside. Could be one of the guys headed for the latrine. Or could be someone intent on hurting Kari. He slid silently out of his sleeping bag. Unfortunately, he couldn't open the tent zipper without making noise and might alert the person on the move.

He lifted it. Inch by inch. High enough to shimmy under. On his belly. Eating the dust. Moving noiselessly. He cleared the tent and rose to his knees to assess. The moon lodged behind thick clouds, bathing the area in inky darkness. He saw no one but had to get closer to be sure.

He eased behind the tents and crept through the night. Kept his ears open for any sound coming from Kari's tent. He'd been out here not more than a few minutes ago, talking to his teammate Colin on his SAT phone. Nothing was wrong then.

A flash of something near the rear. A person? A branch from the mighty Douglas Fir towering over her tent?

He had to move faster. He picked up speed. Gripped the butt of his sidearm. Ready to draw. To take out a foe if needed. He gulped in a breath. Held it.

He crossed the mouth of the path leading to the latrines. Step-by-step closer to his target.

The moon broke free, washing the area in pale light. Good for seeing what was going on. Bad for cover. He spun to the backside of a giant tree, thankful he also carried his backup weapon in an ankle holster.

Jamal stumbled out from behind Kari's tent. Glanced around. Started across the campsite toward his tent.

Micha stepped out. "What are you up to, Jamal?"

He spun, his mouth hanging open. "Oh, hey, man. Had to take a leak and got turned around in the dark."

Really? "That's why we each brought a headlamp like the one on your head."

"Didn't turn it on. Thought I'd try it old school." He grimaced. "You know. Like what would happen if I got stranded and didn't have anything for light? Could I do it? Guess I got my answer."

Micha wasn't sure he bought this guy's response, but he couldn't prove he was up to no good.

The zipper on Kari's tent rose.

Micha spun, hand to his sidearm.

She slipped out, knife in hand, her expression tight in a band of moonlight. "What's going on?"

Jamal rubbed a hand over his face. "I got lost on my way back from the latrine."

"He was behind your tent," Micha stated plainly.

43

She shuddered and eyed Jamal. "What were you doing there?"

"I was coming back from the latrine, but the moon wasn't out. Lost my way. When I saw the tent, I knew I was back. I was about to go to my tent when this guy came out from behind a tree." Jamal tipped his head at Micha. "Maybe the real question is why is he skulking around the area?"

Ah, deflect the issue on Micha. A solid method to hide guilt.

"Not skulking," Micha said and tried not to sound bothered at this guy's insinuation. "I heard a noise and was keeping an eye out for the safety of my clients."

"Well, your clients don't have to worry about anything from me." He yawned. "I'm gonna hit the hay again. See you at O dark thirty." He chuckled and strode toward his tent.

Micha turned to Kari. "You look worried."

"He was by my tent far too long for simply finding his way back."

"So you knew he was there?"

"I heard him. He touched the fabric several times. On several sides. So he was circling the tent. Not sure why." She lifted her knife. "Had this at the ready. I could've defended myself or cut a hole in my tent and escaped."

He frowned. "I hate that you were put in that position. I won't let it happen again."

She planted a hand on a curvy hip. "How can you stop it?"

"I'll be bedding down outside your tent."

"You won't get any sleep that way."

"Don't worry about me. Won't be the first time I missed a little sleep."

"It's not necessary." She lifted her chin. "Not at all."

"It is for my peace of mind." He held up a hand. "You won't change my mind, so let's move on."

"Fine." She didn't sound happy about it. "I'm going to try to get more sleep."

He took a few steps closer and lowered his voice in case anyone was listening. "You can't keep avoiding telling me the truth about the message in your backpack."

She just raised an eyebrow and watched him.

"What are you not telling me?" he asked.

"Nothing. Now if you'll excuse me, I'm going to stop at the latrine and then get some shuteye." She marched down the path toward the women's latrine that she'd dug for herself.

He couldn't very well follow her. Maybe getting away from him was her real reason for going.

He gritted his teeth and stood sentry. Time ticked by. Minute by painful minute.

One. Two. Three.

A cry of distress pierced the night.

Kari!

He spun and ran down the path. Privacy or not, he was going in.

Please don't let Kari be hurt. Or worse...

5

Ava had hit the ground hard, and her knife went flying. She rolled in the path to search for it and gulped in air to stem the residual fear. Two things had happened all at once. She'd caught her foot in a pothole, only to fall flat on her face. Not the biggest problem though. The real problem was a loud snap and then something whizzed through the air above her.

No way an object would randomly fly overhead with such force. Had to be from a trap or something like it. With this path leading to the women's latrine and her being the only woman, the item had to be meant for her. The object designed to hit her. To take her out. Or to seriously injure her. Thankfully she'd tripped first.

She shuddered, and her whole body vibrated with fear, but she continued to brush across the dirt until she touched the cold steel of her knife. She scooped it up and flipped over in time to see a heavy cloud dart in front of the moon.

Why had she gone storming off without a light? Because that man, that infuriating man, kept prodding, and she couldn't keep her secret from him much longer. Maybe it was time to tell him.

"Kari?" he called out from down the path. "Where are you?"

"Here." She was shaking and terrified and had to admit to being glad he was coming to find her. But what would happen when he started questioning her again? Would she be glad then?

He wore his headlamp and came charging down the path, the piercing light bouncing and swaying as he kept a watchful eye on his surroundings while he moved.

He reached her. "Are you okay?"

Was she? She hadn't even taken inventory. "I think so. I caught my foot in a pothole and hit the ground."

He glanced over his shoulder then looked down. "Where'd that rock in the path come from?"

"Above."

"Above?" His head flashed up, and his light traveled the area. Through the trees. To the side. Over the hard-packed ground littered with pine needles. The bright beam landed on several pieces of carved wood lying by the path. Hidden under a Hosta.

"A catapult." He charged to the spot where his light had settled.

She joined him and pointed at the pothole. "That's where I fell."

He squatted and shone his light on a thin wire. "Trigger point was set here. If you wouldn't have fallen you would've hit this while walking. That rock would've taken you out. Instead, your foot must've caught and triggered it when you fell."

The confirmation of her thoughts left her knees weak. "It flew over me. I heard it."

He swiveled but didn't stand. His light landed on the rock again. He let out a low whistle. "That would've done some serious damage."

She braced her legs to keep from melting into a puddle on the ground. Someone was actually trying to kill her. Or at the very least hurt her. Unless she shared her secret with Micha, she was all alone. On her own to make sure she stayed safe.

She glanced at him. At his rigid posture and his equally tight expression in the moonlight.

This incident stressed him out. Big time. He was a capable guy, but she knew he must've seen the things man did to man in his prior job. Knew the real danger she was in.

Had she been underestimating the risk to her safety? Underestimating her abilities to keep herself safe? Alive?

Yes. An emphatic yes! She couldn't handle this on her own. She needed help.

He glanced down the path. "We need to keep an eye out in case you woke the others when you cried out. I don't want them to see this."

"Understood." She sank onto the cold ground. Looked at him.

He ran an assessing gaze over her. "What do you know about this?"

So, so much, but where to start? Just blurt it out before you chicken out. "My name isn't Kari Curtis. It's Ava Weston."

He drew in a sharp breath and shot a look toward the campsite. Maybe he was checking to see if anyone would come in search after her noisy fall, or more likely, he couldn't stand to look at her.

At least they were in the dark .She didn't want to see his eyes. She knew they would hold disappointment—maybe hurt—over her lies. But that was the easy part. Her next reveal? That would elicit revulsion, and he would likely turn her in to the law.

"I'm wanted for murder in Portland," she said the words before she chickened out.

That breath? Sharper still. His body unmoving, save his fingers clenching and unclenching.

"I didn't do it," she rushed on. "But there's a video that makes it look like I did."

"Who?" he asked, his tone flat and emotionless. "Who did you *supposedly* kill?"

She didn't like how he'd emphasized the word, but at least he was speaking to her. "A woman in my care at a hospice care center. Her name was Holly Boyle. Her son Layne located a security video that makes it look like I poisoned her. He told me to turn myself in within three days or he would kill me. I think he's behind tonight's attack."

"Not likely." Micha looked back down the path. "I doubt he got onto our property unseen. More likely he had one of these guys working with him. Do you think that's what's going on?"

She shrugged.

He dropped to the ground facing the path to the campsite and stretched his long legs in front of him. "That's the only logical explanation. Unless he tracked you to the compound. He couldn't get into the fenced area, but the property out here isn't secured. It's possible he tracked us, though as I said, I doubt it. One of the guys here could've hidden a phone and told him our location."

She knew hiding a phone was entirely possible as she was guilty of doing the same thing. "You're sure about the compound?"

"Absolutely. The secured area is covered by cameras, and Reid would've gotten an alert for any breach of the perimeter. Which he didn't. So no one got in to put the note in your backpack at the cabins. If you're sure it wasn't in there when you arrived at the compound, then one of these guys had to have done it."

"I'm sure it wasn't there when I packed my bag for the trip." She shared the two times the pack was out of her sight.

He didn't speak for a while, then looked at her, his light landing on her face. "Has this Layne guy communicated with songs before today?"

"No."

"He into music?"

"His mother was a concert pianist. One of the reasons we had so much in common." Ava closed her eyes so she wouldn't cry over the loss of the dear woman who she didn't even get to say goodbye to. "Holly said she gave him piano lessons, and he tried to learn the trumpet but had no real interest in either one and dropped out right away."

"That's odd then," he said. "Why suddenly change his communication to include a song?"

"I don't know. Maybe to keep others around me from seeing this was a real threat and wouldn't be inclined to help me?"

"Except I didn't buy that explanation when you gave it." He looked at her long and hard. "Or could someone else be threatening you, and it's not about Holly at all."

Could someone else have a vendetta against her? She ran through the song lyrics again. "No. The song tells me to turn myself in. I have nothing else I need to turn myself in for."

And right now she had an even bigger question to worry about. "Are you going to turn me in?"

He didn't answer but continued to study her. "Tell me about this evidence in the video."

Could this answer mean he might not report her? *No. Don't let hope build. Not yet.*

Maybe her story would sway him in her direction. She made sure not to look away and appear guilty even though the concentrated light left her feeling like a suspect being grilled. "One of Holly's favorite things to eat was raw cookie dough. Of course they wouldn't give that to her at the care center. Raw eggs and all. I shouldn't have either, but she hadn't been eating much. I thought she might've given up even though the doctors said she had at least two more months to live."

Ava shuddered over the memory and looked up at the night sky to go on without crying. "She had to check into the center because Layne refused to care for her. She said her parents were both dead, and she had no one other than Layne. Her heart was broken, and I wanted to brighten her day. Maybe get her to eat something. So on my day off, I made a batch of dough and brought it to her. Even if she only got a teaspoon down, I hoped it would put a smile on her face and get her to eat something else. One of the cameras caught me giving the container to her and her eating the dough. She barely took a nibble, but she got really sick after that. Like food poisoning sick. This was right before she died."

He tilted his head. "What did the coroner list as cause of death?"

"Dehydration and organ failure likely from food poisoning, though they didn't confirm that last bit."

"Do you think it was the cookie dough?"

She shook her head. "Not with the little bit that she ate. But if I'm wrong and the dough caused the food poisoning, it wasn't intentional. I didn't poison her like her son is saying I did."

"Did they take her to the hospital?"

"No," Ava said. "The care center had everything needed to take care of her, and even if we didn't, she would have refused to go. She said, why spend her end days in such a sterile environment when the hospice center was more homey."

Micha's frown deepened. "Why do you think the son has it out for you?"

This was the part she didn't want to tell him, but she had to. "Holly changed her will to include me."

Micha sat forward and stared at her.

"I had no idea she would do something like that. None. Not until Holly told me. Layne was supposed to inherit her entire estate, which she hinted at being substantial, but she left half of it to him and the other half to me. She said I deserved it more than Layne. I don't even want it and would gladly sign it over to him. I tried to tell him that, but he blew me off. Saying I was lying."

"I told you I worked criminal investigations in the military, right?"

She nodded.

"If I was the local detective assigned to this investigation and this information was presented to me, I would have secured an arrest warrant for you, and you would be sitting behind bars."

Her turn to suck in a breath.

"I'm just telling you like it is."

"I appreciate that, but you didn't say if you planned to turn me in."

"What I'll do is sleep on it and give you a decision in the morning." He stood and offered his hand to help her up, but kept his gaze locked on her. "What I don't understand is why you're taking this course."

That she didn't mind answering except for disclosing the location. "My cousin left an old cabin to me. There's no online connection to me and no way anyone would track it to me. It's a primitive place out in the middle of nowhere. He used it for hunting and fishing. I needed to learn how to live off-grid so I could hide out there for as long as it took for the truth to come out."

He rested his hands on his waist. "Where's this place located?"

"About thirty minutes from here," she said, purposefully being vague.

"And the property address?"

Right. She was coming to see he was a detailed guy— probably a great investigator—and he would ask that. She didn't know what he might do with the information, but she had to be forthcoming if she wanted him to take her side and not report her. But she couldn't get the words out. "Why do you need to know?"

He turned that light on her again. "So if you decide to bail tonight, I know where to find you."

She held her tongue for a moment as she squinted into the light. Fine. She had to say it. Be all in for him to trust her. But that meant her fallback plan was gone, too, and her life truly was in his hands. She shared the address.

He gave a sharp nod. "No point in trying to run. I'll be sleeping outside your tent. Not only to protect you, but to be sure you don't try to take off."

"I wouldn't."

He met her gaze. "See that you don't. But if you don't heed my warning, just know I'll hunt you down and turn you in."

"I won't run." She fled the area, hurrying down the path to her tent. She ripped up the zipper and dropped onto her sleeping bag. Pulling up her legs, she wrapped her arms around them. This man terrified her, yet at the same time, his strength and convictions exhilarated her.

No matter her feelings about him, her future was in his hands.

He would do the right thing in the end, she suspected. Meaning this could be her last few hours of freedom.

Micha shifted on his sleeping bag. The sun filtered a reddish light at the horizon. Forecasters predicted a beautiful day, but would it be? He still didn't know yet. Didn't know what he planned to do about that woman just on the other side of a thin nylon wall, his thoughts fixed on her for hours.

He hadn't slept the rest of the night and was tired. Maybe cranky. He'd been more tired in the past, and he would try not to let his fatigue factor into his decision making. But this monumental decision was weighing on him. Heavy. A woman's potential freedom depended on him.

He also couldn't let his attraction to her factor in the decision, but how did he pull that out of the equation? He liked her. More than that. Would like to get to know her. He thought she liked him, too. Ditto on getting to know him if she wasn't running from the law.

"Hah!" How had his life come to the point where he was considering dating a woman who was wanted by the law? Plain craziness. He was as straight as the proverbial arrow when it came to the law. He'd worked too many years upholding and enforcing it to suddenly change, hadn't he?

But he believed her story. Believed the cookie dough wasn't meant to kill but to bring joy to a dying woman. Maybe a badly misplaced idea, but one done out of love.

Still, accidental death or not, he could see charges being brought for involuntary manslaughter, and she would not only serve time, she would never practice as a nurse again.

And if she ran? She couldn't practice as a nurse then either. So at least he wouldn't be ruining that part of her life.

Movement sounded from inside her tent, and the zipper came up, the ripping sound ringing through the morning quiet. She stepped out carrying a toiletry bag.

She flashed her gaze to him.

The vulnerability he saw there cut him to the core. He couldn't be responsible for sending her to prison for something she'd intended for this woman's good. But what if the dough hadn't killed this woman? What if someone wanted to murder her? Her son, maybe. He didn't know if the police would look into things or just assume she was guilty, and he couldn't let a woman's potential murder go unsolved either.

He stood. Looked her in the eye. "If you promise to stick by my side, I won't turn you in."

"You won't?" Tears glistened in her eyes.

"No, but you stay with me so I can make sure you're safe. And we get my team involved in investigating Holly's death to see if it might've been the cookie dough or if someone else wanted to end her life."

She swiped her free hand over her eyes. "You think they'll agree to that?"

"I can convince them to help. But if we do our very best and don't turn up another viable explanation for her death, then you'll agree to turn yourself in."

She nibbled on her lip. A very kissable lip.

Stop thinking that way. Will only get yourself in trouble, especially if this thing goes south.

He held out his hand. "I think of a handshake as a verbal contract, so shake on it."

She clasped his hand. He expected touching her to set fire to his emotions. It did, but not in the way he expected. The icy cold fingers spoke to her fear, and the touch raised a chill instead.

"We should find a secluded place to talk about our next investigative steps, and I can get my team working on it."

"But we'll stay out here at the campsite?"

"For now. I don't like it, but I have an obligation to finish the class. That said, I'll see if one of the other guys can take over for me."

"Thank you, Micha." She rested a hand on his forearm. "I mean it. You can't imagine how relieved I am."

"Since we're both up early, we should take advantage of the time alone and plan."

"Okay." She dropped her bag into her tent and grabbed a down vest. "I guess I can clean up afterward."

Did she really think cleaning up was more important than staying free? Surely not. Maybe he was placing too much emphasis on the disappointment expressed in her *I guess* part.

He glanced at his tent. "I need to grab something. Come with me and then we can go look at that catapult to see if we can get a lead on who might've placed it there."

They crossed to the other side of the campsite to where he'd pitched his tent yesterday to be as far away from her as possible. *Hah!* Yesterday he hadn't wanted the temptation she presented for him, and he'd just ensured she'd be glued to his side for the foreseeable future.

Help me to do the right thing at all times. Please.

He dug the SAT phone from his pack and shoved it into one of his cargo pockets, then went back to Kari. No Ava. *Ava.* He hadn't even given her real name much thought. Would be hard to start thinking of her that way, but Ava fit her better. More regal sounding. Less casual.

"After you." He pointed at the path to her latrine.

She led the way, moving at a fast clip. Her cargo pants appeared to be new and a blue turtleneck clung to her every curve. Thankfully it was a chilly morning, and she'd slipped into her vest and zipped it to her neck. Too bad she hadn't put it on before he'd seen the curves.

Didn't matter. The moment they reached the catapult area, all thoughts of Ava as a woman fled from his brain. Well, except for thinking of her as a vulnerable woman who needed his protection.

Facing the trail in case anyone followed, he crouched and studied the catapult. "Whoever built this knew what they were doing. Had to be made in advance as these don't look like scavenged pieces."

Ava squatted next to him. "Jamal and Buck said they'd attended several of these survival sessions. Maybe they learned how to make a catapult there."

"It can be used in hunting to bring down an animal, so it's possible, I suppose." He pointed at a boot print in the mud. "Fresh and definitely not your size."

"Not at all." She leaned closer to it. "Could be from Jamal. Maybe this is why he was wandering around last night, because he set this up."

"Could be."

She stared at the wood. "Too bad we don't have phones to take a picture of it."

"I got it covered." He retrieved his phone and snapped several pictures.

She blinked at him. "You said phones were off limits."

"They are for class participants, but I need one for safety reasons. What if one of you got injured, and we needed urgent medical assistance?"

"Good point."

"But I don't let anyone know I have it, or they'd ask to use it, which defeats the purpose of the no phone policy." He checked the quality of his pictures and considered other places a catapult might show up other than as a hunting device. "Catapults were often used in medieval times and could be used today in Live Action Role Playing. Anyone mention being into that?"

"I don't know if anyone is into LARPING." She tapped her chin. "We could subtly question them."

"Like you did last night at the fire?" Satisfied with the photo detail, he shoved the phone into his pocket.

"Guess I wasn't so subtle if you caught on."

"No, you did a good job. The others didn't seem suspicious at all, but my years in investigations make me more attuned to what's going on around me."

"I could see that. Which is why you knew I wasn't being honest with you."

"Exactly."

"I'm sorry about that. I'm not one to lie. I just..." She looked away, but not before he caught the pain in her expression.

He couldn't let that sway him. "You should know the first thing I'll do is have our IT expert do a deep dive on your real name. If there's anything you need to tell me, now would be the time to do it."

"There's nothing. I'm really a boring person. Work and home. Some social events, but that's pretty much it."

"No boyfriend? Someone you're dating?" Now why did he have to go and ask that?

"No one right now, but if we can prove my innocence, I do hope to find the right guy someday and get married. I especially want to have kids."

He did too, and he wanted to find the right woman. But not at this time in his life, which was even more reason to ignore his interest in her. "So at breakfast you could bring up hobbies. If we have a LARPer, he might mention it."

"Or not. I've worked with a few guys into LARPing. I think other people don't understand it, and my coworkers were hesitant to mention their involvement."

"I could see that. It's kind of dress up for adults and not something others might take seriously."

"Still, I'll do my best to learn more about each person today."

He nodded. "We'll be finding sources of food, along with hunting and trapping today."

"Hunting." She shivered. "The part I've been dreading, but I know it's necessary."

"It is. You need protein, but you can get protein from beans. It just takes time to grow and harvest them. I'll also discuss gardening and preserving produce. Necessary for sure, but especially if you decide to go vegan or vegetarian."

"I honestly don't know the difference," she said, though if she wasn't able to stomach hunting she wouldn't be eating any meat.

"Vegetarians might eat eggs and fish, but vegans don't usually eat any animals or food products that come from them."

"I could never live without cheese for a long time. I think I'm part mouse." She grinned.

He chuckled and liked that she could find some humor in all the stress. He took his phone from his pocket. "I want to grab a picture of Layne from the internet if I can find one so I know what to keep an eye out for."

"That's easy. A tall, buff guy. Blond buzz cut and startling blue eyes."

"Sounds like a lot of guys, but it's a start. I'll also call Colin now to do that background on your name and get deeper backgrounds going on everyone here. I'll ask him to specifically look for a link to Layne and Holly Boyle."

"Thank you."

He stood. "We need to get a hold of the autopsy report, and the hospice care center security feed, too, which I assume the police don't have or Layne couldn't be threatening you with it."

She got up, too. "He probably turned it over to the police after I took off, and now they're looking for me too."

He nodded. "We'll try to get the police report and figure out if he turned it in, then plan accordingly."

"Once you know for certain that I'm a fugitive, you can't

hide me, right? You'd be guilty of harboring me. I can't let that happen."

"Let me worry about that. I'll deal with it if we learn an arrest warrant has been issued."

"If you want a copy of the security footage, Layne sent it to me. It's on the phone I surrendered to you at the compound."

"Good. I'll want Colin to look at it to see if it's been altered. And of course, I'll want to study it too. But we should still try to get the original from the facility to confirm it's complete and hasn't been changed." He held out his phone. "Now I need you to stand watch down the trail a bit. Stay within eyesight. If anyone heads my way, give me a shout-out so I can end my call."

She gave a quick nod and marched off.

He kept his focus on her and dialed Reid.

"Problem at camp?" Reid asked.

"Yeah." Micha shared the situation. "I wanted to ask if someone could relieve me, and I could bring Ava back inside the secured compound for safety."

Reid hissed out a breath. "Let me grab the schedule."

"And can you have someone other than Colin do it? I hoped you'd let him do some investigating for me."

"If I can work the schedule out that way, you got it. Now let's see what we have here." Reid went silent.

Micha imagined him sitting in the lodge office behind the big rolltop desk that once belonged to his dad. The Maddox brothers had grown up in the lodge, and their parents had remained there until recently, when they moved into town. Reid now lived there with his daughter Jessie, his wife Megan and her daughter Ella, plus Poppy their cook, who'd been with the family since Reid was a kid. She was like family, as were all the team members, all adopted by

Barbie, mother to the Maddox boys and a throwback hippie with love for all.

"Okay," Reid said. "I can get Ryan up there after the training he's conducting this morning. That is, if I can pry him away from Austin for a few days." He laughed.

Ryan was a devoted father to his baby boy, but he was also a team player, and Micha believed he would say yes.

"When you get back here, I'd like to talk to Ava," Reid said. "Sounds like her assailant knows where she is, and we'll need to gather the team to brainstorm safety protocols. And I'm assuming you won't only have Colin do a deep dive on everyone involved, but you'll be running a full-blown investigation yourself."

"Colin's already started, and I'd like the team's help on the investigation if you can swing it."

Reid didn't reply right away. "What's your take on this? You believe she's innocent?"

"I do."

"You're a great judge of character—might even do a better job than most of us—but I've been picking up on a vibe that says you have a thing for this woman."

Micha's first instinct was to deny it, but he sure didn't like being lied to, as Ava's recent actions confirmed, and he tried never to tell a lie himself. There were times he had to omit things on the job, but this wasn't one of those times. "I admit it, but it's not a big deal and isn't swaying my opinion. I promise."

"If that changes, be sure you tell me. Until then I trust you have this in hand, and I'll figure out how to find time in our schedule to keep the business moving forward and help her get her life back."

Micha appreciated his boss's confidence in him. "I'll collect the pieces from the catapult for evidence processing. If you can pull some strings and get it on the Veritas Center's schedule, I'll drive the evidence up to Portland overnight and be back before the morning. I'm glad to pay for the work, too."

"I might be able to do you one better. I've got a former agent friend who works at Blackwell Tactical in Cold Harbor. They have a chopper and make regular flights to Portland. Maybe we can get the evidence on one of those flights."

"I'd appreciate that," Micha said, and he would. Cold Harbor was only an hour away, which would be a much shorter drive than the three-hour one-way trip to Portland. "Call me as soon as you know if Ryan can make it. If I don't answer, I'm with a client and please leave a message."

"Will do, and you keep your head on a swivel out there."

"Always do." Micha ended the call and silenced the phone. When Reid's call came in he didn't want anyone to hear the ring.

He shoved the phone into his pocket and joined Ava, who was pacing the trail.

She cast a hope-filled look his way. "Can they send someone to replace you?"

"Likely Ryan. But he has a young baby and will need to arrange to leave his family for a few days. Reid will get back to me with a final answer."

She frowned. "I hate taking Ryan away from his family."

Micha waved a hand. "No worries. We take turns teaching this session. I'll take the class for him when his name comes up in the rotation again."

"I wish I could help too."

"You can by listening to me and staying safe. That, more than anything, will be a big help."

"Of course."

"Now I want to get back to the camp for a plastic garbage

bag to pick up the catapult and take it to a lab for forensic testing."

"Oh, wow. Yeah. Very CSI of you." She gave a nervous laugh.

"CSI, huh? Don't tell me you're one of those people who watch TV crime shows." He started down the path and waited for her to move into place by his side.

"Guilty, but why?" She blinked those thick eyelashes up at him. "Is it bad?"

"They don't exactly follow law enforcement protocol, and a lot of the forensic science they use doesn't exist—very futuristic that real law enforcement labs could only dream of employing."

"Makes for good TV though."

"I suppose it does. I just can't get past the inaccuracies." He fell silent, and as they approached the camp where the others were up and sitting around the fire with coffee in hand, he stopped to look at her. "You'll have to keep going by Kari until we leave here. We don't want to raise any suspicions."

She frowned at that. Too bad, he wouldn't change his mind. He could be flexible on some things, but this was too important.

"When will you tell them we're leaving?" she asked.

"Not until right before we depart. That will keep the questions to a minimum." He ran a hand through his hair. The strands were going every which way, making him think he had a bad case of bedhead. "I'll say you have a medical complication and have to go back to base, but that you hope to return tomorrow. That way if we do have someone in our group working with Layne, he'll stay put and not try to accompany us."

"Sounds like a solid plan." She drew in a long breath

and let it out. "What about a cover story for why we were out here?"

Yeah, what about that? "We don't have anything with us, so we can't say fishing. Or gathering berries. We don't have any, and when we go foraging after breakfast, we could locate some, and I would look incompetent for missing them."

"Then one-on-one training in something?"

"Sure. I can say I helped you identify trees and shrubs that might work better for fire-starting. But I warn you, they might see through that and think we're trying to cover a romantic thing developing between us and wanted to get away."

She shrugged. "I can handle that if you can."

"It might come across as unprofessional, which I don't like, but it can't be helped. We don't have any other good reason for being out here together. Especially when we come back from your latrine area where I shouldn't have a reason to go."

She gave a firm nod. "Then we'll go with the trees. But on the way, fill me in on what you might've told me."

"Glad to." He started naming trees and only hoped she would remember them. He didn't like coming across as unprofessional for any reason, but when it came to keeping her alive, he would compromise his needs and so much more.

6

The sun battled with clouds to break free. Ava sat near the still-roaring campfire while Micha led a first-aid training session. As a nurse, she didn't really need the session, but it never hurt to have a refresher. Especially when it came to wilderness survival. She'd like to say she was paying full attention to him, but she kept checking the trail for Ryan's arrival. He should be there any minute, and she was both looking forward to seeing him walk up the trail and dreading it.

Dreading, because Micha was right. The others had snickered when they explained where they'd been. Now, when she left with him, that would raise all kinds of questions. Still, she doubted she would be finishing out this week with her classmates.

But she also was looking forward to Ryan getting there so she could leave whoever was trying to hurt her behind. She'd been trying to catch a glimpse at boot patterns whenever a guy lifted his foot, but so far she didn't see one that resembled the print they'd spotted on the trail. She'd especially focused on Jamal as his late-night wandering put him at the top of her list.

Micha clapped his hands, the sound reverberating through the trees and sending birds in flight. "Let's take a quick break. Hit the latrines. Get some water. Then we'll finish up."

"How long until we actually do something?" Buck asked. "I mean this is good stuff, but man, a guy can only sit around so long."

"You like to stay active?" Ava asked, hoping to get him to tell her the brand of his boots.

"Like? Not sure that's the word for it, but I'm used to being on the go. Off-grid lifestyles guarantee that if you want to have food, water, and decent shelter."

"I was wondering." She looked at Micha. "Do you plan to talk about good brands of clothes and boots to purchase for off-grid living?"

Micha shook his head. "Not something we cover here. Maybe the guys here who are already living the lifestyle could share with you."

Buck lifted his boot. "No hikers for me. Steel-toe work boots all the way. These babies are Redwing. Won't wear anything but American-made, and they're made in Red Wing, Minnesota, where I grew up."

Jamal lifted his boot and swiveled it. "I prefer hikers because I do a lot of hiking for the fun of it. These are Lowa Camino, but I have a pair of Jim Greens in the tent. I like to let my boots dry out each day."

"I checked out the Lowa's, but they're way out of my league for price," Ernie said. "Went with a store brand from a discount store."

"If you really do go off-grid and wear them every day," Buck said, "you'll probably regret getting the cheapies."

"You could be right," Ernie said. "For now I'll stick with these. If the wife agrees to leave her creature comforts and move to my cabin with me, I might change my mind."

"Enough talk about boots." Fritz picked a hunk of wood from the stump he sat on and shredded it. "We all have our favorites, and you'll figure it out. Same with clothing. What fits, is comfortable and affordable is my motto. If that's not enough advice, maybe you could get some more extra tutoring from the big cheese here." He smirked.

Micha opened his mouth to speak but then must've reconsidered and snapped it closed.

"I have an odd question," she said to draw attention to herself. "Anyone here involved in LARPing?"

"LARPing." Buck stared wild-eyed at her. "Who in their right mind wants to play dress-up at our age?"

"I don't even know what it is," Ernie muttered as if embarrassed that he wasn't in the know.

"Live Action Role Playing," Ava said. "The participant physically portrays a character in a group. They wear costumes and use props."

"So it *is* dress-up then," Ernie said. "Sounds fun."

"I thought so, too," she said. "And figured it might be something inexpensive I could get involved in when I move off-grid."

"I do a medieval combat one." Jamal lifted his chin, issuing a challenge at Buck. "But I live close enough to go to Portland and doubt you'll find anything out in a rural area."

"Combat?" Buck sat forward. "Maybe I'm missing out on something. Wouldn't mind getting into a few battles."

"We use foam swords, and you seem more bloodthirsty than that." Jamal laughed.

Buck raised an eyebrow. "Do people get hurt?"

"Sometimes."

"Then I might be down for it. Who's in charge of the group?"

"Guy's name is Phoenix Preston."

Buck scoffed. "Seriously, is that his real name?"

"Yep."

Buck shook his head. "No wonder he does weird stuff like LARPing. Must've been teased like crazy as a kid."

They were getting off track here, and Ava needed to reign them back in. "Do you use medieval weapons other than foam swords, Jamal?"

"We don't use anything dangerous." He looked over her shoulder as if ending the subject.

So Jamal had another factor to move him up the suspect list, but then, with Buck's eagerness to engage in combat, that could put a checkmark in his suspect column, too.

She couldn't very well come out and ask about a catapult without alerting the one who set it. Besides, Ryan rounded the corner and stepped into camp, taking everyone's attention. She kept an eye on the suspects to see their reaction.

Jamal startled and sat back, his gaze assessing. Buck didn't move but raised an eyebrow as he watched Ryan. Ernie shifted and ran his gaze over Ryan as did Garrett and Fritz, but they didn't seem to be worried about a stranger arriving in camp.

"Meet Ryan Maddox, one of the Shadow Lake Survival owners," Micha said as Ryan joined him at the campfire. "Give me a second to talk to him, and then we'll get back to it."

Jamal stabbed a toe into the dirt and watched the cloud of dust rise up. "Hey, maybe he can answer my website question."

"You can ask him when we get back." Micha walked away, and Ryan followed him down the path that led to the men's latrine.

"Wonder what he's doing here," Buck said, his eyes narrowed. "Must be some sort of problem to bring him all the way out here."

"Or he's just here to do some of the training," Ernie said.

"If you'll excuse me." Ava stood before they asked her any direct questions. "I need to hit the facilities."

"Like there are any facilities here." Fritz shook his head. "We might be living off-grid, but the latrine way of life is really off-off-grid."

Ernie rolled his eyes. "I for one am thankful to learn how to have a proper latrine to stop the spread of disease."

She left them discussing latrines and slipped away, hurrying down her segregated trail into the forested area. She reached the catapult area and cringed at the sight. But she couldn't afford to get distracted now, so she moved on, exiting the trail and plunging into the deep shade of the thick evergreens.

She circled back, easing over needles and leaves, hoping she wouldn't get lost in this small area before she found the guys. Voices filtered through the air, and she followed the sound, until she spotted Micha and Ryan deep in conversation on the trail.

Micha caught sight of her and raised a brow. She couldn't tell if he was glad or mad to see her.

Ryan watched her approach, his expression sardonic. "So it's Ava, is it?"

Her face colored at his tone. "Yes, sorry for misleading you."

"A little more than misleading, but hey, I get it." He cracked a slight smile.

"Thank you for understanding," she said and resisted fanning away the burning heat on her face and only drawing more attention to her embarrassment.

"Micha was just filling me in on leads, and he said you got several of the guys to tell you about their boot brands. That along with the pictures he took should help the staff at Veritas narrow down the boot style."

Micha's gaze flashed to Ryan. "You got them on board to process our evidence?"

"Reid did. They'll expedite your catapult, and you can give them the boot print pictures, too."

"That's wonderful," Ava said. "Your team's connections will really help, won't they?"

"Let's hope so," Micha said. "But don't get too excited yet. The person who built the catapult could've worn gloves. And there's no way we can afford to get a Veritas staff member up here to process the area and look for additional evidence."

"True that," Ryan said. "But the catapult and boot print are a good start. And we should grab the rock, too."

"Already done."

"Figured you'd have taken it. Some investigators think you can't get prints off such rough surfaces, but Sierra isn't just any forensic tech, as you'll see when you meet her." Ryan looked between her and Micha. "I'll keep an eye on these guys for the next few days. Might learn something else helpful."

"Be careful," she said. "This person could be dangerous."

"Ryan can handle himself." Micha laid a hand on Ryan's shoulder. "He's a former police officer, and he's carrying too."

She'd forgotten about that fact as the men always concealed their weapons well with an overshirt or jacket.

"Besides," Ryan said. "Your fellow participants might all be innocent, and someone else located you up here."

"But how and who?"

Ryan shrugged. "Depending on time, the person after you might've joined us for an earlier session to see where we went during this week. Or one of these guys is in on it and brought a phone along so you could be tracked."

She shook her head. "This is all getting complicated."

"Not overly," Micha said. "Not compared to some of the investigations I've handled. At least not yet. But don't worry. No matter what we learn, we'll figure it out."

"You'll have our whole team working with you, and you can't ask for better investigators." Ryan brushed his knuckles across his chest and cast a playful grin at Micha. "'Course some of us better than others, but..."

Micha rolled his eyes, then looked at his watch. "We should get going. I want to leave plenty of time to get back before dark. Never know when we could encounter a problem."

"You mean from someone coming after me?"

"No. Your stalker likely doesn't know you're leaving so hasn't planned to follow us. I'm thinking more like rough terrain. Animals. Things like that."

"Watch out for those sneaky spiders out to get you too." Ryan grinned. "Wouldn't want you screaming like a little girl."

Micha clenched his fingers. "I know you're just trying to lighten things up, but thanks for throwing me under the bus like that."

"So you haven't told the group about your spider phobia?" Ryan kept his gaze pinned to Micha. "You usually do that day one when you tell them to be careful near wood piles."

"Well, I didn't, all right?"

"It's okay," Ava said, wanting to ease his discomfort. "I already figured it out."

Micha gritted his teeth.

"We might all joke about it, but he has a legit reason," Ryan said. "He was bit by a poisonous one in the service and almost died."

She looked at Micha. "I'd say that was legit."

"I suppose," he said. "But I should be able to overcome it."

"You're not superhuman, you know?" Ryan grinned again. "Go ahead and leave that to me."

Micha laughed, and just like that, peace was restored between the men. Micha made eye contact with her. "When you get back to the campsite, leave your tent for Ryan to pack out. I'll leave mine too. I want to make it seem like we really are coming back. Take only what you absolutely must."

Like my cosmetics.

"Hey, thanks for the added weight in my pack," Ryan said.

"You going soft on me now that you got a dad bod and can't handle it?" Micha laughed.

"No dad bod yet." Ryan pounded his abs. "I can still handle everything you can, but doesn't mean I want to." He laughed and looked at Ava.

"Sorry," she said. "You already came all this way on short notice, leaving your son and all, and I hate that I'm even more of an imposition."

"Don't worry about it. Your tent won't weigh much, and I didn't bring one for myself as I can use Micha's. So no biggie. Just giving this dufus a hard time." He punched Micha in the arm.

Micha shook his head, but a fond smile for his teammate had found his face. "After you. I'll tell the group we're leaving. You grab your backpack while I do. Make sure to fill your water."

She nodded and hurried back to the trail and into her tent. She shouldered her pack and heard Micha tell the others that Ryan was taking over. Fritz complained, which was seeming to be his go-to thing, but the others didn't say much.

She lifted the flap of her tent and mentally prepared herself for the hike. Not only the physical exertion it would bring but the hours alone with Micha in the wilderness.

~

Ava and Micha had come straight back to the compound, stopping twice for a break, and Reid was waiting on the wide, wraparound porch of the lodge to greet them. Seriously, how did he know exactly when they would arrive? Micha hadn't called him, that she knew of. She did take a bathroom break twice so maybe then, but she'd thought he was doing the same thing.

Reid stood tall and in charge but was still dwarfed by the large log structure set at the end of the compound driveway. His dark hair was even darker in the shadows on the porch, and he wore an intense expression on a face with a wide jaw. Tall fir trees towered over the building, and smoke whispered up from the chimney, the smell of burning wood comforting her.

He jogged down the steps and ran that intense gaze so like his brother Ryan's over her, head to toe. "I have to say you seem more like an Ava than a Kari."

Micha had said the same thing, but she really didn't get it. "I'm sorry to mislead you. It's not my nature to lie, but I..." She ended with a lift of her shoulder as she couldn't really explain the innate desire to remain free. Alive, yes. Most everyone would understand that, but unless a person faced incarceration, she didn't think they could fully understand that flight urge.

"The team's waiting in the conference room," he said. "We should head straight over there."

"Oh, wow," Ava said. "You don't waste any time, do you?"

"Not if I can help it."

"You tracking my phone?" Micha asked as he set off.

Ava fell into step beside him, nearly running to keep up with both guys' long strides.

Reid took her other side. "I was. Wanted to get this going as soon as possible since Ava's life might depend on our actions."

"I appreciate that." Micha glanced at her and slowed his speed, heading down the driveway toward the guest and staff cabins.

Maybe he slowed because he'd seen her struggling to keep up. After the long hike, she didn't mind slowing the pace down. And a shower. How she craved a shower.

The cabins were located near the building where she'd run into the team the night she'd foolishly tried to flirt with Micha. If she thought about that failed attempt, her face would burn bright. Better not to try the flirting route ever again in her life and simply be herself.

"Are you worried we're not safe here in the compound?" she asked and didn't care which guy answered.

"I'd like to believe that our fencing and cameras don't leave any blind spots," Reid said. "We've never had a break-in we didn't know about right away, but you never know how cunning this guy is."

"Technology like the cameras are good, but no system is foolproof." Micha glanced at her. "Which means you still have to be aware of your surroundings, and we won't ever leave you alone." Micha looked at Reid. "Or at least I figured the team would agree."

"Roger that," Reid said. "But I have some ideas about it to discuss, too."

Micha got moving faster again, his long legs taking him the last distance to the building. Was he so eager to resolve this? Or was he desperate to have help with her protection so he didn't have to spend twenty-four/seven with her?

He opened the door for her, and she entered the large building and went straight to the conference room where Micha had held orientation the night they had all arrived for the training. It was just a few days ago but felt like a lifetime.

Colin and his brother Devan, who she'd also met that night, had kicked back by the table. Cheese, crackers, and pepperoni sat on a plate near them, along with bottled water and a bowl of mixed nuts. The guys were laughing, but when they saw her, they both came forward in their chairs and watched her.

Talk about uncomfortable. Both men were eyeing her up like the wolf in Little Red Riding Hood. Colin's gaze was especially sharp and assessing. Devan a little more relaxed as he tossed nuts into the air and caught them with his mouth.

"Russ won't be joining us unless absolutely necessary. As the sheriff, he would have to report you, Ava." Reid pointed at a chair. "I have made him aware of a security issue and that it's not in his best interest to join us."

"And he was good with that?" Micha asked.

"Considering I didn't share any details, he was surprisingly okay." Reid went to the head of the table. "Thanks to the softer, gentler version of Russ we now see since he married Sydney."

"The change in him is big." Devan held his arms wide out. "I mean monumental big."

"A good woman can do that." Reid got a dreamy smile on his face, erasing all the hard lines and angles and replacing them with a softness that Ava could see any woman would find attractive.

"Guess you're thinking about Megan." Micha glanced at Ava. "His wife of a few months."

"I am." Reid's smile widened. "Maybe you guys should try finding someone."

Devan feigned a shudder. "Not a good time for that for me, but more power to you all."

"I'm with Dev," Micha said. "But I'm glad you're both happy."

Ava had gotten a vibe that said he wasn't looking for a romantic involvement. Not that he'd said anything, but she sensed his reluctance, and he just confirmed it. Oddly, it stung. Not a little but a lot. Not that she was looking for anything right now either, but if her issue was resolved she would be glad to date again, wouldn't she?

"Help yourself to the snacks and water, Ava," Reid said. "And let's get down to it."

She was too anxious to eat, but she took a bottle of water. Now that she was back in civilization with running water instead of a latrine, she wouldn't mind hydrating to the max to make up for sweating on the hike.

She took a seat in one of the comfy chairs with a reclining back and thickly padded arms and looked at the room again. The far wall held a dorm-sized refrigerator. Another wall, two whiteboards. The third, a door and a map of the compound. The last wall, a large screen TV. All of which Micha had used on their orientation and welcome night.

"So about those safety ideas." Micha dropped into a chair across from Ava and kept his attention on Reid.

Reid picked cashews out of the nut bowl. "I'd like to think this place is secure, but nothing is a hundred percent secure, and we have to act as if Ava's stalker knows where she is."

"Agreed," Micha said.

Reid had dropped the nuts in his mouth and finished

chewing them. "So we discussed you delivering the evidence to the Veritas Center in Portland."

Micha's eyebrow went up. "We did, but you mentioned getting a helo to help us out."

"I got ahold of Gage Blackwell. He's good with it, and I still think it's a solid idea." Reid snagged a few more cashews and leaned against the wall. "But I also think the two of you should be on that flight with the evidence and don't come back here right away."

Ava picked up her water bottle. "Because our suspect won't know where I am then?"

He shook the cashews in his closed hand. "That, and while you're in Portland, you could run down some leads."

"It would be good to get a copy of the original video from the hospice center," Micha said.

"Or what you think is the original file," Colin said. "It could've been altered, and I'll need to confirm that it hasn't been."

Micha picked up a cracker and loaded it with two slices of cheese with pepperoni between them and topped if off with another cracker. "Tell me what you need so I know what to ask for, and I'll meet with the facility manager."

"Will do."

"I'd like to go with you to the center." Ava raised her hand before anyone could argue. "I know I can't. Not without being arrested, but I just wanted to put it out there."

Micha swallowed the bite of his little snack sandwich and peered at Colin. "Maybe you should come to Portland too. You can get a look at the actual server files, and that frees me up to stay with Ava at the apartment."

Colin faced Reid. "You able to make the schedule work?"

"It'll be tight, but I'll manage it." Reid turned to the whiteboard and noted security video and Colin's name as the responsible party for retrieving it. Then he added the catapult and boot prints and assigned Micha's name.

"I'd really like to get a look at Holly Boyle's autopsy report." Micha glanced around the group. "Anyone have a source in the ME's office?"

"I do from my deputy days," Devan said. "Old college buddy. I can give him a call."

"Good," Micha said. "Get back to me the minute you know anything."

Reid added the information to the whiteboard.

"While you're writing, put me down for a deep dive on all of the class participants," Colin said. "I've done most of the work. Unfortunately, I haven't turned anything up, but I've got a few more searches I can run." He leaned forward to look at Ava. "Oh, and you'll all be happy to know my search of Ava's real name came up squeaky clean."

"I wasn't worried it wouldn't," Ava said when no one else said the same thing. Not even Micha. Had he doubted her? Probably. After all, she'd lied to him. Why would he trust her?

"What about a visit to the main suspects' homes?" Micha asked. "We know they're with Ryan, and we should be able to get in without getting caught."

"And who exactly are your main suspects?" Reid held his pen, ready to write.

"I think it's Ernie, Jamal, and Buck," Ava said.

Micha set down his water bottle and swiped the back of his hand over his mouth. "Jamal and Buck are strong possibilities. Both have violent tendencies, and Jamal's into a medieval LARPing where catapults could be used."

"And Ernie?" Reid asked.

"I'm not liking him for this," Micha said. "Just a gut feel. I don't want to rule him out based on that. We can't rule out the other two either, but they're not setting off my radar."

"The three of them are familiar with music and the threatening note to me was a song," Ava said.

Devan narrowed his eyes. "But couldn't Layne have written the song and given it to whoever put it in your backpack?"

"He could, but the song's actually well written," Ava said. "And he doesn't have the musical knowledge to do something like that."

"He could've hired someone," Colin said, "then did as Dev suggested. Gave it to one of our class participants."

"I could see that happening." Micha picked at his thumbnail, his expression thoughtful. "But getting someone else involved could leave a link back to Layne. If he means Ava harm and has an ounce of sense, he'd try to avoid any connections."

"It's all possible, though. we don't know enough about Layne to know what he's capable of." Reid lifted his marker and rested the tip on the board. "There has to be a connection with one of them to Layne, and we need to find it."

"Trying, boss man," Colin said. "To that end, the minute Micha called me, I went into storage and cloned the other participants phones to search for Layne's name and number. Nada. I need to give them a deeper look, but it would help if I could just focus at first on the three you named."

"Hey, man," Micha said. "Great work on the cloning."

"Would you expect anything less?" Colin laughed.

Micha rolled his eyes.

Ava glanced around the group. "I hate to add more work, but shouldn't we also add Jamal's LARPing group leader to the list? Guy's name is Phoenix Preston. He might have info that could help us."

"Then let's start with the three suspects and Preston." Reid noted their names on the board.

"Will do," Colin said.

Reid glanced back. "Checking out the suspects' homes is a solid plan, too. We might find that connection to Layne there."

"I can give you the addresses," Colin said.

"Ernie mentioned he's married, and his wife's a real homebody," Ava said. "So it might be a problem to get a look at his place."

"Let's skip his house for now," Micha said. "We can always go back there."

"About that chopper ride," Colin said. "As much as I'm all for it, Buck and Jamal live on rural properties. By the time the chopper lands, we get a rental car, make the trip to their places, we might as well have road-tripped it from here."

"Then road trip it is," Micha said, but didn't look all that thrilled about it. Maybe he didn't want to be in a car with her for the three-hour drive to Portland. Especially not after a two-hour hike at her side.

Colin grinned. "I call dibs on any tunes played."

"Say it isn't so." Micha groaned.

"You snooze, you lose, buddy." Colin laughed.

Micha looked at Ava. "He's been into seventies disco lately."

Ava laughed. "Well, he said on any tunes played, so we just don't play any."

"Wise woman when traveling with any of these guys," Reid said, a sarcastic smile forming.

"Hey, now." Colin grabbed his chest in mock horror. "My taste is very refined. It's the rest of the world that's out of step."

The group laughed and offered more pointed barbs in jest. What a team. They were dealing with something serious like murder and could joke to relieve their tension. She supposed they had to do something. Some nurses did the same thing, but in dealing with dying patients, she'd never been able to crack a single joke, and this break was actually good for her mental health in that respect. In the respect of being terrified someone would kill her or she would go to prison? Not so much.

When the laughter died down, she looked at Micha. "Can I get my phone back? You'll want to see that video and maybe Layne left a message that could change our plans."

"It's in the office. Let me grab it." He got to his feet and took long strides out of the room.

The team went back to joking around and snacking, likely not wanting to move on without Micha. Only a few minutes passed when he returned with her phone in hand. "I turned it on."

She set it on the table in front of her and watched with expectation laced with a heavy measure of dread until the screen flashed a light, displaying readiness. She woke the device up and looked at it with one eye as if side-eyeing the screen would mean she wouldn't have a message from Layne.

No display of a missed call or voicemail, and she let out a relieved breath. "No messages. Not sure if I'm glad about that or not."

"I get it." Micha leaned against the wall. "Direct contact from Layne could've helped, but we'll just move on with our plan."

"I have the video from cloning your phone and will check for changes," Colin said. "If we score the original, I can compare to see if Layne altered it."

"I'll text everyone's contact info to you when we finish up here, and you can send a copy to the rest of us," Reid said and faced Colin. "I assume you looked into Layne and Holly, too, and not just a connection to the others?"

He nodded. "Nothing helpful as of now, but I'm still

running a few things. I'd suggest we go to Layne's house too, but we can't be sure where he is or guarantee he won't walk in on us like we can with the others."

Micha crossed his feet at the ankle. "Let's get eyes on him as soon as we get to town and put a tracker on his vehicle."

Tracker? Ava had heard of them and seen them on TV shows and in books, but..."Is that legal?"

Reid shook his head. "One of the reasons we excluded Russ from our investigation. But it's our best bet if we want to get into Layne's place without a confrontation." Reid added the information to the board, and the marker squeaked, grating on her already raw nerves.

Micha leaned forward and scanned his team. "We'll need a safe place to stay in Portland. Any ideas?"

"Already got it handled." Reid turned. "Gage came through on that too. Blackwell Tactical's protection business has really taken off in Portland, and he leased an apartment for his men when not on protection duty. He's not using it this week and offered it to us. With no connection to any of us, and if you're not followed, which I know you'll be sure you aren't, it'll be a great safe house for Ava."

Ava tried not to look shocked at the kindness of this man called Gage, but it was a rarity in today's world when a person went out of the way for a complete stranger. "I don't even know him, and he's offering so much support."

"That's just the kind of guy Gage is," Reid said.

"The way you all are." She smiled at him. "You all have blessed me so much, and I thank God that I decided to take this survival course. I might not be learning survival skills right now, but you all are guaranteeing I survive Layne's revenge."

"We're glad to be of assistance," Reid said.

"Thanks for arranging that, bro. I owe you." Micha

planted his hands on the table. "One final thing before we hit the road. Layne could be watching this place, so we need a transport plan."

"Decoy vehicles should do the trick," Reid said.

Devan sat up. "Better yet, why don't we combine the decoy with a boat transport to the public ramp. Even if he has us under surveillance, there's no way he could follow us in time to see where we go from there."

Ava had learned that Devan and Colin had grown up on a lake and were familiar with boating. Devan had also been a former Clackamas County deputy specializing in water rescue, which she assumed was why he proposed the idea.

"I like that." Colin faced Micha. "I could go ahead to the ramp, and you could bring Ava in the boat. Then we take off for Portland."

"We'll have to cover our license plates in case he's watching so he can't track that vehicle," Micha said. "But we can do that. I'll let you drive, and I'll ride shotgun. Don't want a wussy former federal agent in charge of our weapon choices."

Colin laughed. "We did use firearms in the FBI, you know."

"Like when?" Micha smirked. "Once every five years."

"Hey, now," Reid said. "More like every three years."

The guys laughed. Ava would join in, but she'd never even held a gun or wanted to. Ever. She didn't even want to think about guns, much less joke about them.

"Sounds like a solid plan," Reid said. "I think we're done here, and you can go pack. While you do, I'll get the decoy vehicles set up."

"I'll need time to visit our armory to prepare for the trip, too." Micha looked at Ava. "Ready?"

Was she? Her stomach cramped hard as she stood. "Just

a quick thank you for all your help. I will forever be in your debt, and I don't know how to repay you."

"As long as you truly are innocent of the charges, we don't need repayment," Micha said.

And just like that, at the mention of her potential guilt, the pain twisted her stomach. She wasn't guilty of murder. She knew that. Hoped these guys knew it too. Even if they didn't, they might be able to keep her alive.

Good. Great, even. But that didn't mean they could prove she was innocent of all charges. She could still be looking at life behind bars with real murderers.

7

Micha remained fluid and rode the chop, piloting the aluminum fishing boat across the rough waves on the small lake. The public boat ramp sat in the distance under the cloudy afternoon skies, but he kept his gaze moving for any sign of a stalker. Micha wasn't hooked on the boat idea. Not that he thought it was a bad one, but as he'd known would happen, they were sitting ducks on the water. On land they had a better escape route, but it was also the most likely route staked out by her stalker and therefore more dangerous.

At least Ava was hidden under a tarp, and as far as any stalker might think by the fishing poles stacked in the bow, Micha was going fishing. Of course, Micha was carrying as always. Sidearm and ankle backup. Plus, he'd lodged a rifle at his feet just under the tarp in case they came under fire. Again, something he doubted would happen, but he had to be prepared for anything.

He really had to forget his investigative days and revert back to the Marines, when his main training was how to stay alive and keep his teammates alive as well. He needed that training more than anything right now. The investigative skills would come in handy once they arrived safely at the suspects' properties.

He aimed the boat toward the shore, where Colin stood by one of the company SUVs. They'd turned the license plates around when he hooked the boat trailer to the back of the SUV. They could change the plates back when he loaded the boat, with Ava under the tarp, back onto the trailer. Reid's good friend owned a property down the road a few miles where they could park the trailer and let Ava out in a more secluded and defensible area.

"Just about to reach shore," Micha said over the puttering of the small motor so Ava knew where they were.

"Good," she said. "I can't wait to get in a warm car. The metal got colder than I expected on the water and is seeping through the quilts you put down."

"Sorry."

"No worries. I'll be glad to be safely out of here. But I have to warn you, I might beg you to keep cranking up the heat in the car until you can't breathe." She chuckled.

He laughed with her, careful to keep it down as sound carried over the lake, but he was glad she could still have a sense of humor. Still, it might not be the best idea. "Laughing is good, but make sure when we move you from the boat to the SUV that you stay alert and move quickly."

"Aw, talk about a buzzkill." She laughed again.

"I'm serious, Ava," he said. "Your life could depend on it."

"I get it." Her tone bordered on dire now. "You should know I laugh when I get stressed, but I know what to do and how important it is, and I won't let you down."

"Thank you." He fell silent as the water lapped at the ramp, and he pointed the boat toward it.

A flash of the video he'd reviewed before they departed came to mind. Ava on the veranda of the care center with

Holly, handing her the cookie dough. But he couldn't see the cookie dough, only that she handed something to Holly, and then Holly got sick that night. Didn't look good for Ava. Not good at all, and Micha had an even greater desire to help her.

So focus, man. Do your job right now. Get her safely out of here.

He killed the motor and let the craft glide into shore.

Colin sloshed down the ramp in his rubber boots and attached the cable for the trailer winch to the boat. He soon had the motorized winch humming, and the boat moved forward. Micha ignored the movement and kept his gaze roving over the area. No sign of another person. No one at all for as far as the eye could see, which Micha put at a football-field-sized area before the shoreline curved south.

Cabins were few and far between on this lake as most of them had been built in the fifties on large plots and had stayed with the original families who didn't give up their land. He didn't know how Reid's parents had scored their property when they did in the nineties, but they must've paid a pretty penny for it.

The boat slid onto the trailer, and he jumped down but stayed near Ava so he could come to her aid if needed.

Colin secured the boat and came alongside Micha. "Ready for us to get on the road, Ava?"

"Ready," her soft voice came from under the tarp.

"Stay put unless one of us clears you to move," Micha added.

"Of course."

"Then let's hit the road." Micha gave Colin a pointed look, warning him to take care too.

He locked gazes with Micha. "I got this, bro."

"I probably should've asked if you were a good driver before I agreed to this." Ava chuckled.

"Better than the bozo riding shotgun." Colin socked Micha in the arm.

"Let's roll," Micha said, ignoring the humor and heading to the vehicle to climb in. He secured his door, then checked his side mirror to keep an eye on Ava as he clicked on his seatbelt.

Colin got the SUV climbing from the ramp and onto the road. They'd all visited Reid's friend with him at one time or another, and Colin knew where they were headed without directions.

Micha wished he could report not being nervous, but his heart was thumping. Maybe he'd been out of action for too long. Or maybe the stakes were higher than he imagined. Not the actual danger but the stakes brought on by these unwanted feelings for Ava.

Had he fallen for this woman in less than two days? Was that even possible, when he knew now was not the right time to get involved with anyone? If so, he better watch himself. He didn't want to give her the wrong impression. Didn't want her to think he hoped to start something with her. Not when that was the last thing he needed. Right?

They reached the driveway, and Colin backed the trailer into location. Micha opened his door, birds chirping above the only sound.

"I'll grab my rifle and set up a perimeter," Micha said. Though he would like to be the one to free Ava from the tarp, he was the better marksman, and they had to play to their strengths to ensure her safety. "You unhook the boat and move Ava into the vehicle."

"Got it." Colin slid out.

Micha went to the boat. "We're at the transfer location, and Colin is unhooking the boat. I'm going to grab my rifle now."

"That wasn't such a bad trip," she said. "Remind me to praise Colin for his driving skills."

Micha ran his fingers under the tarp to locate his rifle, and her hand came over his and gently squeezed. Her fingers were cold. He wished it wasn't so, but he loved the gentle touch that went right to his heart.

He squeezed her hand, then promptly ignored the way the simple touch brought all the wrong kinds of thoughts to his brain. "Colin will be back for you as soon as he unloads the boat and changes the license plates."

He lifted his weapon and found the most strategic location under a tall maple tree where he could see in all directions and keep an eye on Ava at the same time.

Colin worked fast to crank the trailer jack stand down into place, then pull the vehicle forward to free the SUV and turn the plates. Back at the boat, he hefted his body over the side and flung off the tarp. He took Ava's arm, and she jumped down, then stretched her arms overhead.

Micha joined them. "Straight to the vehicle. Get down on the floor until we're on the main road, and we're sure we aren't followed."

She moved quickly to the back seat and slid in. Colin closed the door and ran around the front to the driver's seat. He pulled the SUV forward to Micha, who backed inside. "Move. Move. Move."

Colin peeled out of the driveway and onto the narrow road. They had about a mile to go to reach the main highway, and Micha wouldn't relax until they were cruising down the road without a tail.

Who was he kidding? He wouldn't relax even then. Not until Ava was one hundred percent safe.

~

Ava had counted down the time until they reached their destination, and she eagerly scanned ahead through a jungle of plants and trees to see Buck's house hidden on the far side of an open space ringed with tall evergreens. If you could call the dilapidated structure a house. It was more like a makeshift shack that could fall down with the slightest wind.

Colin shifted into park. "His place doesn't exactly serve as an advertisement for off-grid living."

Micha leaned forward. "Wonder if he built it himself or if it was an existing structure when he bought it, and he hasn't had a chance to reinforce it."

Ava squinted against the falling sun out the side window. "Either way, it hardly looks safe to go inside."

"The good news is it's so small it won't take long to search," Micha said. "And I don't see any outbuildings."

"We should get moving." Colin opened his door. "The sun is setting fast, and we'll soon lose all light."

Micha reached under his seat, his hand coming out holding a flashlight and headlamp. "I always come prepared."

"Well, aren't you the regular boy scout?" Colin slid out.

Micha glanced over his shoulder. "Colin will stand watch out here, and you'll still come inside with me as planned, but be careful."

"Roger that," she said, getting an odd look from both guys at her response as they got out of the vehicle.

Micha opened her door and took disposable gloves from his pocket. He gave a pair to her. "Put these on, but I'd still rather you wouldn't touch anything without asking me first."

She resisted saying *roger that* again, but why would she when she'd gotten such an odd response the first time? She nodded instead and struggled to get her fingers into the tight gloves. He didn't have a hard time at all and drew his sidearm. She slid out.

He handed over his flashlight. "Stay behind me in case he's booby-trapped the place."

"Buck seems like the kind of guy who might do that."

Micha drew his weapon and started through tall grass in an area that should've been mowed. Or at least an area she would mow. No telling what was living in this grass and could come into the house. But then again, with the house being more of a shack, just mowing the clearing wouldn't stop critters from joining you inside.

"Hopefully, this grass will spring back up before Buck gets home." Micha picked up a long stick from one of the many towering trees on the property, one leaning precariously over the shack. "Don't want him to know someone's been here."

"Might not matter if we find something to implicate him in working with Layne. Then he might not be coming home at all."

"That would be too easy." Micha continued to move slowly through the grass, poking the ground with the stick and occasionally pausing. "Besides, even if we locate a connection today, we'll still have to prove his involvement in another way."

"Right, because entering his house without permission isn't legal."

He nodded. "Just like using the tracker. If we locate something, the police won't be able to use it unless we can legitimately obtain the information."

"Good thing we have you on our side to remember all the rules."

He didn't say anything, but his shoulders raised a fraction at her compliment. He was a strong man and probably didn't need to be complimented on his abilities, but strong or not, all people needed positive feedback.

They reached the front door Buck had locked with a heavy metal hasp and padlock. Micha felt around the door and then took a small tool kit from his pocket. "Strong lock, but with the way the wood is splintering, it wouldn't hold if someone wanted to get in here."

He glanced around the area, then holstered his weapon. He removed a couple of metal tools from the case and inserted them in the lock. The padlock soon dropped open.

"Is there anything you can't do?" she asked.

"I can sew on a button and stitch up a wound, but beyond that I wouldn't win any sewing prize." He laughed. "And forget knitting or crocheting."

If he weren't opening the door, she might continue this conversation, but his laughter had faded, and his shoulders tensed. She didn't need to be hit over the head to know it was time to be even more vigilant.

"Stay here and stay alert," he said. "Let me sweep this place inside for tripwires."

He turned on his headlamp and eased through the door. She shone her flashlight ahead of his feet, too.

"Thanks," he said but didn't look back.

She took in the small, one-room place. Wood everywhere. Walls. Ceiling. Floors. All wide boards with big gaps between them. An old wood stove sat on rocks that looked like they were harvested from the property and mortared into place. Next to it, Buck had created a towering stack of wood that balanced precariously, and a wooden rocking chair rested in front of the stove.

A small kitchen held only three cabinets painted a shocking green, plus a white cast-iron sink with a red hand pump. The other corner held a narrow twin bed with a vintage plaid quilt that looked very much like the WWII-era memory quilts she'd seen on an *Antiques Roadshow* episode. Rain gear and heavy work clothes were hung on pegs pounded into the wall beside it.

That was it. His entire life in this small space. An extremely simple life for sure, but it had sounded like he enjoyed living this way. Compared to this place, her cabin seemed like a palace, with running water and electricity should she decide to risk connecting to the grid. And it wasn't falling down. Her cousin always maintained the property in top-notch condition.

"You're clear to enter." Micha stepped back. "Still watch your step. I found a few bad floorboards you could go through."

She nodded and went inside. She didn't know where to look when there wasn't much to check out. The old boards creaked and groaned under her weight as she went ahead of Micha, swatting away the cobwebs for him.

"You don't have to do that," he said from behind her. "The cobwebs, I mean. Actually makes me feel even dumber about having such a lame phobia."

She looked back at him. "I don't think any less of you for it, and I don't think others would either."

"Tell that to the guys I served with. Got razzed all the time. Same thing now."

"But the teasing's in the form of affection, right?"

"For most guys, yeah, but I don't like it. Not one bit." His sharp tone told her he was done discussing spiders, so she went directly to the kitchen.

The sink was surprisingly clean, and the small counter free from any dirty dishes. The place might not be livable by her standards, but at least Buck kept it clean, with no visible signs of rodents.

"Can I touch the cabinet doors?" she asked.

"Go ahead," he said from over by the bed. "Let me know if you want to pick up anything inside."

She opened the first door with a silver handle in the shape of a small spoon, the latex on her fingers feeling odd against the rusty metal. She found only home-canned foods in dusty jars. The next cabinet, this one with a fork handle, held a few dishes along with big pots and a bulk load of canning supplies. She couldn't even imagine having to can without a stove. Perhaps he used the top of the wood stove.

The last cabinet, with a knife handle, held canned foods, predominately baked beans.

"Anything?" Micha asked.

She faced him. "Guy loves his baked beans, but other than more food and dishes, nothing else."

He lifted the mattress. "Nothing here either. He said he didn't like nutso preppers, and I think he was right. No sign of him being slightly off other than living in a place in such bad condition. He's just an average Joe living off the land by himself."

"Seems like you're right." She started across the room toward a basket sitting on the floor by the rocking chair, but her flashlight caught dark spots on the front wall.

She hurried toward them and focused her light on the area. "I think I have blood here."

Micha rushed over to her. He leaned closer and his light mingled with hers. "That's blood all right."

"He could've cut himself."

"The blood hit this wall with a strong force, so if he injured himself, it had to be a bad cut."

"How can you tell?"

"See how the drops aren't circular but point to the right? That's due to impact force." He got out his phone. "I don't pretend to be a forensic expert, but we had one testify at a trial about this very thing. I'll take pictures for the Veritas forensic expert and bring her a sample."

She flashed her gaze back at him. "Can you do that? Isn't it disturbing a crime scene?"

"We have no reason to believe it's a crime scene. Besides, I'll take such a small amount it won't be missed." He snapped photos with his phone and then got out a swab and plastic bag.

She watched him. "Do you routinely carry these things in your pockets?"

He shook his head. "Figured we might want to collect some evidence, so when I got the weapons together, I tucked a few supplies we had left over from an earlier investigation into my pocket."

Was there anything this guy didn't think of? She doubted it. "Once again, I'm thankful for your expertise."

"Let's hope it pays off in the long run." He glanced at his watch. "I'll grab this sample, then we should do a perimeter check in case he has a bunker."

"That seems likely if he's an unhinged prepper, right?"

"It does. Or could even be just a root cellar to store his provisions." He took out a tiny bottle of liquid and dampened the swab. "With dried blood, I have to use sterile water to collect it."

He touched the swab on the tip of a tail and came away with a speck so small she couldn't see how it was enough to run any tests, but he knew what he was doing, so she didn't question him.

He bagged the swab and pocketed it, then pointed at the door. "I'll go first, just in case."

He took off across the floor, skirting two questionable boards as did she. Once outside, he took a long look in both directions, then cupped his hands around his mouth. "Done inside, Colin. Doing a perimeter check."

"Roger that." Colin's voice came across strong through the trees.

That reply sounded right coming from him, and she vowed never to try using their lingo again.

"Stay behind me again." Micha motioned for her to exit. He picked up his stick, drew his gun, then started to the right, plowing down the grass and making her steps easier. He tapped the ground around him as he moved, as he'd done on the way to the cabin.

"Do you really think he set boobytraps?" she asked.

"Never know with survivalists. Might not be meant to injure or kill but could simply be in place to let them know someone was here when they were gone."

They reached the back of the shack, and he came to a stop near an old stained tarp lying on the ground. He gently tapped it.

"Something hard under there." He lifted the tarp to reveal a pair of metal cellar doors that opened in the middle. He dropped to his knees and felt around the edges like he'd done at the front door. "Checking for tripwires."

"I'm assuming you learned that in the military."

"Once a Marine, always a Marine." He cocked a cute grin.

Her heart took a tumble. Despite the tense scene. Despite their situation. Despite not being free to pursue a relationship.

She tightened her hand around the flashlight to ignore her thoughts and watched him open the doors. What little light remained in the sky illuminated the top three steps. Rough, earthen steps.

"Stay up here until I say otherwise." Headlamp back on, he took the stairs down, the light reflecting against solid cobwebs. He didn't hesitate but swung the stick as he entered , sweeping the webs out of the way, and descended the steps.

Her mind raced over what he could be seeing, and she tapped a foot to ease her anxiety.

"You'll want to check this out," he yelled. "Come on down."

The Price is Right flashed into her brain to finish the sentence, but this wasn't a game show. No game at all. Could be life or death.

She slowly descended and clicked on her flashlight. But she needn't have done so. Micha shone his lamp on a pile of crates in the corner. Crates filled with items that stole her breath, and she stumbled back.

8

Micha moved a few boxes and let out a low whistle under his breath as he stared at crate after crate of weapons and ammo. "We're looking at quite a stockpile here. Not only pistols with enough rounds for a long standoff, but automatic rifles that would quickly annihilate anyone who came onto the property."

He looked back at Ava. Even in the dim light, he could see she'd paled, but he wouldn't sugarcoat things. She needed to know what they could be up against.

He lifted out a rifle. "An AK-47. One of the deadliest weapons ever built."

She let out a long breath. "And not something someone like Buck should have a need for unless he was expecting an assault."

"Correct. This is the automatic version, which is even worse than the semi-automatic that so many bad guys own these days."

She narrowed her gaze and stared at the gun. "You can tell by looking at it?"

"The average person can't, but I spent years working with weapons." He pointed at the right side of the gun to a trapezoidal-shaped metal latch. "Wear shows me this latch has two positions, which is only true of the fully automatic. It's in the down position, and that's this manufacturer's setting for a full auto. I can't prove it until firing the thing, but my gut says I'm right when I don't want to be right."

She arched an eyebrow. "And is this legal to own?"

"Sort of. Companies can't make auto versions in the US for private citizens anymore, but you can legally buy one. That is, if the weapon was registered with the feds before May of 1986. It has to be registered before that date when the law changed. Makes them rare, and they could cost a cool ten grand or more at a minimum to buy."

She continued to stare, the reality seeming to settle in. "Not something you would think a guy like Buck could afford, but maybe he bought it when he was still working in the corporate world."

"Could be." Micha set down the weapon and picked up a gun dealer's business card for Atlas Armory to hold out to Ava. "Could've bought it here or gotten it in a less than legal deal."

She shivered and turned away. "You look at what's under that tarp in the corner?"

"Not yet." He placed the rifle back in the box and lifted the tarp to reveal a ham radio set-up.

Micha studied the equipment. "It's connected to the solar power station on the table. He has to have solar panels somewhere."

She pointed in the right corner. "And that looks like a solar camera."

"I didn't see other cameras when we arrived. Colin and I wouldn't have missed them. Maybe he hasn't installed them yet. Either way, he was expecting and prepping for trouble. TEOTWAWKI even."

"TEOTWAWKI."

"The end of the world as we know it. A term survivalists use, especially online."

"So Buck might not be quite as normal as he let on."

"Maybe not."

She gnawed on her lower lip. "Is there anything we can do about the weapons?"

"I'd like to report them, but then we'd have to say how we know about them, which we can't do. Even then, the authorities might not do anything about it."

Her mouth fell open. "Why in the world not? No one needs to own this many guns."

"It might be illegal to own a machine gun in Oregon, but he could still legally own all of these, even the AK-47, as long as it's registered with ATF before the date I mentioned."

"Do you think it's likely that he registered it?"

"No." Micha turned to take in the back wall filled with canned goods and a large water bladder along with a cot and sleeping bag. He pointed at the bladder. "That's a lot of water."

"Meaning he planned to spend a good bit of time down here."

"Indeed." Micha got out his phone and snapped pictures of everything in the room. "We should get going. Never know if he has someone checking on his property for him."

She turned to depart.

He followed, moving a little slower. He hated to walk away from such a major cache of weapons and ammo, but they had no choice. Didn't mean he wouldn't check in with Reid and the team to see if they had thoughts on how to handle this. The last thing he would want was to leave such a deadly supply available for an apparently unstable man to turn on other people in a potential massacre.

~

Ava couldn't let go of her thoughts of Buck's weapons, but as they pulled up to Jamal's large piece of land, she had to prepare herself for what they might find here as she'd thought Jamal was more dangerous than Buck.

Jamal had posted numerous keep-out and no-trespassing signs at the property entrance, raising Ava's unease even more. Micha jumped out of the vehicle to unlock a heavy-duty gate to give them access to the place. Instead of getting back into the SUV, he moved on foot in front of the vehicle. He hadn't said what he planned to do, but he had a stick in his hands again, and she guessed he was looking for any booby traps.

They reached the log cabin, which was much better maintained and twice the size of Buck's place. He'd mowed his yard, and a large garden plot, mostly dormant now, was located just past the building. Ava had studied gardening when planning to vacate the city for her hideaway, and even in the waning light she recognized garlic, kale, and other cool-weather crops, along with herbs like rosemary and thyme. Looked like Jamal had a green thumb, something that surprised her, but then she'd been told Oregon was a fairly easy place to garden as long as she could provide water in the dry summer months.

Colin made a three-point turn, facing the vehicle toward the exit and shifted into park on the driveway that continued past the house toward a large pole barn.

He leaned over the wheel. "Don't see any cameras. Odd for a prepper who wants his privacy."

"Maybe he hasn't connected his electricity as he doesn't want his information tracked that way."

"Could be. Guess you'll see when you go in."

Micha came to her door and opened it. "Same drill as last time. I go first. Get the place open and tell you if it's safe to come in."

She got out and followed him across the green lawn. The sun plunged below the horizon now, a slight drizzle settling in. She needed to turn on her flashlight. She swept the beam of light over the lawn, the beam occasionally intersecting with Micha's light.

He lifted a hand. "Stay put until I clear you to move forward."

He climbed the steps and she tracked him with her light. He ran his fingers around the door, reaching the top plate. He suddenly jerked back and spun. "Back to the car. Now!"

She turned and started to move, but he grabbed her hand and ran for the vehicle, towing her along. She couldn't keep up and stumbled. He swept her into his arms without missing a step, and carried her as if she weighed no more than a bag of sugar.

"Get this vehicle moving," he said to Colin as he shoved her in the back door and climbed in behind her.

Colin had slid in and cranked the engine. He peeled over the gravel, spitting it in all directions as the SUV raced down the drive. She scooted onto the seat behind him and clicked her seatbelt in place.

"Get us away from here. At least a half mile, then pull over when possible." Micha fastened his seatbelt but kept his focus out the window.

She wanted to know what he'd discovered, but his rigid and alert body language told her not to distract him. If he should be disturbed, Colin would've asked, right? She could wait a half mile, couldn't she? But even with Colin moving the SUV at top speed, it seemed to take forever for him to pull to the side of the road at the end of a wide driveway.

He lifted an arm over the seat. "Explosives?"

"Not sure," Micha said. "Tripwire at the door. Could be explosives, or could be to warn him someone had been there, but I couldn't take any chances with Ava behind me."

"Want one of us to go back and check it out?" Colin asked.

He didn't waffle but answered right away. "It's not worth the risk. If he has one tripwire, there are likely others."

"You're right, and it would be hard to explain to the locals why one of us went kaboom." Colin grinned.

Ava could hardly believe his laid-back attitude.

"We joke as a way to get rid of stress," Micha told her as if he could read her mind. "We'll go ahead and drop our evidence off at Veritas."

Colin turned to the wheel.

"Hold on, and I'll take shotgun again." Micha reached for the door handle, but that inquisitive gaze of his searched her from head to toe. "Sorry about the rough handling. I didn't hurt you, did I?"

"Don't worry about me," she said. "I'm fine."

Micha let his gaze linger, then he squeezed her hand and pushed out of the vehicle to get in the front. He entered the Veritas Center's address in the GPS system. The female voice announced a thirty-minute drive.

Ava settled back and watched the scenery pass by under the bright moonlight from above and tried to recover from the shock. The night would be picturesque if they hadn't found a massive cache of weapons, then just run from a potential bomb, and if her heart wasn't still wildly beating.

Her phone rang. She got it out and looked at the screen. "Not a number I recognize."

Micha leaned between the seats. "Answer it."

She moved closer to him so he could hear better and tapped the speaker button. A haunting melody played in the background as an altered male voice sang.

In the darkness whispers fall,
I've found you again, now heed my call,
Turn yourself in and don't you bail,

Or in the stillness, nightmares will prevail.

She gulped in air, panic having its way into her body.

She wanted to run. To flee. Go anywhere. To get as far away from her phone as possible. She tossed it down ahead of her.

"Breathe." Micha picked up the phone. "Take slow, easy breaths."

She did. *One. Two. Three.* Deep and cleansing before she could speak. "Do you think he found me again?"

"Not likely."

"But who made the call?" she asked, her mind racing.

"I think it's from Layne, but not that he's found you." Micha pocketed her phone and looked at Colin. "I'll need you to track this phone number as soon as possible."

"If the class participants' phones weren't still locked up at the compound, I'd say it could be from one of them," Colin said.

"They could own a second phone," Micha said.

"True that," Colin said. "I'll request records for the number, but odds are good it'll be from a burner."

"Yeah, but we still have to try." Micha glanced back at her. "You look deep in thought."

She nodded. "I was thinking Jamal was our guy because of the explosives, and he could've written the song too. But I don't know if any of this moves him higher on my list than Buck. I can see a guy with a stockpile of weapons like Buck's being willing to fire a rock at my head."

"Yeah," Micha said, but his tone held a healthy measure of caution.

He opened his mouth as if he wanted to add something but stopped mid-thought.

What was he going to say? Was he going to put voice to what she was thinking?

That if given a chance, a guy with explosives could do even worse damage, hurting not only her but others? Even ending all of their lives in one fell swoop.

～

Nearing eight p.m., Micha let Ava and Colin go ahead of him to the big glass door of the Veritas Center. The door opened to a single-story building located on the ground floor between two four-story towers. Light glowed through windows from inside, highlighting the empty parking lot. Not likely coming from the labs as they wouldn't have windows, but maybe offices. He knew some of the staff lived on-site in condos located in the tower on the right side and that they also often worked late hours.

A guard, whose gray, buzz haircut said former military or law enforcement, met them at the door. He wore a security uniform and sidearm. Not surprising they had an armed guard what with the amount of evidence this lab housed at any given time.

The guard pushed open the door. "You must be the folks coming to see Sierra."

"We are." Micha shifted the evidence into his other hand to shake the guard's outstretched hand. "Micha Nichols."

"Pete Vincent." His firm grip pinched Micha's fingers. "Come on in. I'll let Sierra know you're here. Then I'll need to see some ID to make security passes for you. You're not allowed beyond these doors without passes and an escort. Not for any reason."

Micha nodded, but even if he didn't actually agree with the rule, the intense stare this older man was giving him would encourage most people to fall into line.

Pete led the way to the reception desk in a large, neutrally decorated lobby and stepped behind it to pick up the phone. "Sierra's guests have arrived."

He tapped a finger on the desktop and listened. "Okay, I'll tell them."

He set the handset in the cradle. "She's sending an intern to take you to her. Now those ID's." He held out his hand.

Micha placed his driver's license on Pete's palm and looked around the lobby, which looked nothing like a lab. The calming beige paint left the room feeling light and airy, and the space held a contemporary seating area placed under a stairway. The center's logo—Connecting Loved Ones Around the World—was painted on the wall above photos of happy, smiling people. They'd used bold red color to paint the letters, and they circled a black globe. The pictures could be stock photos, but more likely they were clients the lab helped reunite through DNA matches.

Private clients didn't likely know about the criminal work processed here. They only wanted to find the truth about their ancestry. He'd once looked them up online after they'd opened, just to check them out and learned the name Veritas meant "truth" in Latin. They helped find truth by processing criminal forensics for law enforcement and for running DNA for their private clients.

"Here you go," Pete said.

Micha looked back to see him holding a plastic pass with a metal clip.

Vincent eyed him. "Wear it at all times and turn it in before you leave."

Micha clipped it on his shirt, and the others did the same when handed theirs. As they waited for the intern, Micha walked around the lobby with Ava, but Colin leaned against the counter, his attention fixed on his phone.

He frowned and sidled up to Micha and Ava, leaning close. "The phone number used to send the song came from a burner like we thought. I'll do a more thorough look when we get to the apartment and let you know if I learn anything else, but don't hold your breath."

A door in the back wall opened, and a young woman with black hair and blue streaks came hurrying forward. Her nametag read Delcie Carter. "Sierra is just finishing up a class in our crime scene house, and I'll take you to her."

She spun, and her athletic shoes squeaked. She pressed her fingers against a reader near the door she'd come through and led them down a hallway. They passed a glass-walled conference room and an elevator, then traveled down a long hallway where the firearms lab was located. Micha couldn't walk past it without glancing in the window. He stopped to find display cases lining the walls. They held different firearms and ammunition neatly labeled with their details.

He let out a low whistle. "I'll be needing a tour of that lab."

"I'm sure our firearms experts, Grady or Trent, would give you one if we asked," Delcie said.

Oh yeah. Could be the one bright side in this whole situation. "Then let's ask."

They moved outside, and he caught sight of a firing range in the distance, but what really caught his attention was a two-story house built right behind the center. Not a model. Not a false front, but a real house.

Delcie entered the front door and held up a hand. "We wait here for Sierra."

Micha took in the two-story entry with a sparkling chandelier and sweeping staircase. A warm and inviting vibe came from the brightly patterned wallpaper. Only if he ignored the blood spatter on the paper and the pool of blood on the floor, along with several pieces of evidence noted by bright orange evidence numbers.

"What is this building, anyway?" Ava asked.

Delcie shoved her hands into the pockets of her white lab coat. "It's a sixteen hundred square foot house, where we set up mock crime scenes to provide new hires with a hands-on experience in unique crime scenes. Sierra also uses it as a teaching facility to instruct all of her staff in the latest forensic breakthroughs so we can live up to our reputation as a cutting-edge lab."

"Wow," Micha said. "Quite an investment for that."

"As I always say," a woman with long blond hair and bangs stepped into the foyer, "you can't put a price on greatness." She chuckled, her eyes warm and friendly. "Sierra Rice. Forensic expert and partner here."

Micha held out his hand, and they shook. "Thank you for agreeing to see us last minute like this."

"Of course." She turned to Delcie. "Can you help the staff get this crime scene cleaned up?"

"Sure thing." She hustled into the other room.

Sierra offered her hand to Colin. "Nice to see you again, Colin. How is everyone doing at Shadow Lake?"

"They're all being their usual bossy selves." He chuckled.

"And I'm sure you just go along with everything." Sierra laughed and shook hands with him, then Ava. "Sorry I'm not in my lab, but I have evidence bags here, and I can take possession of your items now if you'll follow me. Careful of the blood. It can be slippery. Especially on tile."

She stepped into a living room where full blackout shades had been lowered making the room darker than normal. "Our home is pretty normal except for the intense blackout shades used in our shooting scenarios. Helps with the laser-trajectory rod usage that Grady and Trent do. And blood stain analysis for the various lights we use in evidence collection too. We've also placed cameras in several areas to allow us to do a better job of training, too."

Micha took it all in. "This place would be great to train law enforcement too."

She nodded. "We agree and take our role in enhancing law enforcement and forensic science seriously. So we allow access for area agency trainings as often as they like."

"Impressive addition since I was last here," Colin said.

"Thank you." She stepped into a kitchen and moved behind an island. From a drawer she took out bags and markers. "Now what do we have?"

Micha placed the bag holding the catapult on the counter. "I did my best to preserve the evidence. None of us touched it. I wore disposable gloves from the first aid kit to handle it and the bag was clean."

She slipped on purple gloves. "Sounds like you know what you're doing."

"Former military intelligence," he said.

"Ah, that explains it." She pulled out a roll of white paper from under the island and covered the counter with a long sheet, then took out the catapult and studied it. "Wood is quite smooth. Lifting any prints that it might hold should be pretty straightforward."

"Good deal," Micha said.

"Well, partially a good deal anyway." She narrowed her eyes. "I can find the prints for you, but if you're expecting me to submit them to AFIS, I can't do that. Not without an official law enforcement investigation."

Micha's good mood evaporated. The Automated Fingerprint Identification System managed by the FBI contained prints from known criminals, which was the most likely way to find a suspect. "We aren't working with law enforcement. At least not yet."

Sierra raised an eyebrow. "Not even Russ Maddox?"

Micha shook his head but didn't elaborate as he didn't want her to refuse to process the evidence when she heard they weren't handling everything on the up-and-up. "We have five potential suspects, though. Three more likely than others."

She rested her gloved hands on the paper. "Then do what you have to do to get their prints to me. That way I can do a manual comparison to see if they touched this device."

"That might be a problem," Colin said. "They're out in a campsite in the boonies on Shadow Lake property."

"But we can do it," Micha said quickly. "Ryan's with them, and he'll find a way to get samples from them. It'll just take time we don't really have to spare."

"Sorry, I wish it were different, but without an official case number and an agency contract, we don't have access."

"Let me call Ryan right now," Colin said. "To get things moving."

He took out his phone and stepped toward the door.

"Did you have additional evidence?" Sierra asked. "I thought I heard something about a boot print."

"We have pictures and a video of that." Micha got out his phone and opened the photo app for her.

She narrowed her eyes and flipped through the photos, enlarging them and studying each one before handing the phone back to Micha. "Text those photos to me. We're part-nering with a university in the UK who's doing 3D scans of footwear in hopes of creating an extensive database. We can quickly scan a suspect's shoe or even a cast or photo of the footprint to see if it's a match. It's sort of like the way DNA is run through CODIS for a match."

The Combined DNA Index System was another FBI managed database, only this one contained DNA instead of fingerprints.

"Speaking of DNA." Micha swiped to the picture of

blood on the wall. "We found blood at one of the suspect's homes."

She squinted at the photo. "Oh, wow, this blood isn't from an ordinary injury. The spray pattern and blood tails would indicate a forceful puncture wound. Could be accidental or someone could have been attacked by another person."

"Do you have any thoughts on which it might be?" Ava asked.

"I would find it odd to hurt yourself badly enough to create such spatter, but say you stabbed your hand or arm with a scissors or screwdriver and hit the right vein, it *could* happen."

"Sounds like you doubt it though," Micha said.

"I do, but I don't like to commit in a situation without more evidence."

"In any event, I brought a sample for you to run for DNA." Micha got out the zipper bag with the swab.

"How long has it been in that bag?"

"A couple of hours."

"Good you got here when you did. Blood stored wet in plastic for more than two hours can have a contamination problem." She studied the bag. "But letting it sit out to dry when you all were on the move could've caused an even bigger contamination issue, so I think you made the right call."

"Thanks for understanding," he said.

She took out the swab and laid it on the paper. "I can get this to Emory to run the DNA, but we'll have the same issue as the prints in that we won't be able to compare to CODIS without proper authorization."

"But we could do the same thing with comparing to the suspects?" Ava asked.

"If you get me samples, yes." Sierra wrote on a small paper bag.

"What about the prints we collect," Ava asked. "Can they be used for DNA?"

Sierra looked up. "Yes, but it would be better to have a separate sample. I have to collect the DNA from the prints first, and you always risk ruining the print."

Micha spun to look at his teammate. "You hear that, Colin?"

"Heard it and on it," he said.

Sierra took off her gloves and pulled a laptop close to her with an evidence log and receipt on the screen. "I'm sorry I can't do more for you."

"I get it," Micha said. "We're very appreciative of anything you can do."

"Then get the print and DNA samples to me as soon as you can, and I'll start working on the items you brought in." Sierra smiled.

"How long might it take?" Micha asked.

"I should have the evidence processed by the time you bring in the suspect samples. And I can handle the prints you provide right away. But you should know DNA will take a minimum of twenty-four hours to run."

"That long?" Worry lifted Ava's tone high as she expressed the same thoughts Micha was having.

"Sorry." Sierra rested a hand on Ava's arm. "I went through an ordeal like this too and completely understand how you feel. But we can't speed DNA up any faster. In fact, you should be prepared for it to take a bit longer, though I assure you we will get it running as fast as is humanly possible."

"Thank you." Ava placed her hand on Sierra's for a moment and shared a knowing look with her.

"In the meantime let me finish up this evidence receipt."

Sierra went back to her computer. "I'll call you if I learn anything from the boot print that might help."

"I should've mentioned that I questioned the possible suspects about boot brands they wear," Ava said. "They gave me company names. Would it be helpful if I texted them to you?"

"Absolutely." Sierra's smile widened in earnest now. "It could make it faster to determine a match."

Ava got out her phone. "Your number?"

Sierra provided it.

"Texting now," Ava said.

Micha hadn't been sure about Ava questioning the men about their boot choices. He'd feared she would slip up and alert them to their suspicions, but she'd done a good job of it. Now her quick thinking could be the key to figuring out which of the men—if any of them—had set the catapult that could've ended her life.

9

Nearing eleven, Ava was restless. Not sleepy in the least and no point in even trying. She would just toss and turn and likely raise her anxiety. Colin had gone out to put a tracker on Layne's vehicle, and after coming back, he'd headed to one of the bedrooms to investigate the validity of the video from Layne. Micha sat next to her on the sofa, a laptop on his knees as he looked up Atlas Armory, and she was left to figure out what to do while she waited for him to finish his research.

Move. Just move. She got up and wandered around the apartment. The place wasn't what she expected. She figured it would be like a hotel suite or a rental apartment, stark and sterile, but there were homey touches, like colorful pillows on the buttery-soft leather sofa and scenic coastal pictures on the wall. The kitchen was well stocked with cooking supplies, too.

She opened a tall cabinet near the living area and found toys and games for various ages. She could imagine being here with family and sitting at the round dining table, playing any one of these games. Maybe *Chutes and Ladders* with a young child. Her child.

Don't even go there.

Thankfully Micha looked up at her to save her from her wayward thoughts.

"You see this?" She stepped back for him to see the games and toys. "Seems like odd gear for a protection team."

"All the team members are married with kids, so maybe the families use this place too."

"Could be." She'd looked Gage up on the Blackwell tactical website and had seen his photo. Instead of thinking of the kids she'd have someday, she pictured him with a wife and children and was overwhelmed by the man's generosity again. "I'd love to thank Gage in person, but if not, maybe on a video call."

"I'm sure that can be arranged. If..." His words fell off.

She looked at the dark line of concern in his eyes, and her stomach roiled. "If my stalker doesn't get to me or I'm not sent to prison, right? You just didn't want to say it."

"Yeah."

She appreciated his honesty, but maybe he could learn to keep things like this to himself. Still, her brain might've gone there all on its own. She crossed the room and joined him on the sofa. "Do you have a gut feel for which of our suspects is the guilty party?"

"My gut says Buck, but the facts don't really support one guy over the other right now."

"I hope the evidence we turned in provides a lead."

He didn't answer right away, stowing his phone and shifting to face her. "I want the same thing, but having worked investigations for so many years and being disappointed a lot of the time, I'm not holding out hope."

More brutal honesty. "But you didn't have the Veritas Center experts helping you."

"True that."

"I was very impressed with Sierra."

"Me too, and the entire center has a solid reputation. Maybe you're right and hoping a little might not hurt." He smiled at her and held her gaze. His angst vanished, and his eyes warmed to a honey brown.

Her heart flip-flopped. "Now you're just trying to make me feel better."

"I am," he admitted.

Reality did its very best to settle into her body and grab a firm hold. "I could really go to prison, couldn't I?"

"It seems possible, but remember we're just beginning the investigation. When Colin gets the original video tomorrow, it could very well contain info to prove your innocence."

"You really think he'll be able to persuade them to give it to him?"

"You said the administrator's a woman, right?"

"Right."

"Then yes. This might sound sexist, but when Colin turns on the charm, women are hard-pressed to say no to him. Not that he abuses it, but he does use it to his advantage in investigations."

She could see that as Colin had proven to be quite the charmer. "You probably do too."

"Probably, but he's more charismatic than I am."

"I don't know. You have your moments." Relishing the change in mood, she grinned at him.

His expression remained serious. "You think so, huh?"

"I do," she said sincerely.

"Then if I turn all my wiles on you, does that mean you'll fall for me?" he asked, sounding very unsure of his abilities to charm her.

She wasn't sure how to answer his question, but she would take a stab at it. "Is that what you want to happen?"

He went so still she didn't know if she'd offended him.

"I do." He looked her in the eyes. "And I don't. I can't make a commitment. My sister needs me more than ever right now, and I have to focus on her first."

Ava appreciated his dedication to his sister—very admirable—but she wanted to know more. Know everything she could about this wonderful guy. "Can I ask how she was injured?"

He grimaced. "A freak accident. She fell from a step stool and injured her spine. Became paralyzed. Verdict's still out on if it will be temporary or permanent, but her husband couldn't handle it, and he walked out on her and their daughter. The poor kid is really suffering from the situation. She's barely talking. So you see why I don't have time for dating, especially not seriously. I can't make another commitment."

"How awful for her. For them." She reached for his hand and held it, his skin rough and calloused against hers. "I'm sorry they're having to go through such a traumatic situation."

"It's hard." His voice cracked.

"I can't imagine her exact situation, but I grew up much like the two of you and can understand how very important your bond with her must be."

"You grew up in the system?"

She nodded. "Not something I like to talk about, but yeah. My mom was into drugs and ended up becoming estranged from our entire family. Her choice. Kept them all from me. But then someone reported how she neglected me, and she was deemed unfit. She didn't want the family to know she'd failed and lied to her caseworker about having any family. So I went into care at ten years old. She refused to let me be adopted, wouldn't relinquish the rights."

Micha gritted his teeth and reversed their hands so his cupped hers. He held tightly. "That's rough."

"Which is why I don't like to talk about it. Best to leave it in the past."

"I understand that, as long as you don't let it fester and cause problems."

Did he speak from experience? Could be as she'd known a lot of foster kids who carried their issues with them. "I can't say that it hasn't had a part in who I've become. Maybe even why I'm still single."

"You said you want to get married and have kids, right?"

"I do, but only if I can do it the right way. I want to be sure whoever I marry will be a forever husband. I don't want to put a child through divorce."

"I get that. I want the same thing. Which is why it's so hard to see my sister's husband take off when a big problem struck. We all thought he wasn't the running kind."

This man's actions made her stomach turn. He was exactly like the guy she hoped to avoid. "How can a person ever really know?"

"They can't, which is why any relationship is a risk."

She loved how much Micha had thought about this and that he was willing to sideline himself while he had to turn his commitments elsewhere. Proved he wouldn't want to hurt a woman by neglecting her.

Was he a risk or a sure thing?

She let her gaze linger on his face, searching for answers. Finding only one. He'd already found his way into her heart. "I could fall for you, Micha Nichols. Quite easily, I think. You have to know I'm very attracted to you."

His eyes darkened. "But you won't do anything about it because you don't think I can be that guy you're looking for?"

"No, I think you have the potential to be a forever kind of guy." She smiled when her heart was aching. "But I'm not a forever woman right now. Not with this murder charge hanging over my head. No point in starting anything until that's resolved in my favor." Her mood darkened. "*If* it's resolved."

He cupped the side of her face. She should pull away but leaned into his affectionate touch and reveled in the tenderness coming from such a powerful man.

"I'll solve it and won't fail you." His words came out on a whisper. "I promise."

No way he could promise such a thing, but his touch and his utter confidence gave her enough hope that she let go of everything, including her common sense, and leaned forward to kiss him. Just a soft pressing of her lips against his before sitting back and releasing his hand.

Oh, wow, she hadn't expected such surprising emotions from a simple kiss. Her thoughts. Heart. Body. All jumbled up with something she couldn't name. Not when she'd never felt like this before.

He drew in a long breath and let it out. "Does that mean you believe I'll help you?"

Oh, she did. Sure, she did. But that didn't mean he could keep his promise. "It means I know you will do your very best, and that's all I can ask."

~

Micha had just made a promise he had no idea if he could keep. But how could he not with those big eyes trained on him? The soft, gentle kiss pressed against his mouth, firing off all of his senses. And now he wanted to sweep her into his arms and promise her the moon.

Cheesy, he knew, but she brought up feelings new to him, and he felt like a teenager with his first crush, though more intense and driven. But she'd made it clear he was to stay at arm's length right now, and he would respect her wishes. After all, that was what he wanted, too. No *needed*, too.

Before he did something she wouldn't appreciate, he opened his computer and notified the team of an impromptu meeting. "Let's follow up with the team. See if Dev got an appointment with the ME and if the guys have any idea what to do about the major cache of weapons we had to leave behind."

She looked at the wall clock. "Isn't it getting late for a call?"

"No worries. We work all hours." He arranged a video conference call and sent the link to the guys. Whoever was up, which was bound to be most of the team, would answer soon.

Colin came out of the bedroom and plopped down on a swivel chair, moving it around to face them and setting his laptop on his knees. "I hope this is important."

Micha ignored his comment and nodded at Colin's laptop. "You find something?"

"Yep." He tapped the closed computer. "First, the video seems legit. Not altered at all, and I suspect the one we get from the center will match."

Ava pounded her fist on the arm of her chair. "I hoped he'd modified it somehow, and the police couldn't use it."

"Sorry," Colin said.

"And second?" Micha asked, hoping to hear something that might boost Ava's morale, not take it down even more.

"I made some progress on the suspect background checks. Specifically Buck. I found posts he made on the dark web. Subversive, anarchy kinds of posts. They're from last year, and I haven't found anything current, but it was all about overthrowing our government and white supremacy."

Ava cringed. "Makes me want to have Ryan ditch the guy in the wilderness."

Micha couldn't agree more, but... "Obviously we can't do that. But we need to make sure Ryan is informed. Buck could be carrying and dangerous."

Ava looked at Colin. "Did you find any connection to Layne?"

Colin shook his head. "Which is probably good. Buck seems unhinged, and if Layne has him coming after you, who knows what the guy might do."

"Sounds like he could go rogue and enjoy it," Micha said.

Ava shuddered.

Micha didn't care if Colin was sitting across from them, he squeezed her hand. "Don't worry. We won't let anything happen to you."

She looked at him with a boatload of trust, churning his gut.

"Guess I should get connected to the call, so I'm ready when the others are." Colin opened his computer.

Micha's computer dinged and he looked at the screen. Colin successfully accessed the meeting Micha had set up. Another ding.

"Yo." Rubbing his eyes, Dev came on the screen below Colin. "I was just going to hit the hay."

Micha shared his screen with Ava and wasted no time explaining their situation to Dev. "You arrange that appointment with the ME?"

"I did you one better." He grinned. "Just finalized you for eight a.m. with the assistant I know. Guy's name is Toby Wetzler."

Say what? "How could an assistant be better than the big honcho?"

"He's a college buddy of mine, and he's more likely to give you the info you need than the ME, who I think you'll strike out with."

Reid joined the group on screen, looking alert as usual. "Problem?"

Micha told them about the weapon's stash, and Colin chimed in, explaining his dark web discovery for Buck.

"And you should also know we found a tripwire at Jamal's front door," Micha added. "Could simply be set up to tell him someone has been there or could be for explosives. I didn't stick around to find out but got Ava out of there."

"As I would want you to do." Reid flexed his jaw muscles. "I don't like the sound of those two and don't want to risk them out in the wilderness with Ryan or the other participants."

"You want to cancel the class?" Micha asked, as he'd never seen Reid do that, but then they'd never had a dire situation like this before either.

Reid nodded. "But I hate to. Especially when participants often make arrangements months in advance and take time off work. But it's too high of a risk to have these guys on site. I'll get on the phone to Ryan so he knows what he's dealing with and have him bring the group back to the compound first thing in the morning. Then we'll help them clear out their cabins and escort them off the property."

"I get your reasoning," Micha said. "But from a protection standpoint for Ava, if one of them *is* the guy after her, knowing where they are at all times has been a good thing."

"Sorry, Ava." Reid cast her an apologetic look. "But I have to think of the greater good, and this now involves other people. Others could get hurt if one of those guys lost it out there."

"I completely understand and would have you do nothing less." She smiled at Reid.

Micha didn't have such an agreeable attitude, but he would get there. He had to. Besides, once Reid made up his mind, there was no changing it. Time to move on. "Can someone search their vehicles before they return?"

Reid nodded. "Odds are good they have vehicle alarms, but we can try."

"Thanks," Micha said. "And what about the weapon stash? Any idea on what to do about that? I didn't feel good about leaving it behind, but now that we know Buck's a little unhinged, I like it even less."

"We have to figure out a way to get the authorities out there without implicating any of us." Reid tipped up a water bottle.

Ava moved closer to the laptop. "And how do you suggest we do that?"

"Make them think he's hoarding illegal weapons," Dev said.

Colin's gaze flashed to his brother. "We don't know that they *are* illegal."

Micha agreed, except..."The AK-47 is suspicious for sure."

"You said you found a gun dealer's business card," Dev said. "Maybe we've dealt with them in the past and can check in with them. What's the company name?"

"Atlas Armory," Micha said. "In Beaverton."

Reid set down his water bottle. "Never heard of it."

"Me either," Micha said. "But I looked it up online. Both a store and firing range. Seems to be fairly new."

Dev tilted his head. "Wouldn't have thought there'd be enough interest in an upscale suburb like Beaverton for a shooting range and gun dealer."

"You'd be surprised who's carrying these days." Reid looked straight into the camera. "Still, a trip to the store might get info we need to go on."

Micha scoffed. "You know gun dealers are notoriously closemouthed."

"It's been my experience as a deputy," Dev said, "that legit ones who are offended by someone breaking the law could be willing to help."

Ava darted her gaze to Micha off-screen. "It's worth checking out, right? Especially since there doesn't seem to be any other reason we can get law enforcement to visit the property."

"I'd recommend a welfare check," Dev said. "But your name would be on that report, and you'd have to be okay with Buck finding out about it."

"I'm not good with that," Micha said.

"You could phone in an anonymous tip," Colin said. "But not sure they would take that seriously, and unless you find a payphone, the call could be tracked back to you."

"I think it's better we wait to see if we can find a legit way to get the police out there." Micha peered at the group. "Any other ideas besides visiting the gun dealer?"

They shook their heads.

Micha clapped his hands, startling Ava. "Then I'll hit the store tomorrow after my visit to the ME's office."

Reid frowned, reminding Micha of Russ, who used to frown a lot before he got married. Now he was a pussy cat. Well, a pussy cat in Russ's terms, which meant more like a semi-feral cat.

"Even if the store owner does give you info," Reid said, "we'll still need to figure a way to get it to law enforcement without implicating any of us in the process."

Micha nodded. "The kind of info we get could inform our next step, so let's think on it tonight."

"Agreed," Reid said. "I'll let you know when Ryan is safely back in the compound and Buck and Jamal are packed and on their way out of here."

"Hey, wait," Dev said. "What do you think about putting

trackers on Buck's and Jamal's vehicles? That way we'll know where they are at all times."

"Not a bad idea," Colin said.

"Maybe for the average guy, but a paranoid prepper like these two?" Micha asked. "They might inspect their vehicles every time they leave their property."

"Micha is right," Reid said. "Might not be worth the risk to tip our hand. Don't want Buck to move that stockpile or escalate any further attempts on Ava's life."

Ava sucked in a sharp breath, but the others nodded.

"If that's all, let's get after it." Reid looked at them for a moment, then clicked off.

"Hang on a minute, Dev," Micha said. "I have something to talk to you about."

Micha looked at Ava and stood. "Be right back."

He stepped into the hallway where she couldn't hear the uncertainty in his tone as he questioned Dev. "You really think this Toby guy will let me look at the autopsy report?"

"Sounded like he would, but then you never know when it comes down to violating policy. Some people come through. Others freeze and bail on you. If he balks, I know you can be persuasive. Still, you might have to resort to talking in hypotheticals and approach him that way."

"Yeah, I can be persuasive if I need to be."

"I'm not talking force here, dude." Dev laughed.

Micha didn't find any of this funny. "You have any hints on what might tip him my way?"

"Hmm." Dev drummed his fingers on the table in front of him. "He's really big into military battles. Wars. Especially World War II. You find a way to work that into the conversation and it could get you some brownie points."

"Are you kidding?" Micha gaped at his teammate. "I studied battles in the Marines, but how does a guy causally bring World War II into a conversation?"

125

"That's a tough one. But you have all night to figure it out 'cause I know you won't be closing those eyes while Ava's in any danger."

Dev was right. Micha wouldn't be closing his eyes. But then, that didn't at all mean he could come up with a way to mention World War II to Toby. Still, he had to figure it out.

Especially when Ava's life could depend on it.

10

Micha didn't want to leave Ava behind at the apartment the next morning, but he couldn't risk someone at the ME's office recognizing her. He trusted Colin to watch over her, but he trusted his own skills more. He could've let Colin interview Toby, but Colin had work to do on his computer. Micha knew deep down Ava was safe. He just needed to suck it up and relax a notch on that protective stuff.

He pulled into the lot of the large building located on the far east side of the Portland metro area. The Clackamas County Medical Examiner's Office took up the right side of the modern building while the Oregon State Crime Lab filled the other half. He'd had a chance to tour both facilities in the past and was most impressed, but not as impressed as he was with the Veritas Center.

He parked and entered the small vestibule to ring the bell for admittance. Smiling up at the camera that he knew the receptionist would be watching, he waited until the buzzer sounded and the door popped open.

He entered the industrial-looking reception area. A woman with her hair buzzed short on the sides and sticking up like a scrub brush on top, gave him a tight smile. "We only have one appointment on the books this morning, so I suspect you're here to see Dr. Wetzler."

He nodded. "Micha Nichols."

"I'll need to see some ID for my log. While you get it out, I'll give him a call." She lifted the receiver on her phone and relayed the information to Toby.

Micha fished out his driver's license and provided it to the woman.

She studied it. "Shadow Lake, huh? I grew up in that area of the state. Lovely place, but not a lot of jobs and opportunities, so I came to the big city to make my fortune. Not hardly doing that here." She chuckled and started writing down his details in a formal-looking logbook. "Where do you work there, if you don't mind me asking?"

"Did you know the Maddox family?" Micha asked. "They owned a resort on the lake."

"Boy, did I." She lifted her head to stare at him. "I was two years ahead of Reid in school, and those boys were involved in everything. Including making a lot of young girls' hearts swoon. Is their family still running the resort?"

Micha shook his head. "Their parents moved to town, and the brothers run a wilderness survival group out of the family lodge. That's where I work."

"And you're here to see Dr. Wetzler, so you must have a big problem." She handed back his driver's license and watched him expectantly.

"No problem at the resort. Just need some background information." He felt like he was lying, though, in fact, he *was* here to get background info. The cause of death.

The back door opened, and a guy in his early thirties with unruly red hair and a freckle-covered face stepped over to them. He wore scrubs and white sneakers, a risk in Micha's book. Even wearing protective booties didn't likely protect them from all the body fluids they must deal with.

He shot out a hand. "Toby Wetzler."

Micha shook and winced at a punishing grip he didn't expect from the slender guy.

"Come on back. You can catch me up on what Devan is up to as we walk." He led the way to the door that he released with a key card.

As they strode down a hall with doors to offices, Micha told him about Shadow Lake Survival and Devan's role in the company.

"I'm glad he was able to get out of law enforcement." Toby opened the door to a small office. A glorified closet really. "He was burning out. This place is a pressure cooker, and I totally get how the demands of a job can affect your life."

The opening Micha needed. "So what do you do to relieve your stress?"

Toby slipped behind the small desk that held a pair of glasses, a laptop, and a pencil cup filled with stick pens. "You'll probably find this weird. I know I do. With all the death I deal with here, you'd think I'd look for something like yoga or meditation. Something more life-affirming, but my real passion outside of work is battles from World War II."

"Not odd at all." Micha dropped onto the chair and resisted gloating at his success on what he'd expected to be a nearly impossible task. "That war fascinates me too. I mean, how can one man be responsible for waging a war where an estimated sixty million people were killed? Sixty million. That just blows my mind.

"Exactly." Toby scowled. "I know the estimates are all over the place. Some saying as low as thirty-five mil, but still. That number is too hard to really even comprehend. One guy. Just one guy."

He shook his head and sat staring for a moment as if

he'd forgotten Micha was in the room. He suddenly blinked. "How'd you get interested in it?"

"Served as a Marine, and for a while, I was obsessed with all things military. What about you?"

"Family. We lost a lot of family members to the Holocaust, and in high school, I wanted to try to understand it. Then I got hooked on the military strategy. From that day on, I've tried to create other scenarios that might've changed the course of the war. Shortened it perhaps." He clasped his hands on the desk. "I figure I keep doing it because I still can't make any sense of it, and my brain is trying to process. Sort of like I do here. With homicides or victims of violence."

"I never understood how medical examiners like you can do this job, but I have all the respect in the world for you."

"I feel the same way about service members. Not sure I'd be willing to risk my life like you all do." He waved a hand. "Listen to our mutual admiration society. So what did you need from me?"

Micha figured he'd buttered the guy up enough, and he should be straightforward in his approach. "I was hoping to learn the official cause of death for a Holly Boyle. She recently died in a hospice care facility, and my friend told me it was from dehydration and organ failure."

He lifted a thick eyebrow. "And who is this Holly Boyle to you? Family?"

"No. My friend cared for her in the facility and thinks there was perhaps a cover-up on her cause of death. Because I served in military investigations, she thought I could figure out if there was foul play and asked me to try to get to the bottom of it."

"Let me see what I can find." He grabbed the mouse for his computer.

Please let him give me the answer I need.

"Okay, I see it. Only one Holly Boyle in our system." He picked up the glasses and settled them on his nose. "It's as you said. Organ failure from severe dehydration. Food poisoning was suspected but not confirmed."

"Can you test for that?"

"Yes, there are tests to confirm food poisoning."

"Did they test for it?"

"No, it wasn't done by the center, but we sent in samples."

"Why wouldn't the center test for it?" Micha asked.

Toby looked at Micha through the glasses, and his pupils were much larger through the lenses. "Says here no one else at the facility got sick, and so food poisoning wasn't considered. Not surprising, I suppose. Usually you see more than one case in an environment like this where the same food is prepared for most residents. If the center had considered it, they could've tested for the offending food." He glanced back at the computer. "I see results for our samples are still outstanding."

"Can you put pressure on the lab to get the results?"

He shook his head. "I'm not listed on this case, so they would refuse. Plus, any request outside of my assigned cases would raise red flags that would escalate to the ME, and I don't want to lose my job."

"But a source other than food poisoning could've caused her illness?"

"Sure." He squinted at the screen. "Hmm. Not sure why this wasn't looked into, but then she was in hospice care, so it wouldn't be unusual."

Interest piqued, Micha sat forward. "What wouldn't be unusual?"

"We located a small puncture wound on her leg with a surrounding bruise consistent with a needle. The bruise wasn't fresh, which means the injection wasn't given on the day of death, but before that."

Injection. Oh wow. That could be significant. "Could someone have poisoned her?"

"Poisoned?" He leaned his chair back and looked up at the ceiling. "Her food poisoning symptoms might suggest that, but why? Her cancer was at a very advanced state and would've taken her in a short time, so why not just wait?"

"To exact revenge, maybe," Micha said. "I don't know, but the needle mark could mean she was poisoned."

"Or could simply suggest an intramuscular injection given by a doctor or nurse."

"Wouldn't she have had an IV or a PICC line to administer all of her drugs?" Micha had seen the PICC—peripherally inserted central catheters—used in the military for various reasons, but most often for chemo.

Toby snapped his chair forward and stared at the screen. "She had a PICC line and IV. But some drugs are still administered into the muscle or subcutaneously."

"Might it be worth having a tox screen done, just to be sure she wasn't poisoned?" Micha phrased it as a question, but he wanted to demand Toby arrange to have one done.

"I suppose." He sucked in his lower lip and held it. "But that could only happen with the ME's approval."

The answer Micha expected but didn't much like. "But if Holly were your patient, wouldn't this evidence make you want to order that now?"

"It would, but even if I was willing to go to the ME, which I'm not, her body was released some time ago. I have to assume she's already been interred, and we can't take a tissue sample. Besides, some poisons aren't detectable for as long as she's been gone."

"What about exhuming the body?"

"No. No." Toby planted his hands on the edge of the desk

and looked like he was going to get up and end the conversation, but he removed his hands. "No way anyone would exhume her based on this information. Especially when I can't give the ME a logical reason why I'm even questioning one of his autopsies."

"What about her blood?" Micha asked. "Might the lab still have a sample of it? Could you look for toxins there?"

"It's possible." Toby took off his glasses and dropped them on the desk with a loud clink. "But again, the ME would have to order the tests."

Toby was starting to sound like a record. A broken one that Micha didn't like. "What about checking her chart notes at hospice care? See if there's a record of an injection into the muscle where the needle mark was located?"

Toby rested his elbows on the desk and steepled his fingers. "That I could probably get away with doing."

"And would you be willing to do it?"

"Yeah, I suppose."

"Soon?" Micha pressed.

He glanced at his watch. "I'm off in an hour, if no emergencies come in, I could go by the place on my way home."

"Thank you." Micha stood as he wanted to get out of there before Toby changed his mind. Right now this lead was the best one they had, and Micha didn't want to do anything to jeopardize it.

Ava swiveled in the car seat to look at Micha. They were on the way to question the gun dealer who might've sold weapons to Buck, and Micha had just shared his conversation with Toby Wetzel. His tone was flat—emotionless—and she couldn't tell what he thought about the outcome.

She desperately needed something to pin her hopes on.

Anything, no matter how small, that moved them in the right direction. No way she would let the information he'd just shared go without discussing it.

She shifted even more to face him. "Do you think Toby will actually follow through and ask to see Holly's records?"

"I do." Micha exited the highway onto a busy four-lane road.

Not what your body language is saying. "Why don't you sound more enthusiastic about it?"

He came to a stop at the red light and glanced at her. "The same old thing. Years of experience where leads don't pan out. But also I'm concerned that a visit to the hospice center twice in one day—Colin and Toby—might raise suspicions and they could somehow lead back to you."

She hadn't even thought of that, but Micha's investigator brain did, and she was thankful. Still, she wished he didn't feel a need to be so suspicious. Must be unsettling. "You think it's possible?"

He shrugged. "You learn in the military to plan and prepare for the worst possible scenario and be glad when the outcome is better. A holdover I don't know if I'll ever lose."

With his neatness, organization, and dedication to service, she could easily imagine him as a Marine. "Did you like being a Marine?"

"I mean, it had its downsides like low pay and moving often, but yeah, the jobs I held were great and so were the people. Overall, I'd recommend it for sure." The light changed, and he punched the gas.

She waited until he swerved around a car that came to a quick stop before saying, "I don't think you mentioned why you left."

"My sister needed me to be stateside full time and nearby for her."

"You're a good brother, and she's lucky to have you."

He cast her a brief smile. "I do my best."

"And I'm guessing your best is more than most people's best." She squeezed his hand that was resting on the gear shift. "I think you're an amazing guy, Micha, and I'm glad I got the chance to know you. Even if it is in such a trying situation."

"Backatcha." He twined his fingers in hers but didn't say anything else.

She leaned back, her heart at peace despite her circumstances. She was sure that would change once they reached the gun shop, but for now she would savor his touch and the warm feelings it brought.

They made the last few turns in silence. The exact opposite of the firing guns that greeted them at the gun shop and range. She didn't want to be in a place like this, but if Buck had purchased at least one of his weapons here—maybe the AK-47—they could learn something to help.

Inside the place, an aroma from fresh building supplies greeted them, and the fixtures looked new, too.

She stepped in. "Doesn't look like the store's been open long."

Micha frowned. "Which means we could be out of luck, and Buck didn't buy many, if any, of his weapons here."

She looked up at him. "Do you mind if I take lead here? Maybe the guy won't be as suspicious of me as he would of a guy who knows his weapons as well as you do."

"I don't think it much matters." Micha's shoulders drooped. "He's already sized me up and made me for military or law enforcement and could clam up."

"Still, I could try."

"Sure." He smiled. "Just don't expect a miracle."

She headed straight for the guy standing behind a display case. He had dark hair graying in a weird pattern around his head like below where a ball cap might've sat. Wrinkles creased the sides of his eyes, and his stomach hung over his belt. He had a gun at his side and several tattoos on his hands and arms.

Behind him, the back wall held a display of rifles. She quickly counted nine rows of five different guns and couldn't believe they needed such an assortment. Glass-enclosed cases sat in front of it with handguns mounted upright in impressive displays.

The man planted wrinkly hands on the polished glass. "Help you?"

"Hi." She smiled. "First let me say I don't know a thing about guns and need to rely on your expertise."

"No worries, little lady." His shoulders lifted. "I'm Rob. I own this place, and I got enough knowledge for all three of us." He fired a challenging look at Micha.

Micha tightened his hands. He obviously wanted to come back with a comment disputing Rob's superiority to his military weapons knowledge, but held his tongue.

"So I have this friend I'm worried about." She clutched her hands together to emphasize her concern, though Buck was far from a friend. "He's kind of gone off the deep end into conspiracy theories and prepping for Armageddon."

"Sorry to hear that," Rob said, sounding sincere.

"I don't want him to get in trouble for owning anything illegal, you know?"

"Sure, I get it." Rob rested a hip against the counter.

"So when he showed me his cache, he had an AK 47 he was extremely proud of. I don't know anything about them, but I heard you can't own one in our state."

Rob came upright, his eyes wide now. "Well, yes and no. Oregon would count a fully automatic version as a machine gun, and for the most part, it would be illegal to own." He went on to explain the gun registry before May of 1986, just like Micha had reported to her.

"He had your store's business card in his stash," Ava said. "Could he have bought it here?"

"We've had a few for sale." Rob pursed his lips. "I sold all of them except one. Tell me what this friend looks like."

Ava described Buck the best she could.

"Nah, he's not one of the guys I sold to, but could be the sale I didn't handle."

"Might you be willing to look his name up to see if he did get it here and if it's legal? I would feel so much better about it." She ended with a beaming smile she hoped might gain his compliance.

"To put your mind at ease, little lady, I'd be glad to." He returned her smile. "What's his name?"

"Buck. Corey Buck. I can give you his address if you need it."

"Might if I find more than one CB in my system." He stepped down to the end of the counter and started typing on his keyboard, using the one-finger hunt-and-peck method. He focused intently on his work.

Ava gave Micha a quick glance.

"You're doing great," he leaned down to whisper.

His breath on her cheek made her nearly forget her task. Not good. She stepped away to keep her mind on Buck.

"Nope." Rob looked up. "Didn't buy anything here. Not even ammo."

She worked hard not to let her disappointment show. "Is there anywhere locally that might've sold the gun to him on the QT?"

He stepped back down their way, trailing his finger over the edge of the counter. "I hope you aren't insinuating that I mighta done that because I didn't."

"No. Of course not." She met his gaze to make him believe her. "I can tell you run a reputable shop."

"I do, and I'm glad you can see that." He planted his hands on the counter. "So anything is possible if he was willing to pay the price. And if he bought it before February of last year, he could've gotten it from the worst offending dealer of all time. Slimy as all get out. Big into straw sales. That's where he made all the money he's now forking over to lawyers to keep him out of prison."

"Straw?" she asked.

"When firearms are purchased with the intent to resell them. They're usually sold to someone who the law prohibits from purchasing guns. Like felons or underage kids."

Ava shook her head. "That's just all kinds of wrong."

"Exactly. But Squib didn't care?"

"Squib, huh." Micha chimed in for the first time. "Interesting nickname."

"But fitting." Rob grinned.

Ava looked between them. "Will one of you mind telling me what a squib is?"

Rob turned his gaze back on her. "A squib is when a bullet gets lodged in the barrel."

"Never heard of that," she said, but Micha bit his lip, and she could tell he wanted to explain it but held back.

"Not surprising if you don't know about guns." Rob gave her that patronizing look again. "The two biggest reasons a squib occurs are when there isn't enough gunpowder to eject the bullet from the barrel or contamination stops the powder from fully igniting. So when the bullet is fired into the barrel, it gets lodged. If not fixed before firing the next shot, it can destroy the weapon, injure the shooter or even people nearby."

Okay, but..."And that fits this dealer, how?"

"A squib fouls the weapon, and he's run afoul of the law for so many years that he earned the nickname."

Ah, now she got it. "Sounds like a great guy."

Rob clenched his jaw. "You don't know the half of it. Gives all of us reputable dealers a bad rep. The feds finally closed him down in February. He didn't file any of his paperwork. No record of background checks. Blatant disregard for the law and he's gonna stand trial for it. Hope they throw the book at him."

She did too, but..."Too bad it won't help me find out if my friend's gun is legal."

Rob leaned on the case. "I didn't say that it wouldn't. Squib might not have filed the right paperwork, but he had a security camera that recorded all of his sales. The feds found years' worth of files on his computer. Maybe you could somehow get a look at them."

"Sure. Yeah, maybe," she said, trying to convince herself that it was a possibility when she doubted it would be. "Thank you for your help, Rob. Can I give you my number in case you think of anything that might help?"

"Sure." He grabbed a paper and pen and slid them across the counter. "If I was twenty years younger and single, I would've already asked for it." He cackled with laughter.

She forced a grin and jotted down her number before saying goodbye. She stepped outside with Micha.

He let out a long breath, acting like their visit was a bust.

"You did good not commenting or questioning," she said as they walked to the SUV. "I saw you have to bite your lip at times."

"I did, but you did a great job of managing that guy, and me chiming in on weaponry might've made him clam up."

"So why do you look so down? Is it because you know there's no way the feds will let us look at these files?"

"Yeah, but don't lose all hope. With Reid and Colin as former FBI agents, they might have contacts who could make it happen for us."

"Will they do that for us?"

"I'm certain they'll try. They know if we can prove Buck bought the gun illegally, the police will have a reason to search his home and find the stash of weapons. Not only could this prevent the guy from taking potshots at you, but equally as important, it could prevent a mass shooting event."

Mass shooting. Ava sucked in a breath, but she had no reason to be shocked. She'd seen the pile of weapons. No person needed a stockpile like Buck had amassed. He could only be planning to use it in a nefarious way. They had to stop him and stop him soon.

He would be coming home tomorrow and would once again have a major cache of weapons at his fingertips.

11

Back at the apartment, Micha followed Ava to the sofa where he got Reid, Colin, and Dev on a conference call. Ava clenched her hands and tapped a nervous foot. She'd been jittery like this for the entire drive.

He hadn't spoken with her much because he was disappointed in their result with Rob and was thinking about how the team could best help now. Especially Reid with his federal contacts. Micha didn't know why Ava had been quiet, though. She was likely disappointed as well. Maybe worried about Buck and Jamal coming back to civilization. Coming after her again.

Colin stepped out of the bedroom, laptop in hand as usual. "Got your video file from the hospice administrator."

Ava shot forward on the sofa. "You did? You really did?"

"Don't be so surprised. I'm one of the best." He grinned. "I emailed a copy to the rest of the team, too, so they can see the same thing we're looking at."

"Is it any different than the one Layne sent me?" Ava locked a nervous look on Colin.

"Take a look." He pushed his way between them on the sofa and set the computer on his knees. He started a video playing. "This one begins sooner than the one Layne sent to you, and it has two different angles that I spliced together."

Ava scooted closer. "This is in the common area outside the facility, and that's Holly in the wheelchair with the plaid blanket on her legs."

The gaunt woman with eyes sunken into deep sockets leaned back in her chair parked on a wide veranda near three other residents. She'd closed her eyes, the sun beating down on her face. She might be ravaged by disease, but she emitted a peaceful vibe.

Ava stared at the screen, her eyes welling with tears. "I made sure to take Holly outside whenever we had a sunny day. She loved to feel the heat on her face. It reminded her of a psalm in the Bible where it says God is a sun and shield, and the rays helped her know everything would be all right. She said feeling the warmth from the sun God created was like He was pre-welcoming her to heaven."

If Micha were in her shoes, could he rest in God's assurances like that? He had no idea. If he took into consideration how he was handling Tristin's paralysis, *no* would most definitely be the answer. What he needed to do with his worry for her was give it to God and rest in His peace. His worry for Ava, too. Needed to do it, but could he?

"Here's where I found a different angle recorded at the same time," Colin said.

"There! That's me." Ava pointed at a woman climbing the hill from the back of the property. "This one shows the way I arrive. It was my day off, so I came in the back way to avoid any questions about why I was at the center. I have the cookie dough in a container."

"Coming in that way could make your visit more suspicious looking," Colin said.

The opposite of what Micha hoped this video might show.

In the video, Ava moved closer to Holly, and he took in Ava's curvy figure in the jeans and purple fleece, open in front to reveal a body-hugging knit top. She looked at peace, too, not like the stressed-out woman he'd seen so far. And so filled with vitality compared to Holly.

He glanced at her. "You're so amazing to be able to work with terminal patients."

"Not amazing. I just feel called to do it." She gave him a quick smile. "I figure it's a great time to introduce a nonbeliever to God. I have to be careful about it or I could lose my job, but they usually ask me about my faith first, and then I'm free to share."

Movement on the screen caught his attention, which was a blessing as he was letting himself get down again and wanted to call out so many questions to God that He previously hadn't answered. And really, it wasn't Micha's place even to be questioning God.

Ava walked up to Holly in the video and knelt next to her.

Colin pointed at the screen. "Back to the other camera angle which is what the video Layne sent Ava shows."

Holly sat forward, and her gaze landed on Ava. Holly's eyes glowed with affection for Ava, and she grasped Holly's hand. If Micha had any doubt that Ava would have killed this woman, he didn't after seeing their connection.

The moment was over in a flash, and Ava held out the cookie dough container. Holly grabbed it and tried to open the container but faltered.

"She didn't have enough strength to get the container open, and I had to do it for her." Ava frowned. "She didn't have long to live. Why, oh why, couldn't whoever killed her let her pass in peace instead of making her so very sick at the end?"

"People can be very cruel." Micha took her hand. "But you know she's with God now."

"And she's not suffering any longer, so that's a good thing." Her tone didn't reflect her words. She missed this woman. That was obvious.

On screen, Ava handed Holly a spoon. Holly scooped out a large chunk of dough but only nibbled on the edges.

"Her desire for the dough was great, her appetite not so much," Ava said. "And she hadn't been eating a lot before that. Which is one of the reasons I made the cookie dough. I thought it might spark her appetite, but she didn't end up eating much of the dough. I left it with her but don't know what happened to the container as no one ever mentioned it to me."

"We should see if it's in the police report," Reid said, speaking for the first time. Micha had almost forgotten he and Dev were there. "I'll put out some feelers for that file."

"Just be careful," Micha said. "We don't want the police to think we're working on Ava's behalf. Then they'll think she might be with us and come looking for her."

"I got it." Reid sounded a bit testy at the reminder.

Too bad. Boss or not, Micha wouldn't take any chances with Ava, and Reid would get over it.

Micha shared their visit to the armory. "I know you're already checking with the locals, but can you check with your fed contacts to get us a look at those videos from Squib's business, too?"

"I'll look into it," Reid said. "But don't hold your breath. This is bound to be an ATF investigation, and I only have one contact there. She's a by-the-book agent, and I doubt she'll break any rules for me. For anyone actually."

Micha assumed the Bureau of Alcohol, Tobacco, Firearms, and Explosives would handle this investigation, but he'd hoped Reid had developed more than one contact with them over his years as an agent.

"If I strike out with her," Reid continued as if he'd read Micha's mind, "I'll check in with a few buddies still in the Portland office to see if they might have someone who can help."

"What about you, Colin, or Dev?" Micha glanced between them. "Either of you have someone you can go to?"

Colin shook his head. "We didn't deal with ATF in the cyber division very often."

"Not me. I was just a lowly deputy, not some hotshot agent." Dev chuckled.

Reid rolled his eyes. "We all had our jobs to do and you did an outstanding job."

"Oh, I know." Dev blew on his knuckles and rubbed them over his chest. "Just can never resist the chance to mess with a fed, even if it's a former fed."

The guys laughed.

Micha wanted to join in, but he couldn't. Not when he felt like he was striking out at every turn. He couldn't keep letting Ava down all the time. There had to be something else he could do. "Maybe *we* don't look at the files."

"Not look at the files." Colin squinted at him. "I don't follow."

"Yeah, what then?" Reid asked.

"We find a way to make it worth an agent's effort to look into it for their personal gain and do the work for us," Micha said, warming to his spontaneous idea. "If Buck is busted with that cache, it would be big enough for the local media to cover, and the agent could spin the story as a *look at what we did to stop a mass casualty event* kind of thing."

"That might work." Reid's eyes lit up. "Yeah. Yeah. It actually could be the ticket. Not for my contact. She's established herself and will probably blow me off. Still, I'll float the idea with her. And then, if she doesn't bite, I'll find a young, hungry agent."

"You think that's really doable?" Ava asked. "Because I would feel so much better if someone in law enforcement knew about that stockpile of guns."

"I do," Reid said. "But it might not go as fast as you would hope, and you will continue to need a protection detail."

Reid wasn't telling Micha something he didn't know. "You still good with the two of us staying here in Portland with her?"

He nodded. "I can work with it."

"What about the suspects' vehicles?" Micha asked. "Find anything?"

"No, and surprisingly they didn't have security systems, so we were able to do a thorough search."

"What happened with your visit to my guy Toby?" Dev asked.

"He was cooperative. I owe it to the WWII connection, so thanks for that." Micha explained what transpired in their meeting. "But I won't know if he'll actually follow through on his visit until he gets back to me later today."

Dev gave a sharp nod. "Toby's good at keeping his word."

"I'll let you all know what he has to say."

"Any updates on forensics?" Reid asked.

Micha shook his head. "What about Ryan? Was he able to get DNA and fingerprint samples?"

"He came through. Made the guys use disposable cups and marked their names on them for reuse. Then he collected them before they departed under the guise that they couldn't dispose of them back at the campsite."

"And they were good with that?" Ava asked. "No questions or suspicions raised?"

"Yeah," Micha said. "I could see them complain about using things they won't have access to out in the boonies."

"Oh, they questioned that aspect, but Ryan simply told them we keep them in our kitchen supplies in case of unforeseen emergencies and they should too."

"When will they be back to the compound?" Micha asked.

"I expect them back any minute." Reid frowned. "They complained about the class cut short far more. I'm giving everyone their money back for sure, and I'll give a free future course to everyone except Buck and Jamal. Even if it turns out they're not involved, they still won't be invited back."

"Good call," Micha said. "Especially on Buck. I can't be sure Jamal had explosives at the end of his tripwire, but we can't be too careful with the safety of our other participants."

"I can really see now why you do background checks before you allow people to take your classes." Ava curled her arms around her stomach. "I will never forget the sight of all of those guns. Never."

Was she worried the weapons would be used against her or worried about the implications of a man possessing such an arsenal? A man who might be unhinged.

Because Micha was. More now than when he'd discovered the stockpile, as the guy would soon be out of the compound and on the move. This raised the stakes to a whole new level, and Micha had to up his protection game.

~

Colin had gone back to his room to take a call, leaving Ava alone with Micha, who'd been staring straight ahead since he ended the meeting. His behavior, coupled with a downcast expression, had her taking a breath to prepare for more bad news.

"You know," he said, still not making eye contact, "I was thinking about how you said the patients you care for often ask about your faith."

What? This wasn't about their update meeting? "And?"

"And I don't doubt that they ask because you're a role model for how a strong Christian behaves. I wish the same could be said of me, but it can't. I want..." He looked up and shook his head.

Wow. This was coming out of left field. Or maybe not for him. Maybe he'd been thinking about this for a long time and God was working on his heart. It seemed like he needed to open up about this, and she wanted him to. Wanted him to trust her with such important information.

She resisted taking his hands in hers but smiled at him. "I try to live my faith but don't put me on a pedestal. I fail all the time. Especially when I let my anger get to me over things like insurance and Medicare or Medicaid dictating a patient's meds and care. As if they know better than the doctors."

He looked at her then, the anguish in his eyes painful to see. "I'm not putting you on a pedestal. Just being realistic. I don't see you questioning God like I am. I used to do better. Be better. But my sister..." He shoved a hand into his hair, running it over his head and leaving little tufts standing on end. "I don't get it. Why did she have to fall? Why did her life have to change this way? Why couldn't she continue as she was? Happy, and living the life she'd always dreamed of when we were in care, instead of struggling physically."

"I wish I could tell you how to stop questioning," she said. "I've learned not to ask why, but that doesn't stop me until I realize it doesn't help. Second-guessing God is never a good thing, but then, even when I know that, I fall back into it."

"I don't want to, you know?"

She nodded.

"But then I see Tristin struggling to learn how to do basic tasks in a wheelchair and how everything is so much harder for her now. Especially in a house that wasn't built for life in a chair. Then there're her finances. I give her most of my paychecks—I don't need much to live on—but she doesn't want to take the money. She does, for Charlotte's sake, but keeps a tally of what she has to pay back."

"I can understand that last part," Ava said. "I would do the same thing."

"Me too, but I don't want her to have to worry about that when I don't need it."

"I guess the bottom line is it doesn't matter what we like. It's a matter of what's right for us right now, and only God knows that. Doesn't mean we'll stay in the same place. We can even work with God to change it. But accept that it's the right place for right now."

Oh, wow, she needed to listen to her own words. She'd just complained about waiting when she should be thanking God for directing her steps and embrace whatever He had in mind for her.

Colin marched into the room, and Ava had to admit to being glad he interrupted their conversation as she felt like a real hypocrite at the moment. She hadn't even noticed how much she'd been questioning her current situation when her questions should be reserved for figuring out who killed Holly.

Colin set his laptop on the coffee table and gestured for Micha to join him on the far side of the space. A private conversation. They talked in hushed whispers, but Ava caught the gist of what they were discussing. They mentioned the type of weapons Micha had seen at Buck's place and their calibers. High-powered weapons, he said. Far more deadly from a distance.

She swallowed. Swallowed again. Her fear returning, and that exact moment she'd just talked with Micha about when she wanted to question God coming into play. She meant what she'd said. She would never forget seeing that giant stockpile of weapons. Not only because of the quantity, but she could imagine them turned on her. On others. One or more of them.

So maybe discovering the weapons was the reason God put her in this situation. So that someone found the cache and perhaps stopped a mass shooting. If she ended up going to prison so they could stop such a horrific event, she would have to accept that.

The right place for right now. She would keep that in the forefront of her thoughts.

Colin's computer beeped. He hurried across the room. "Most likely one of my background check alerts."

He dropped down next to Ava and tapped his trackpad. His mouth fell open, and he stared at his screen. "Well, lookie here."

He turned the laptop to face her, and Micha came to stand behind them.

Ava looked at a photo displaying a LARPing group. Layne was in the front row, and he was dressed in medieval attire. "Looks like Layne's into LARPing too."

"Look closer," Colin said. "You're missing the key thing."

She bent forward to study the group. She counted eight individuals all in similar medieval role-playing costumes. She ran her gaze over each person. Stopped in the back row. Flashed a look at Colin. "Is that Jamal?"

Micha leaned over her shoulder. "Yeah, it's him all right.

Wonder why this didn't come up on your earlier searches, bro."

"His social media presence is almost nonexistent," Colin said. "Also, since he's in the picture he didn't take it and probably wasn't his to share. Unless he used a timer on his camera."

"Where did your search turn it up?" Micha rose back to full height but didn't move away.

Colin swiveled his laptop to face him and tapped a few keys on his keyboard. "Ah, that's it. I added Phoenix Preston's name in my searches, and he shared the photo in a private Discord group he manages."

"Discord?" she asked.

"It's a chat app. Voice, video, and text. Mostly used by gamers, but lately it's become popular with like-minded people who form private groups of all sorts. The data is harder to mine, but I've found a way to do it."

Micha clapped Colin on the back. "Good work."

"I know, right?" Colin laughed. "I'll dig into the group and see what they might be sharing that could help us."

She swiveled to look at Micha. "No matter what else he finds, we now have Layne's connection to one of our suspects, and hopefully it will move us forward."

Micha and Colin parked down the road from Jamal's house, a light rain wetting the property in the hazy, late afternoon. Ryan had returned to base with the disposable drinking glasses and drove them to Portland, but headed right back home to his family. Reid also had freed up Dev to make the trip to Portland to aid Micha in any way he needed. Right now, Micha needed him at the apartment to protect Ava so he and Colin could both question Jamal.

Micha killed the engine and looked at Colin. "You ready for this?"

"Are you kidding? I was made for this." Colin grinned.

Micha rolled his eyes, but Colin was right. He was made for this. He was known for walking the fine line of legal. Never straying over the line, but pushing the boundaries. He might be a crushed idealist, but he was also charismatic and street smart, where his brother Dev was the natural charmer of the family. Colin had burnt out on the job, and maybe that was what crushed him, or it was his natural personality to walk that fine line. Either way, he was usually up for a good fight to try to right the scales of justice.

"Be on alert," Micha said. "We can't know for sure if the guy has explosives."

"I got this." He opened his door and drew his weapon. "I don't want to have to save your sorry butt, so you just worry about yourself." That grin came back as he slipped into the dark of night.

Micha joined him at the front of his vehicle, and they headed up the driveway. The skies were overcast. What remained of the sun was hidden. Good for cover. Not so good for seeing, but at least the big rain storm meteorologists were predicting hadn't started yet, and heavy rain wouldn't hinder their search for any boobytraps.

They moved slowly. Silently. Micha caught sight of the house and flashed up a hand to tell Colin to stop. Jamal's battered white pickup truck was parked next to the cabin where the front door stood wide open. Not a good sign.

Micha searched the area, but no sign of Jamal outside.

Colin came up next to Micha. "What's with the open door? A trap to lure us inside?"

"We were careful, so I doubt he knows we're here. Unless there's a hidden camera in the trees." Micha glanced up, searching nearby trees. "Nothing."

"I didn't spot one when we were here last time either, and you know I gave it a good look."

Micha gripped his pistol tighter. "If we missed one, the open door could very well be a trap, like you said. We need to be doubly careful now."

Colin gave a sharp nod. "Want me to take lead?"

"Why would I want that?"

"You're sounding like a scared little girl." Colin chuckled. "But seriously, yeah. I won't make a step without your approval."

Micha eyed his friend. "Hand signals from this point on in case he's listening for us."

"Roger that."

Micha eased toward the house and kept his head in constant motion to scan for a threat. He rested a hand on the pickup. Cold. Jamal had been there for a while. He took one last look to the side and behind. The trees swayed in the heavy breeze but no other movement.

He moved on, toward the light shining inside the house.

He slowed his pace. Creeping closer. Looking at his feet before each step. He didn't want to trigger any kind of boobytrap.

Step. Look. Step. Look. Over and over. Closer and closer.

He reached the bottom stair. Safe and in one piece. He signaled for Colin to stay put, and that he would climb the stairs. The first one had groaned on their last visit.

He skipped it and started on the second one.

Listened. Took the next one. Waited. Climbed the last one.

Fine. No movement or attempt to take them out.

He crossed the porch to the door. Scanned the frame again. Felt for tripwires. Gone.

He dropped his gaze to the porch floor. No wires. No signs of explosives.

Now the risky part. Penetrating the cabin. Crossing the threshold. But not without taking a quick look.

Prepared to jerk back if Jamal waited with weapon in hand, Micha poked his head inside. He took a quick look around the room.

What in the world? He lurched back and rushed down the steps, the sight reverberating in his brain.

This wasn't what he expected to find. Not at all.

12

Ava paced the gleaming wood floor at the apartment, and she felt Devan watching her. He'd tried several times to help her forget about the danger, and she had. For the moments he'd entertained her with his humor. But then she pictured Micha at a house that might contain explosives and booby-traps, and she couldn't remain sitting.

She got up, paced, hoping each step would relieve her stress. She tried to employ her newfound discovery, believing Micha was in the right place for right now. Tried to trust God. But Micha's life was too big to test her on something she'd only just realized, right?

What might it have been like to know him when he was in the military? To love him when he might be hurt in the line of duty? She could never be a military spouse. Never.

This was showing her that her faith was so weak she couldn't trust God to keep Micha and Colin safe. Honestly, she wanted God to change this whole situation. Change the *right now* part. Deliver her and Micha from it. But He allowed her to be in this situation for reasons only He knew. It could be as simple as meeting Micha. That God wanted this attraction between them to go forward. She would have to give it some careful thought and prayer.

The door opened, and she flew to the entryway. Micha and Colin stepped in, their expressions both somber. *No. Oh, no.* Something bad had happened. But what?

She ran her gaze over Micha. Let it travel head to toe, found no blood or injuries, and resisted throwing herself into his arms. "You're okay? Really okay?"

"I am, but let's sit down." He frowned. "I have something to tell you."

She didn't like the sound of that. Or his continued tight expression. But she couldn't speed him along without complying. She rushed back to the sofa so he could share their news.

He sat next to her, and Colin perched on the arm of a nearby chair. Devan took a stance behind his brother, looking curious but not questioning his teammates. He'd likely been in a situation like this with them before and knew how to wait for news.

Her, not so much. "You guys are scaring me."

Micha narrowed his gaze. "We don't mean to, but we have some bad news about Jamal."

Okay, not what she expected, but still..."What is it?"

Micha scrubbed his palms over his knees. "When we arrived at his house, we found the front door open. I looked inside and spotted him lying on his back in the family room. There was a strange object sticking out of his neck, and he was dead."

She gasped. Blinked. Gasped again. "Dead?"

Micha nodded. "I didn't go into the house. I didn't want to risk contaminating the scene, so I don't know how long he's been dead."

She could easily imagine discovering Jamal like that. Far too easily as she had found patients she cared for who had passed away in their sleep, but this was gruesome. How she wished Micha didn't have to experience that. "What did the police say?"

"We haven't called them yet."

"No?" She glanced between Micha and Colin. "But why not?"

"I wanted Reid to weigh in on how we should handle the discovery. I called him, and he's consulting with Russ in hypotheticals so as not to get him officially involved. I also wanted to talk to you first and let you know what this might mean for you before I call it in."

She was confused. "What do you mean?"

"Once I report the murder, I'll have to tell them about you and your role in all of this."

"You do? I mean, yeah, I guess you do." She took a moment to let the news really register. "And they'll want to know where I am, right?"

"Right."

"And then they'll come here to arrest me." She jumped up. Paced a few feet away, then turned back to stand over him. "I need to leave. Yes. That's it. The only solution. I'll go somewhere you don't know how to find me. That way I won't put you in the position of having to lie to law enforcement."

"No!" He sprang to his feet and clasped her hands. "I won't let you go off on your own. Not when we know a killer is out there. I'll go with you."

She locked gazes with him. "I appreciate that more than you know. But I'm a fugitive. You'll be guilty of aiding me. You could go to prison."

"Better that than someone hurting, maybe killing you."

"We have to figure out the killer's identity," Devan said, his demeanor calmer than theirs, bringing the anxiety level down in the room. "Starting with figuring out what the murder weapon is."

She let her mind race over anything that could help. "Can you describe it?"

"Better yet," Micha said. "I took a picture if you're up to seeing it."

"Go ahead," she said, but she really wasn't. Still, if she could help identify the object, maybe that would identify the killer. She was all for that. "Show me."

Micha took a long look into her eyes, then released her hands and got out his phone. He swiped a few times and held it out.

She studied the photo, trying to ignore Jamal's wide open eyes staring vacantly at the ceiling. She focused on his neck. Gasped and dropped onto the sofa.

"You know what it is?" Micha asked.

"Yes," she said, panting for air. "But I wish I didn't."

At the paling of Ava's face and the way she was scanning the room as if looking for a way out, every defensive urge in Micha's body sat up and took notice. Gone was any question of trusting God to take care of her. Micha had to do it. She felt threatened. Like an animal facing down a lethal predator. She needed him. Now and until this whole situation was resolved.

He took her hand. Her fingers were ice cold. She really *was* terrified. "What is it? What was used to kill him?"

"It's a bocal." She drew in air, panic lighting in her eyes. "Probably my bocal."

He wanted to help her. To comfort her, but he had no idea what she was talking about and why it frightened her so badly. He needed details. "Your what?"

"A bassoon bocal. The end that holds the reed is what's sticking out of his neck. If it's mine, I might be charged with his murder." She freed her hand and ran it through her hair, then tapped a nervous foot.

Colin held out his phone to Micha. "I Googled it. Here's a picture."

Micha took the phone and studied the diagram holding labeled parts of the instrument. The bocal was a slender silver tube with a crook in the metal. Looked a bit like a shepherd's hook. A reed was affixed to one end, and the other end was mounted into the long cylindrical instrument with a vast assortment of silver keys.

He gave the phone to Dev to look at and focused on Ava. "You're right. That's what it is. Can you tell if it's yours for sure?"

She shook her head. "There are various models and designs of bocals. Many manufacturers, too, but it looks like it could be one of mine. That doesn't necessarily mean anything. It's a basic design and loads of players own ones like this."

"How would the killer have gotten a hold of it?" Colin asked.

She shook her head. "I have some at my house and a few in my case, which is in my cabin at your compound."

"Let's say Layne is our killer," Colin said. "He was at your house the day you fled and could've taken one."

She nodded. "But he would need to have known way back then that he was going to kill someone with it. Maybe me, I suppose."

"You have security cameras on your house?" Micha asked.

"A doorbell one, but the battery died on it a few days after I left home."

"Still, we could have caught Layne on it, right?"

"Yes, but if he came back, we have no proof."

"Or Jamal could've taken one from your case before he left the compound and gave it to Layne," Micha said.

"Not after they got back," Dev said. "Reid said they escorted him and Buck to their cabins to pack and then directly to the gate. I suppose he could've taken it before you all left for the trip. Maybe left the note in your backpack at the same time."

Ava sat staring, like her mind refused to believe what had occurred. "I think my house is more likely. I brought three with me and have them in a separate case made to carry bocals. So if you had someone take pictures of my case at the cabin, I can tell you if one is missing and which one."

"On it." Dev dug out his phone and marched out of the room.

Perfect. Micha's teammates knew just when to step in and take care of matters, and he appreciated it. Not Ava, though. She was frozen. Micha had to handle this for her. "Your house is a different matter. We can't have you going there, but if one of us took pictures, could you tell if anything's missing?"

"Sure, if you take photos of the storage drawers in my music room. I admit I'm a bocal junkie. Always trying a new one. I have over twenty-five of them, so I had custom drawers built to store them and keep them from getting bent. But you can't check them, right? Once the police figure out what was used to kill Jamal and that I play bassoon, they'll be going there."

"We'll take care of it before we report the murder," Micha said.

"And you'll just leave Jamal lying there? Dead." She clenched her hands together.

"We'll have to."

Holding his phone out, Dev came back into the room.

"I've got Reid on a conference call. He's had a chance to talk to Russ about our next moves and is ready to formulate a plan. I sent you the link if you want to open it on Colin's laptop."

"I got it." Colin got up.

Micha slid over to make room for Colin, and he sat. He slid his finger over his trackpad, and Reid appeared on the screen. His eyes were tight with worry.

"Uh-oh," Colin said. "You don't look happy, boss man."

"I'm not unhappy. Just concerned." Reid took a breath. "We need to be sure we avoid any possibility of jail time for anyone and also that we *do not* lie to the police."

"I don't see how we can avoid it," Micha said.

"Stay with me here." Reid leaned back in his chair. "You go back to the house. Park where you did when you first arrived. Call the police. Your story will remain the same. The truth. You went to Jamal's house to question him, but you'll be vague if they ask for times."

Micha looked at his teammate. "We can do that, right, Colin?"

"Absolutely."

"But then they'll ask why you wanted to question Jamal," Reid said.

Ava swallowed hard. "Which means bringing me into the discussion."

Reid gave a sharp nod. "We'll have to tell them how we came to meet you and that we brought you back to Portland, hoping to confirm your story. All that is true."

"That's when they'll come to arrest me." She shifted on the sofa, looking like she needed to pace again.

"Yes," Reid said, but sounded as if he didn't like having to say it. "Micha and Colin will have to tell them that the last place they saw you was at the apartment and that they instructed you to stay put. But while they were at Jamal's place, they wouldn't know if you decided to leave."

"And if you did go, we wouldn't know where you went," Micha said, not liking the sound of not knowing where she was located but also knowing it was the right solution.

"Hypothetically," Reid continued, "if anyone remained at the apartment with you with Colin and Micha gone, and that someone left with you, that person would be able to talk with Micha after he finishes his interview with the police. That person might request for Micha and Colin to meet up with him."

"Okay, I get it, but won't clarify details and put you all in an impossible situation." Ava feigned zipping her lips. "What happens from there?"

"Well, since I don't know what we'll decide to do once Colin and Micha depart the apartment, I couldn't even begin to speculate. Not even hypothetically."

She frowned.

Micha wanted to take her hand but resisted in front of Reid. If his supervisor caught how much he had fallen for Ava, he might pull him back to the compound and let others handle keeping her safe.

He did look deep into her eyes to reassure her. "He's distancing himself and us from any legal repercussions, but I assure you, we'll make sure you're safe."

"I suppose I could—"

"No." Micha flipped up a hand. "No details at all."

"Exactly," Reid said. "Russ did say a good detective will think of this same scenario and know you are in essence lying to them without lying to them. So don't expect the detective to be happy with you. And we better pray that you weren't caught on CCTV anywhere on your arrival back at the apartment just now."

"We knew the location of this building's cameras, so we

were able to avoid them." Micha met his boss's gaze. "Besides, all I care about right now is making sure Ava is safe and finding this killer before he strikes again."

Ava sat forward, her leg falling away from his. "So you'll leave now? Go back to Jamal's place?"

"First we'll get pictures of the music room at your house. Hopefully that will clarify things, and we'll know how to proceed in apprehending this killer."

~

They were still on the call with Reid when Micha's phone dinged. He grabbed it while Ava held her breath. She couldn't handle any more bad news, could she?

Just breathe. Believe. The right place for right now.

Micha leaned over Colin and held out his phone to her. "Photos of your bocal case."

Yeah, it could be bad news all right. The final straw to ensure she spent her life in prison.

She studied the photo. Micha, Colin, and Devan looked on in person, and Reid over the computer. Three bocals lay in the case. She let out a breath but looked at the close-up pictures holding details to confirm the shapes, lengths, and manufacturers were right.

She glanced up. "My case is fine. Nothing missing. If the bocal is mine, it had to have come from my house."

"Then we definitely stop at your house before we return to Jamal's place."

"Keep me updated," Reid said. "Especially if the detective decides to detain you. Make sure I'm your one call."

"Of course." Micha got up and looked at Colin. "We should get moving. Don't want anyone to find Jamal and call it in before we can work this in our favor."

Get moving. Meaning get ready to leave Ava alone with

Devan as her protector. She trusted him, but she sure wished Micha weren't leaving her. At least he wasn't going into danger like before.

Colin looked up. "No way I'm leaving my computer behind, and I need to get my backpack to protect it."

"Yeah," Devan said. "He's like married to that thing. No wait, maybe he's married to the big one at his place and this one is his kid." He laughed.

Colin rolled his eyes and turned his attention to Micha. "We should both pack anything we don't want the police to take into evidence."

Micha didn't answer right away as if waffling on what he wanted to do.

"Leave clothing and toiletries behind," Reid said. "You don't want it to look like you moved out in advance of going to Jamal's place."

"Roger that," Micha said.

"Be careful," Reid warned. "Our killer could be watching for Ava to come home and could be staking the place out."

Micha nodded and looked like he wanted to say something but didn't speak for a moment. "We'll check in with you after we finish with the police and let you know what happened."

"Before I go, you should know I struck out on getting a copy of the police report for Holly's investigation," Reid said. "I might have stood a better chance if I could've given my source more info but had to leave Ava out of the details."

Her heart fell. Another strike against them. How many was that? Surely they'd struck out by now.

Let it go. Let go of Jamal's murder. Move on to any positive thing it might bring.

You're in the right place for right now.

"Figured that could happen," Micha said, surprisingly calm. "But thanks for trying."

Reid nodded. "I had better luck with the feds and Buck's weapon cache. He should expect a visit from ATF in the near future."

Micha smiled. "Great news. If he's involved in this, it'll take him off the street or at least take away his weapons."

"And even if he's not involved," Colin said, "they'll hopefully find cause to confiscate his weapons."

Devan nodded. "And worst case, if they can't do that, he's now on their radar."

"Exactly," Reid said. "My brothers and I'll be waiting for your call and offering prayers on everyone's behalf." He signed off.

"Be right back." Colin closed his laptop and marched across the room toward the bedroom he'd been occupying.

"I need to grab a few things too," Micha said.

"Wait," she said, feeling panic take over at the thought of them leaving.

Micha probably didn't want to take the time to say a long goodbye, but Ava didn't care. She couldn't let him walk out that door without letting him know how she was feeling about him and giving him a hug.

She held his gaze. "Can I talk to you in private before you go?"

"I know when I'm not wanted." Devan chuckled. "I'll just go bug my older, less attractive brother."

Ava forced a laugh and waited for him to go into the bedroom and close the door.

"If you're going to talk about what you plan to do once I leave, don't say a word."

"Not that." She stood and went over to him. "I want to tell you I have feelings for you. Stronger than I first imagined, and I'm worried about being separated from you when I can't see that you are okay."

He blinked a few times. "I feel the same way. But I trust

Dev with my life, and should something come up and the two of you remain together, so can you."

She nodded but took his hands. "Nothing has changed in our lives, so what are we going to do about these feelings?"

"Pray about it for now, I guess, and when all of this is over and your name is cleared, we'll figure it out."

"You sound certain that my name will be cleared."

"I'm confident but would be lying to you if I said I felt certain."

"I'll take confident for now and hold on to that hope." She smiled up at him. "And it seems like I'll have some time on my hands until I see you again, so I'll devote myself to praying."

He took a breath. "We need to embrace your saying. We're in the right place for right now. Trust that God will bring us both through this and if we're supposed to be together, He'll arrange that too."

Trust. But..."That sounds so simple. Easy. But it's not. Not in my circumstances when I could go to prison. When a man could kill me."

"I know it's easier for me, but it's not easy for me to leave you behind. To let go and let God protect any woman in my world. But maybe if I master it here—trust Him to meet me in every step I take, one step at a time—then I can relax about that deep need to protect people. Especially my sister."

"And if you can do that, you'll be open to a relationship?" She heard the hope lingering in her tone. Felt it in her heart. Just a shadow of hope, but it was there.

"That's what I would like to happen." He released her hands and cupped the side of her face. "Because, honey, a future with you would be worth mastering this issue once and for all."

"Oh, me too, and I'll try harder." Reveling in the fact he'd called her honey and all that it implied, she snaked her arms up around his neck. "For now, how about we master kissing before you leave."

"Colin might think your timing is incredibly bad and we should get going, but I doubt it will ever be a bad time to kiss you." His head swooped down, and his lips met hers.

The shock of his touch—her emotions—far exceeding her expectations raced through her body. He slid his arms around her back and tugged her gently closer, but then his arms gripped her with a fierce need she relished. He deepened the kiss. Seeking. Exploring.

Oh, wow. Just wow. Her senses were on fire. Her heart racing. She met him kiss for kiss. Never wanted him to let her go.

She vaguely heard a door open.

"Yeah, just like I thought," Devan said. "A whole lot of mushy going on in here."

He and Colin laughed.

At their laughter she pushed back and smoothed her hands over her top that had risen up when she'd raised her arms around Micha's neck. His forlorn look at the interrupted kiss mimicked her internal feelings.

"I'll just pack my things, and we can go." He stepped from the room, socking each of his teammates on the shoulder as he passed them.

Colin carried his backpack to the door, and Devan came to sit in an armchair, resting his elbows on the knees of his khaki cargo pants and leaning forward.

"You'll want to pack too, but not until the guys have left." He leaned back and scratched his close-cut beard, the only real thing that distinguished him from his brother as they looked very similar in their coloring and facial shape, with wide jaws and nut-brown eyes.

"To keep them from knowing I'm leaving," she clarified.

"Exactly."

"But we *are* going, right?"

"We are indeed."

"Where?"

"Coming back into the room," Colin called out.

Ava clammed up and sat back to wait for Micha's return, too. Seeing him with his duffle slung over his shoulder seemed so final in their separation. Panic settled in.

No. Stop. Trust God. He's got this.

The right place for right now. True for both of you. Keep saying it.

"Time to go," he headed for the door.

She jumped up. Ran to him. Hugged him tight and kissed his cheek. Then turned to Colin. Hugged him, too and almost laughed at his surprised look when she pulled back. "Be careful. Both of you. And good luck with the police."

Micha gave a sharp nod and opened the door.

Colin exited first, and Micha, after a lingering look at her, stepped through the door. She twisted the deadbolt behind them, the click echoing into the space, sounding like a finality she didn't like. She rested her forehead against the door and offered up a prayer for Micha and Colin. Then one for Devan and herself.

She took a hearty breath and joined Devan in the living room. He was looking at his phone, but he glanced up.

"So where will we go?" She settled on the edge of the sofa cushion.

"You won't like this, but I found a motel that will take cash only so we don't leave a trail."

"Probably a dump then."

"Not probably. It's most certainly one." He grinned. "But

we'll only stay there until Colin and Micha finish with the questioning."

"Then where will we go?"

"To the cabin you inherited."

Okay. Much better. But..."Why not just go directly there?"

"You mentioned that cell service was sketchy there, and we can't risk not hearing from Micha. Plus, the police will likely figure out I'm with you and be looking for me. They could get a warrant to track my phone and or download my call history with cell tower locations. I don't want to risk the phone leading to the cabin."

"I'm sorry, Devan," she said sincerely. "I hate that the police will come looking for you too."

"First, call me Dev. Second, it's what we do when an injustice is occurring."

These men. Fine men. Giving. Sacrificing. It was almost beyond her to comprehend after a childhood of takers, and she didn't know what to say. "Saying thanks doesn't sound like enough, but thank you from the bottom of my heart."

He waved a hand. "It's more than I need."

Tears ached to be released at his kindness, so she had to move on before she was blubbering like a baby. "You think my cabin is safe? That they won't find us?"

"They haven't made the connection yet. More importantly neither did Colin. If he didn't, it would be extremely hard to do, so it should be fine." He held out his phone. "Plus, I checked satellite views, and it looks like there're two ways off the property, so we have good escape routes if we are located."

"Three actually," she said. "Two driveways lead to two different roads, and if you count the nearby river, there's a third way out."

Dev's eyes lit with interest. "You have a boat?"

She nodded. "A small aluminum fishing boat with a trolling motor. Nothing fancy but could be used to make an escape."

He frowned.

Why did his interest wane? "Is that a problem?"

"We'll check the boat out when we get there, but it won't be a fast escape. Not with only a trolling motor."

"I've never used a motor of any kind, so I had no idea."

"No worries. We got it covered." He smiled. "Time to get packed."

"Should I leave things behind like you guys are doing or take everything?"

"If you leave items behind to make it look like you're still staying here, the police might think you're coming back. They'll put someone on watching the apartment for your return, and it will take them longer to be certain you're gone and start searching."

"Then I'll leave some things." She got up.

He stood, too. "I'll grab my backpack. Let me know if you need any help."

She nodded, but wouldn't ask for more help from him when he was already blessing her so much. She hurried to her room and threw items into her suitcase, leaving behind the things she didn't care as much about. She tossed an assortment of toiletries into the bag, leaving basics behind, too and laid it on top of the clothing. She had to sit on the case to start the zipper. She should have packed carefully, and she would have room to spare, but she wanted to be ready to go when Micha called to say they'd departed her home.

She got the bag closed and onto the floor when she heard Dev's phone ring. Grabbing the handle, she raced back to the family room where he'd already answered on speaker.

"Go ahead, Micha," Dev said. "Ava's here now."

"I'm sending over the photos I took of the drawers in your music room like you asked. We can review them when we next see each other."

"Thank you," she said, wishing he'd called on video so she could see his face. "Is there any sign of a break-in?"

"None," he said. "We didn't find anyone watching the house either, but Colin is keeping an eye out."

"Are you leaving now, then?" Dev asked.

"We are. Will call when we're free to do so. Take care."

"You too." Oh, how she wanted to see him and communicate her concern for him again. "I'm praying for you both."

"Later, man." Dev ended the call and looked at her. "Ready to hit the road?"

She wanted to lie but would answer honestly. "As ready as someone who's running from the law can ever be."

13

Detective Stanley's skeptical look told Micha all he needed to know. The fifty-something guy, with thinning hair, creases between his eyebrows, and a seriously bad case of chapped and peeling lips, didn't buy Micha and Colin's story. At least not completely. He'd already questioned Colin and left him sitting on a stump near the driveway, getting wet like Micha. The rain had finally started and was pelting them all while the moon tried to shine above them.

Stanley had separated them right off the bat. Standard procedure so they didn't compare stories and make changes. At times witness-story changes occurred on purpose, but mostly it was accidental. In the shock of finding a dead body, the one person could share erroneous details with the other and soon they were taking on the other person's details in addition to their own or replacing what they actually witnessed.

Stanley rubbed his forehead. "And this Ava Weston is at the apartment you're borrowing from a friend?"

"That's right," Micha said but didn't want to. Although she knew he would share this information, he felt like he was betraying her.

"I'll need that address."

"Of course." Micha rattled it off.

Stanley jotted it in his little notebook. "As a former investigator, you know I can't have you calling to warn her that we're coming. Not with the warrant out for her arrest."

"Wouldn't dream of it."

Stanley rolled his eyes. "You know I'll send officers right over there to make sure she stays put until I'm ready to talk to her. If she's not there, we'll check your phone log."

"I know."

"We'll probably check it anyway."

"I would expect as much," Micha said but didn't worry. He'd used the company SAT phone to call her from her house, so there would be no record of that call on his personal phone, and he didn't plan to call her now. "I hope you'll reconsider those charges and investigate until you find the actual killer and prove Ms. Weston is innocent."

Stanley's eyebrows rose. "The evidence does not agree with you, Mr. Nichols."

The opening Micha had been waiting for to advance his investigation. "Care to share details on the evidence in your possession?"

Stanley widened his stance. "You know I'm not at liberty to do that."

Oh, man, this guy continued to be super evasive and had Micha's simmering anger dangerously close to boiling over. He wanted to lay into the guy, but why? This was not new in their conversation. Stanley had been so vague this far. Micha could just chalk it up to the guy being a good detective, and wasn't that what they wanted? To have someone who was capable of solving Jamal's murder in charge of the investigation.

But that didn't mean Micha would be forthcoming with more than Stanley asked for. He had to stick to answering his questions and providing details to clear Ava so he could get out of there soon.

"You didn't mention the victim's time of death," Micha said, knowing that the ME had come and gone and the detective had to at least have some idea of when Jamal died.

"I didn't."

"I would need to know that to tell you where Ms. Weston was at the time Jamal was murdered."

Stanley wetted his lips, maybe something he did often and the reason they were so chapped. "The ME gave a preliminary window of between eleven a.m. and four p.m. today."

Had to be shortly after Jamal got home from the trip and right before Micha had arrived here with Colin. If Reid hadn't canceled the class, might Jamal still be alive or would the killer have gone after him on the trail? They would never know, but if he *had* gone after him, others could've gotten hurt.

Micha preferred to think of this as the best outcome. "Ms. Weston was with us during this time and all day as a matter of fact, giving her a solid alibi."

Stanley watched Micha intently and gnawed on the inside of his cheek. "Or she has someone who's willing to lie for her."

"I'm not lying, Detective. As a former investigator, I wouldn't do that." Stretch the truth. Omit things. But not lie.

"I'll need the contact information for all of your class participants."

"What for?"

"I need to confirm that you or your associate over there," he pointed at Colin, "didn't have a run-in with the deceased and a motive to end his life."

Like Micha said. A good detective. "I'll have to check with the company owners on that. Privacy laws and all."

He flipped the page in his notebook, his pen poised to write. "And who might that be?"

"The Maddox brothers. Ryan, Russ, and Reid. They live in Shadow Lake."

He lifted an eyebrow. "Emerson County Sheriff, Russ Maddox?"

"You know him?"

"Worked an investigation with him. Fine sheriff and I'm honestly surprised he's involved in this."

Micha would not want to have Russ questioned. Not at all. "I never said he was involved, other than owning the company I work for, and Jamal attended one of their company classes. He knows nothing about it."

Stanley narrowed his eyes. "Translated, you know that you're walking a fine line and kept him in the dark."

Like Micha would admit that. "Sheriff Maddox might be a co-owner, but he only pitches in with the company when needed, and he hasn't been needed all week."

"Odd. I would've thought you'd want his expertise on this situation so you don't cross that line."

Micha wasn't about to admit to being anywhere near the line Stanley spoke of, much less cross it. "I hope you'll begin your investigation by talking to Layne Boyle."

He gave an impatient snort, rising to Micha's bait and moving on. "And why would I do that?"

Micha explained Layne's vendetta against Ava. "We know he's been in contact with your department regarding his mother's death, or you wouldn't have reopened the investigation, then classified it as a homicide and issued a warrant for her arrest."

"And you think that vendetta stretches to this man?"

Micha explained Layne's friendship with Jamal. "We believe he joined our class to keep an eye on Ava for Layne, and Layne wanted to tie up loose ends. At the same time, he was trying to frame Ms. Weston."

"I'll take a look at that, but all signs right now point to Ms. Weston."

"Like I said. She has a strong alibi." Micha stopped short of admitting that he knew the murder weapon could be connected to her. "Is there anything else you need from us?"

Stanley locked gazes with Micha, his intense and pointed. "I have your contact info. See that you answer when I call, or I'll be sending someone to bring you in for formal questioning."

"No worries." Micha gave the vague answer. He didn't know if he would be answering the detective's call or on the run with Ava, and he wouldn't be caught in a lie.

Stanley stared at Micha, his expression that of a bulldog. "See that you don't continue to help Ava Weston avoid arrest. If you do, I'll haul you in for obstruction."

Micha didn't respond but waited for an official dismissal.

"And don't go back home without telling me." Stanley jerked his thumb over his shoulder. "Now get out of here."

Micha crossed the yard to Colin. Never had he wanted to pick up his feet and run this badly since he left active duty. To get out of here before Stanley found a reason to hold them, keeping Micha from Ava.

Colin stood. "We cleared to leave?"

"Yeah." Micha didn't stop but barreled toward the driveway and the company SUV parked on the road in the same location as when they'd first arrived to find Jamal.

Colin fell into step. "You think Stanley bought your story?"

Micha marched down the drive, glad to continue to put distance between himself and the nosy detective. "I think for the most part, but he's suspicious. Thankfully we never entered the house the first time we visited, so he won't find any evidence linking me or Ava to this property."

"Still, if he finds the apartment empty and Ava long gone, his doubt will grow."

"Agreed, but at least I didn't have to lie about anything or risk giving her away. He didn't even ask if I knew what the object was in Jamal's neck. Don't think I could've faked an answer to that one without right-out lying to the guy."

"Me either. Surprised me that he didn't ask." Colin said. "But maybe he already Googled it and realizes how unusual it is and figures we wouldn't have a clue."

"Could be, and I think he buys the fact that we didn't go into the house, much less kill the guy. Sounds like he doesn't like us for the murder, but he does want to check with the other class participants to see if we had a run-in with Jamal."

"Did you?"

Micha cast his teammate a testy look. "No, of course not. Only thing that could even be close would be when Jamal complained about having to cook his own food, but I handled it diplomatically, and the others will confirm that."

"Figured as much but had to ask as sometimes it's all I can do not to deck some of these preppers who have doomsday outlooks."

"True for all of us, but they're the ones who put the food on my table." His sister and niece's table, too, which was far more important. "We should head down the road a bit before calling Dev. I don't want Stanley to see us and change his mind about letting us go."

They reached the company SUV, and he headed for the driver's side. His phone rang. "It's Sierra at the Veritas Center." He tossed his keys to Colin. "You drive so I can talk to her and we can get moving."

"Sierra," he answered on speaker and climbed into the passenger side. "Putting you on speaker so Colin can hear."

Colin fired up the engine and got the vehicle moving down the road.

"I have an evidence update for you," she said.

"And what did you find?" Micha set the phone in the console and buckled his seatbelt.

"Your guy Jamal Thomason's prints match the ones I lifted from the catapult," she said. "He has a very unique arch, and it's indisputable. I'd be glad to testify to that. You could get the police to arrest him for that while you continue to investigate."

Arrest. Right. She wouldn't know. "Too late. Jamal is dead. Murdered. Part of a musical instrument stuck in his neck. He bled out."

She gasped. "Oh. Oh. Wow. Oh. I guess the police are involved now."

"They are, but we haven't told them about the evidence that we've delivered to you or that we're using your services."

She didn't respond right away, the silence uncomfortable. "Will you?"

He had no idea what she thought about that, but it didn't matter. He had to tell her the truth. "I have no plans to say anything, but the prints might change things. It shows that the guy tried to inflict harm on Ava or even kill her. That could then open the door to believing Ava's innocent of charges."

"Or it could give her even more reason to want revenge," Colin said.

Micha shot his buddy a grumpy look. He didn't like Colin's comment even if it was the truth.

"Not only that," Sierra said, "you can't say the catapult was set for her alone, right?"

"I suppose," Micha said. "But she would be the only one in the group to take that path."

"I've testified at enough trials to know an attorney could use this to cast reasonable doubt," she said. "He could even say the person set it as a trap to kill his dinner."

"Good point and something we'll consider." Micha shared a look with Colin.

Colin slowed the SUV to take a sharp curve on the narrow two-lane road. "They could even say Jamal only made the catapult, but someone else set it."

"Maybe I can help with that." Sierra's tone brightened. "Now that I know we're looking at Jamal, I can also focus my boot print search to the Lowa Caminos and Jim Greens that Jamal mentioned owning. Put him at the scene. We can't say when, but if I find a match it will at least put him there."

Micha wondered if any of this was going to help, but they could evaluate all of that when he didn't need to make sure Ava was okay. "Sounds like a plan."

"After I finished the prints, I took the drinking glasses to Emory's department to run the DNA. That was two hours ago. She told me DNA from the blood sample you provided from Buck's wall has been completed, and we can compare it to the glass DNA once processing is done."

"We still looking at a minimum of twenty-four hours?" Micha asked.

"Maybe a few less. The samples were straightforward and took only a few man-hours to isolate the DNA. It should complete in twenty hours or less."

"Get back to me the moment you know anything if you can."

"Will do." She ended the call.

Colin glanced at Micha. "I would've killed to have resources like this when I was with the Bureau."

"But I thought the FBI had the best lab of any government agency." Micha shoved his phone into his pocket. "At least that's what agents always spout."

"You're right, but turnaround times are nothing like the support we're getting here. Maybe the big investigations in the public eye get this kind of treatment, but not us little guys in the Portland field office."

"Could be worse," Micha said. "Military turnarounds were legendarily slow and not from the top lab in the country. But yeah, I get what you're saying."

"At least we now know Jamal was the one most likely to try to hurt Ava, and he's connected to Layne." Colin pulled to a parking section for a waterfall overlook at the side of the road. "You think it's time for us to pay Layne a visit?"

"Exactly what I was thinking." Micha looked at Colin. "But first we find Ava and make a plan to keep her out of prison and the killer away from her."

Ava sat back in the car seat, stunned, her phone in her hand with the pictures of her music storage drawers open at home. She blinked a few times and looked again. Yeah, third drawer down, the C2 bocal was gone. Likely now in Jamal's neck or the ME's evidence bag.

"The bocal is mine," she said, hating the sound of it.

Dev glanced at her. "You're sure?"

"I'm sure one of them is missing and it's of the size that fits the one in Jamal's neck."

"That's too bad," Dev said. "Micha's not going to be happy when he hears this."

"I know." They fell silent and didn't talk again.

Dev pulled into the hotel parking lot and Ava cringed but didn't share her thoughts as he had chosen the place for her safety. He parked by the lobby door, and they went in together.

The place wasn't as gross as she'd expected. It was even worse. The building was old and falling apart, and the lobby reeked of something she didn't even want to contemplate. The guy sitting at the front desk behind bulletproof glass fit right in. He had greasy, stringy, long hair and graying stubble on his chin. His white Guns N' Roses T-shirt held dark stains, and he grinned at her with a lecherous smile as Dev forked over the cash and slid it through the small opening in the window and continued until they walked out the door.

Dev escorted her through rain that had picked up beyond their normal spitting downfall at this time of year to their room that they would share until they heard from Micha. The space smelled of old cigarette smoke and mold. She flung back the worn floral bedspread to reveal white sheets emitting a hint of bleach smell, giving her confidence to sit down. The burgundy carpet was threadbare, but looked like it had been vacuumed. She didn't even want to see the bathroom.

She shuddered and perched on the edge of the bed. "Anyone who knows me would never look for me here."

"Sorry about this place." Dev rolled her suitcase in and secured the door. "It's disgusting. I get it, but no one looking for you here is exactly why I chose it. Hopefully the detective won't keep Micha and Colin all night, and we'll be out of here soon."

"What about going to that diner just off the highway for a while? It has to be better than this, and we didn't have dinner. You must be hungry."

He tilted his head, obviously thinking it over. "We could do that, but we'll walk. Don't want my vehicle in the restaurant lot with plates that could be run by a cop who stops in for coffee. You'll need a ball cap, too, for a disguise. If you don't have one, I do."

"For the warrant out on me."

He nodded.

"Maybe we shouldn't risk it," she said, but then spotted all sorts of fluids dried on the walls. "But if you think it'll be safe..."

"We can make it work. We'll get a table in the back and make sure you face away from the door." He smiled. "If I think there's any risk, we won't stay."

"You don't have to tell me twice." She jumped to her feet. "I have a cap I can wear in my suitcase."

He easily hefted her large bag and plopped it on a wooden table. "You don't travel light."

"I like to be prepared to leave if needed," she said but didn't explain how most foster kids were always prepared to depart from the home they were staying in. "I would rather put this in the car so it doesn't pick up any odors, but I'm afraid it'll be stolen while we're gone."

"The SUV has an alarm system, but you could be right, and it's best to leave it here."

She got out her cap that she'd bought when she'd been trying to avoid the police in Portland and tucked her hair inside of it then pulled the brim low over her eyes. "Ready."

Dev produced a cap from his backpack, too and secured it on his head. Outside, they both lowered their heads to the deluge of rain. The rush and low hum of freeway traffic filled the air as they crossed the lot with litter skittering across the cracked pavement in the brisk east wind. The rumble of a broken muffler on a worn station wagon that pulled through the lot covered the road traffic. The back of the vehicle was stuffed with possessions. Looked like someone was living in their car in this parking lot. She'd learned a bit about being homeless before she arrived at the training camp, spending a night in her car. She couldn't sleep a wink and had no idea how people did it.

Sirens wailed in the background, winding closer. She instinctually moved closer to Dev. How she wished it were Micha at her side. She would snuggle up against him for protection. Not that she didn't trust Dev's skills. She did. He could protect her.

She looked up at him. His gaze constantly roved the area. So did hers, landing under the bridge ahead, where a small homeless camp sat at the far end.

"Keep an eye out here," he said. "Listen for any instruction I might give and do it without hesitating. Okay?"

"Yes, of course."

They slipped under the bridge, and she appreciated the lull in the rain. The folks sitting around a cut-down barrel with a fire glanced at them but paid them no other attention. They were probably used to being invisible. She wouldn't be one of the people who walked by without offering to help. She would buy four hearty meals at the restaurant and bring them back to the campers.

They cleared the bridge, and the giant red neon sign with an arrow announcing Fat Eddie's Diner loomed above.

Dev stopped in the heavy rain. Scanned the lot filled with big rigs. She knew that was a good sign as truckers usually knew which diners were decent and avoided the bad ones.

"Okay, we're good," Dev said. "I'll handle choosing the table. You just follow my lead."

At the door, he pulled it open for her, and bells jingled above as the scent of burgers and onions frying on a griddle snaked out to welcome them. A long counter stretched the entire length of the building and chrome stools with bright red vinyl tops were affixed to the floor. Most diners were alone and sat at the counter. She counted five couples in booths near the windows that spanned the front wall.

"Welcome to Fat Eddie's," a young waiter with a nametag that read Braxton said, then offered a ready smile on a face with bad acne. His hair was shaved on one side and long on the other. He wore all black and an apron that sagged with his pants. "Go ahead and seat yourself wherever you want, and I'll come get your order."

They crossed the clean black and white checkerboard floor down the row of booths, also in red vinyl, to one in the back by the restrooms. Not the spot she would've chosen, but it was the only one situated away from the windows and where no one could surprise them from behind.

Dev pointed at the first seat. "You're here."

She slid in and had to admit she didn't like having her back to the door, but she much preferred that Dev could see what was going on than her. If danger lurked, he was far more capable of warning her and handling it.

He grabbed menus and handed one to her. She was pleasantly surprised that the plastic beneath her fingers was clean and not greasy. She glanced down the page to the specials. Meatloaf, mashed potatoes and gravy with green beans. Yes, comfort food, and she didn't need to look any further.

Braxton arrived with a coffee pot. Ava and Dev both turned over their cups.

"Looks like you got inside just before the rain really started." Braxton tipped his head at the window where rain pelted against the glass, and he filled their cups with steaming black coffee. "Supposed to be a real toad-strangler out there. Supposed to last for three days."

Not helpful for them in the least.

He set the pot down. "What can I get you?"

"Is the meatloaf good?" Ava asked.

"Oh yeah. Nothing basic on the menu at all. Eddie's mama's recipe."

Basic, a term this age group used these days to refer to bad. The opposite was extra. Or at least that's what Ava's neighbor, a sixteen-year-old girl, had told her.

"So there is an Eddie, huh?" Dev asked.

"For sure, but he's like the furthest thing from fat as possible." He laughed and looked at Ava, his pen poised over an order pad.

"I'll have the meatloaf and can you add four to-go orders of it, too?" Ava said. "There's a group camped under the bridge, and I want to give them a hot meal."

"Wow, lady. That's lit." He scribbled on the order pad and then looked at Dev. "And what do you want?"

"Burger and fries. Medium on the burger." Dev closed his menu. "Oh, and a chocolate shake."

"Hang tight. Be out in a minute." He spun, his rubber-soled athletic shoes squeaking on the tile.

"I agree with the waiter." Devan smiled at Ava. "Your generosity is lit! I probably should've checked the weather forecast before suggesting we walk over here."

"Maybe Micha will be free soon, and he can pick us up."

Dev got his phone out and laid it on the table.

"You know a watched phone doesn't ring," she said.

"Then I won't watch it." He chuckled. "Tell me more about your cabin property."

She'd be glad to talk about happy memories for once. "It's a small place. Two bedrooms. One bathroom. But I have to warn you. I don't have any utilities turned on and that includes water. Means we have to use an old outhouse that my cousin built before the cabin."

He frowned. "Will be a bear in this rain if it carries down the state. Better than an open-air latrine, though."

"Agreed."

"Let me check on the weather down there." He picked up his phone, and it rang in his hand.

"One of our SAT phones. Likely Micha." He tapped the screen and answered. "You're on speaker, but we're in a restaurant, so keep it down."

"We're good to go." Micha's voice came through clearly, though it sounded as if he was keeping it down as Dev asked.

Still, her heart soared simply at hearing his voice and her pulse joined in over the fact that they hadn't been arrested.

"Where are we headed?" Micha asked.

"Fat Eddie's Diner," Dev said. "Google it for the address."

"Hang on."

Silence filled the phone, and she took a long sip of her coffee to keep her hands occupied.

"Okay, got it," Micha said. "About an hour from us. Hang tight. We're on our way."

The call ended and she let out a breath of relief. She would soon be reunited with Micha.

"Now about that weather." Dev tapped his screen and frowned. "Our waiter was right. This storm stretches nearly down to California. Actually gets worse the farther south you go."

"Then it'll be an even longer drive."

"Looks like it." He set his phone down. "And there are flash flood watches for a lot of the counties which could be problematic."

She didn't want to go out in the cold rain, but it would only be a trip from the warm restaurant to Micha's SUV. Not like the people living under the bridge. She might be on the run, but God had blessed her in so many ways. She had a cabin to run to. Money to spend. And most importantly, this group of fine men committed to keeping her alive, no matter the cost.

14

Five miles to go to the restaurant, and Micha could swear they were crawling. Inch by painful inch. Stomping on Colin's foot resting on the gas pedal would get them moving faster. Micha had considered it, but he wouldn't. They'd hydroplaned several times on the wet roads and speeding up could be dangerous. He might want to arrive faster, but he wouldn't risk not getting there at all.

Colin finally pulled into the lot. "I don't see Dev's vehicle."

Micha scanned the lot. "Only one Fat Eddie's in town, so it has to be the right place."

Colin backed the SUV in close to the door, the rain shedding off the vehicle like a waterfall. Wouldn't stop Micha. He was out of the vehicle in a flash. The rain soaked him before he got a few feet. No worries. He could handle getting wet but not handle Ava getting hurt. So he took time to check out the place before entering.

A deep scan of the surroundings brought up nothing amiss. Through the front wall of windows, he spotted Dev and Ava in a booth near the back. His heart did a happy dance.

He entered the building and resisted shaking like a dog but stood dripping at the counter. Dev had chosen a booth that Micha would've selected too. Everyone on the team would have due to the location providing the most privacy, and it was defensible.

A waiter tried to tell him something, but he ignored the young guy and charged down the long aisle. He slid in next to Dev, where he could not only keep an eye on the door but look at Ava, too.

"You made it." Her words came out on a long breath as she pushed away her empty plate.

She seemed overly relieved to see him.

"Did something happen?" Micha slicked his hair back and grabbed a napkin to wipe the rain from his face.

"No." She smiled, and the warmth traveled directly to his heart. "Dev has taken great care of me, but I was worried the detective would arrest you two."

Colin arrived at the table, dripping rain on the floor.

She didn't seem to notice he was wet and could soak her, but scooted over for him.

He slid in and helped her move her plate and silverware to her new location. "What did you have to eat?"

"Meatloaf, and it was wonderful," she said but didn't take her eyes off Micha.

"So was the burger." Dev tapped his plate only holding a scrap of lettuce. "Highly recommend it."

A waitress whose name tag said Belinda arrived with her coffee pot. "I'm taking over for Braxton, who's on break, and it looks like you two could use some warming up. And before you get the wrong idea, I meant the coffee. Not that it would be a hardship to get close to any of you fine-looking fellas. If only I wasn't old enough to be your mama."

She laughed and held up the pot.

Micha flipped his mug. "Coffee for me, please, and a burger and fries."

Colin tipped his cup and smiled up at her. "I'll have the meatloaf."

"Not a fit night to be out." She gestured at the counter. "Even my truckers are hunkering down for the night."

There was a question in that statement somewhere—wondering why they were out in the storm—but Micha would ignore it. His stomach grumbled.

"Guess I better get your order in pronto." She chuckled and departed.

"We shouldn't stay long," Micha said. "If a cop comes in looking for us, Belinda will remember we were here because of the storm and describe us to them."

"Odds aren't good they'll be searching on this side of town," Dev said. "They have no reason to believe Ava would be here."

Micha looked at his teammate. "Yeah, great job on choosing a random location, but this surely isn't your safe house."

"We got a motel room just down the road." Ava flinched. "It was so gross we opted to come here for a while and get something to eat."

"We can take off from there, then," Colin said.

"Where we headed?" Micha asked.

"My cabin." Ava's eyes brightened as if she were recalling fond memories of the place.

Micha rested his elbows on the table and pondered the location. He looked at Colin. "You think the connection between her and the cousin is hidden well enough?"

Colin sipped his coffee that he'd loaded with cream and sugar. "It's not impossible to find. After all, once I had Ava's real name I did locate it, but I don't think the police have the resources to do a deep enough search on a timely basis."

"I hate to make you spend even a minute more in that motel room." Micha offered Ava what he hoped was a comforting smile. "But I want to question Layne before we leave town. Confront him with Jamal's murder, but also be sure he doesn't have the ability to make the connection to your cabin. I can't have you come with me for obvious reasons."

"We have two vehicles," Dev said. "She could ride with me, and we could park nearby and wait."

"Okay, that might work." Micha played the scenario out in his mind. "But don't choose a spot too close in case the interview goes south. Don't want him to bolt and accidentally discover you."

Belinda came down the aisle with the food and set a large platter in front of both of them. "I had the cook add extra fries for you and more mashed potatoes for you. The coconut cream pie is to die for, so let me know if you'd like a slice."

"No need to wait for me," Dev said. "I'll take one."

The others chimed in, too.

"Four slices coming up. You won't regret it."

"I might not," Ava said. "But my waistline will."

Micha opened his mouth to say one piece of pie would not change that.

No. Keep your thoughts to yourself.

No reason to delve into the personal realm in front of the guys and risk his growing feelings for Ava getting back to Reid. He grabbed up his burger and bit into the juiciness that dripped on the plate. He groaned at the rich beef taste mixed with tangy spices and all the fixings. "Good."

"Told you so," Dev said.

"Yeah, but you're not always right. Especially not about food. You'll eat pretty much anything." Micha laughed.

Colin smiled. "I always say if he found a woman who

could cook, it would be all over. Despite anything else, he would get down on his knee and propose."

Dev cast daggers at his brother, but Micha knew it was all in jest. He didn't have time for joking around, though. He barely wanted to sit here to eat, but they needed to fuel up their bodies for the drive. "Colin, check the tracker to see if Layne's home."

Colin shoveled a huge bite of potatoes with thick gravy into his mouth, then got out his phone. Micha wolfed some fries dipped in ketchup while he waited. Crispy and tender at the same time. This place gave diners a good name for sure.

He felt Ava's eyes on him but didn't look at her. He didn't want to reveal his unreasonable happiness in seeing her. The guys would speculate as to whether he could be objective here. He couldn't. He knew that. But he could still provide the best protection detail she could need and coordinate her escape from town.

"I need to tell you about my bocal," she told him. "One of them is missing from the drawer in my music room, and it's the right size for the one in Jamal's neck."

"Not surprising."

"You expected that?"

He nodded. "I saw some empty spots in the drawers when I took the pictures, so I figured it would be the case."

"Not good news, though," Dev said. "Now we also need to prove that someone stole it."

"Layne's car is home." Colin traded his phone for his fork. "Doesn't necessarily mean he's there, but it's a good start."

Micha grabbed his burger again. "So we finish up here, then get your vehicle and head out to Layne's place."

Ava picked up her coffee cup. "I need to stop at the

bridge on the way back to the motel. I'm taking meals to a group of homeless people."

Ah, yes. Ava showing God's love in action. Caring. Compassionate. Unselfish. Even when her life hung in the balance. That was the kind of person he was coming to know her to be. He not only cared about her in a romantic sense, but he respected her big time.

"I love seeing your faith in action."

Belinda joined them, balancing on her forearm plates of pie piled high with meringue. She set them on the table. "You want those meatloaf meals to go now?"

Ava nodded. "And pie for them, too."

"You got it. You can pick it up at the register on the way out." She scribbled on her pad and hurried away.

Ava took a bite of her pie. "Oh, my. She was right. This is delicious."

Dev shoveled a forkful into his mouth. "Oh, man, yeah. This meal was worth braving that motel room for."

"Then Colin and I are making out great." Micha pushed his dinner plate away and grabbed his pie. "We didn't have to spend any time there and got a great meal."

"No worries." Ava held her fork filled with creamy pie above her plate, an impish grin forming on her face. "I'll let you go in to get my suitcase."

He laughed, and the tight knot in his gut loosened. He had to work harder, faster, to figure this out so he could see if this thing between them could go anywhere, what with his sister and all. He didn't remember wanting anything this badly for a long time. Scary but also exciting.

They finished their pie, polished off the coffee, and headed to the cash register, where Micha paid Belinda in cash, giving her a very generous tip.

"I should at least pay for the extra meals," Ava protested.

"No worries. I'm glad to help."

"I double-bagged the order to keep the food dry." Belinda passed the bag across the counter. "God bless you all for taking care of people down on their luck."

Ava blushed and reached for the bag, but Micha rested his hand on hers before she could. The touch brought a shockingly intense awareness of her, and he had to fight his reaction, sucking in a breath. "You can get into the vehicle faster and not get as wet if I carry it."

"I won't melt, but thank you." She flipped up her hood and zipped the jacket.

Micha took the time to unroll his hood from his collar this time. He grabbed the food, and they bolted through the rain that he swore was coming down sideways in the gusting wind. He opened the back door for Ava, then piled in beside her. Dev got behind the wheel, Colin took shotgun. Dev knew the motel location and could take them straight to it. He soon had them easing onto water-laden streets and pulling up near the bridge.

"I'll be back in a flash," Ava said.

Micha held up his hand. "I'll do it."

She shook her head. "It's something I need to do to help me remember how blessed I am and not focus as much on my problems."

"Then I'll come with you." He could argue with her about getting out of the vehicle, but he wouldn't deprive her of something so important to her. He took the bag and slid out before she tried to stop him.

She exited the other side, and he took her arm to draw her closer and make her a smaller target. Surprisingly, she didn't balk, and they sloshed through standing water to the bridge.

Under the bridge, she swatted at a cobweb.

"You don't have to move webs out of my way," he said,

trying not to let his embarrassment get to him and bite her head off. "I can handle it."

She looked up at him, compassion in her gaze. "But why, when I'm here to help?"

"Because even if you do it out of kindness like I know you're doing, it's embarrassing when a woman has to move a stupid cobweb for me. Makes me feel like less of a man."

"I'll stop then, but you're not less of a man." She glanced up at him. "You're simply a person who's had a traumatic experience, and it's part of your life now."

"Yeah, I get that up here." He tapped his head. "But not in my heart."

They approached the group and he changed his focus from feeling like a loser to protecting her. Three men and a woman huddled near a roaring fire. Ava marched right up to them, a smile on her face. They cast wary glances her way.

"Sorry to disturb," she said, "but I saw you when we walked by a little while ago and wondered if you might like a meal from Fat Eddie's. I got meatloaf and coconut cream pie."

A man with a scraggly gray beard eyed her, his narrowed gaze telling of a life lived in suspicion of other people. "Why you doing this?"

"I wanted to help. No strings." She took the bag from Micha and set it down between them, then backed away. "I hope it brings you some comfort tonight."

"Thank you." The woman hopped up and grabbed the bag.

"You better be planning to share that with us," a younger guy said.

"'Course I'll share." She sat and started handing out containers.

The older man looked at Ava. "Don't understand why

195

you did this, but it'll be nice to get a hot meal with this weather. So, thank you."

"You're all welcome." She smiled. "God bless."

She turned to leave, and Micha slung his arm around her shoulders, then hugged her to him. "You are a very nice person, Ava Weston, and I'm proud to know you."

She blushed in the light of the fire. "It's nothing."

"No, not nothing. I would've likely been too focused on my mission at hand, walked by and done nothing."

She gazed up at him, her eyes warm and loving. "I probably would on a normal day, too, but your team's kindness is motivating me to do more for others. You all don't want or expect repayment. Even if I found a way to do it, I doubt you would accept. But this way I can pay it forward."

He squeezed her shoulders and let go. "Still a very nice thing to do in the middle of your own crisis. But we need to forget that and focus on our surroundings as we head to the SUV."

Her soft expression disappeared, and she set her jaw. "I don't like it, but I know that's what we have to do."

He took a long look around. Saw nothing but rain and the wind battering the moisture at them. "Ready?"

She nodded.

Together, they bolted toward the SUV and got in just as a gust of wind hit the vehicle and rocked it.

"It'll take us forever to get to the cabin in this weather," Colin said.

"We can pick up our other vehicle at the motel and caravan," Dev said. "That way we can spell each other in the driving and won't burn out."

Micha agreed. "Sounds like a plan. But first, we grill Layne, if he's home."

Colin got out his phone. "Let me check on his vehicle location again."

He tapped the screen and studied his phone, then frowned. "Oh, man. He's not home anymore. Looks like he went to the movies."

"Seriously?" Ava asked. "I'm trying to stay alive, and he goes to the movies?"

"He might not be seeing a movie." Colin looked over the seat at her. "But his vehicle is parked at a mega movie complex. Twelve theaters."

Micha looked at Colin, "So if he *is* in a theater, there's no way to tell which movie he's seeing, and we can't grab him there. But if he comes home, the tracker will let us know when."

"Exactly." Colin pocketed his phone. "Looks like grilling will have to wait, unless you want to hang out in Portland until or if he comes home."

"I don't suggest it." Dev held up his phone. "Just checked the weather. The drive will already be a bear, and radar says it's only going to get worse."

"I know we should head back," Ava said. "But why not take advantage of him being away from home to search his place like we did with Buck? We might turn something up that could help."

"She has a point," Colin said.

"Yeah, a good one, and it wouldn't take us that long to do," Dev said. "And then we can get on the road."

"Then the search is on," Micha said. "The next best thing to grilling Layne is digging into his personal space."

Ava sat in the SUV's back seat and scoped out Layne's ranch-style home through the steady downpour pelting the area. If the front spotlight on Layne's house wasn't on, she wouldn't even be able to see the place. But it was, and she took a good look at the white paint that had faded to a sickly gray and the shingles on the roof that had discolored and curled. Couple that with the weather-beaten door and overgrown landscape, and it all made for a dismal-looking property compared to the neatly manicured and well-kept homes nearby.

Ava couldn't believe Micha agreed to let her come here. He even seemed to embrace her request, saying Colin could keep an eye on Layne's movements, and she would be fine. He also believed her knowledge of the man might let her see something that he would overlook.

Dev and Colin remained out front to keep watch, and she hurried up the walkway with Micha. At the front door, he handed her a pair of shoe coverings. "To keep from tracking mud through his house."

She put them on and he slipped on a pair too then took out his lock-picking tools and got them inside. She still was impressed that he could so quickly get through the locks, but it would make her feel less safe in her own home in the future. If she ever got back to her home. Home alone. Without Micha.

Not having him around all the time? That wouldn't make any woman feel safer.

Seriously, why was she even thinking that way?

They stepped inside, and a minty smell like from a muscle cream or ointment filled the air.

"Wonder if Layne injured himself." Micha moved through a small foyer with outdated orange and black floor tile to a small living room painted a drab olive green that clashed with the entry tile.

"He always smelled like ointment when he came to visit Holly." Ava took in the space that held only a large recliner with a small table next to it, a big-screen TV, and large sound system on a fireplace wall.

"What was their relationship like?" Micha handed gloves to her, then put on a pair and opened the drawer in the table.

She slid her fingers into a glove. "Not real close, so it surprised me that he even cared enough to look into her death."

Micha thumbed through the drawer. "By 'not real close' do you mean nearly estranged or drifting apart that can happen in families?"

"Holly never mentioned a rift between them, if that's what you're thinking. She didn't talk about him a lot except when she was reminiscing about when he was a kid." Visions of Holly in the last days Ava had spent with her came back, and she worked hard not to cry. "I've found that people in the end stages of their lives often want to reflect on happy times and forget about the regrets if there's no way to fix them. Some are troubled by the past in any form. Some find peace. It's all a way of letting go."

"But she didn't seem to be troubled?"

"No." She met his gaze. "Why all the questions about their relationship all of a sudden?"

"I was just thinking. What if Layne killed his mother, and the reason he's working so hard to have you confess is so he gets away with it?"

"Layne? Kill Holly?" Ava let the thought settle in. "It never crossed my mind."

Micha closed the drawer and started toward the kitchen. "But now that I mentioned it, could you see him ending her life?"

"I don't think so." She recalled the times she'd seen him with Holly. "No. No. I doubt it."

"We can't rule him out, though." He opened and closed a vintage white-metal cabinet in the kitchen with a checkerboard tile countertop and floor. He looked back at her. "If he's capable of coming after you with threats to kill you, he might be capable of killing Holly, too."

She pulled open the nearest drawer only to find silverware. "I would agree, except that I'm a complete stranger to him, and she was his mother. Blood ties and all of that."

Micha moved to the next cupboard. "You'd think that would hold a lot of weight, and it does for people who have a normal perspective on life, but not for some people."

Was Layne guilty of murdering his mother, and Ava just hadn't considered it? "He didn't strike me as unbalanced or losing control of his emotions. Just the opposite. He gave Holly an outstanding funeral with a very pricey coffin and loads of flowers. Would a son who killed his mother do that?"

Micha closed the door. "If he wanted to cover up his involvement, he might."

She pushed the drawer in and stared at him. "I can't get used to thinking the way you do. Always looking for a person's ulterior motives."

"Trust me." He stilled. "I wish I didn't. Since I left full-time investigations, I'm much better at not considering it on a day-to-day basis, but put me in the middle of a situation like this, and that mindset is often what gets the job done."

"Yeah, I can see that. I just can't imagine it."

"Most people can't. Except law enforcement officers. They get it all too well." He finished the last cabinet and then moved on down the hallway.

She followed, and they entered a small bedroom set up as an office. A worn rolltop desk was perched under the window with a stained white blind, and bookshelves filled the nearby wall. Computer programming and other IT books were crammed in to overflowing. The wall next to the closet held photos in cheap plastic frames.

She stepped over to them, moving from top to bottom.

Not a single picture of Holly or them together, but he did have the LARPing picture Colin had found online. She pointed at it. "Seems like he really was into the LARPing group. Maybe we should follow up with Phoenix to get more info on them."

"We will if Colin's search gives us a reason to." He looked down at the file drawer in front of him and withdrew a folder. "Check this out."

He went to the desk and laid it open. She joined him to see the folder was labeled DNA. It held a DNA report for Layne, along with details on his account with one of the big online ancestry sites.

"Says he was looking for his father. This is dated a month ago, but no information after that."

Micha looked up. "So he didn't know who his dad was. Must've meant Holly kept it from him."

"Or he could've been conceived in a one-night stand kind of thing, and she didn't know the guy," Ava said. "I mean if she did know, she didn't strike me as the kind of person who wouldn't tell her son who his father was."

"Unless the father was trouble and she was protecting Layne."

"Yeah, I could see her not wanting him to know the guy in that case." Micha got out his camera and snapped pictures of the pages in the file. "His login and password for the site are written on the folder. When we get back, we can check out his account to see if he's uploaded his DNA to the ancestry site and had any matches."

"Do you think the father could be involved somehow?"

"Could be, but it's a long shot. I can't see a motive."

"Yeah, surely he wouldn't expect any of the inheritance when he's been an absent father. Nor would he care that Layne only got half."

"Still, I'd like to find out who he is and if he's in the

picture, if we can." Micha finished taking photos. "I'll also send the DNA report to Sierra right now to compare to their results."

He concentrated on his phone, tapping away, then pocketed it and took the file back to the cabinet.

She sat down behind the desk and opened the top drawer. "Bingo. A contact list for his LARPing group members."

She ran down the list. "Jamal's on here, but I don't see any other names I recognize."

"Take a picture of it, and we'll have Colin put them into his search criteria."

"Their specialties are listed next to their names." A cold chill washed over her, and she looked up. "Jamal's specialty is medieval weapons."

"Makes sense with his prints on the catapult." Micha rested his arms on the open drawer and held her gaze. "What does Layne specialize in?"

She turned the page and located his name. "Oh, my goodness. Wow! Tracking and stalking."

She looked up to see Micha's jaw tighten. "Then that makes him a worthy adversary who we need to take seriously if we want to keep you safe."

Her gut cramped, and she looked back at the page to confirm she hadn't made a mistake and read someone else's specialty. But there it was in black and white in the grid pattern that made it impossible to read wrong.

Holly's son specialized in tracking and stalking, the top two skills also employed by the person who was trying to end her life.

15

Four hours later as they approached Ava's cabin, the rain let up, giving her a clear look at the small log building nestled in a grove of tall evergreens. She'd been eager to arrive for the entire drive. Not only to see the cabin but also to check for DNA matches on Layne's ancestry account.

She removed her seatbelt and scooted ahead to look between the seats. Colin sat behind the wheel, and Micha had taken shotgun, but for once she didn't look at Micha. Only had eyes for the cabin. How she loved this place. Her cousin had lovingly built and cared for this property. He was ten years older than Ava, an attorney who worked hard and played hard. He'd never married, and he spent all of his free time here.

Nothing had changed since she'd last stayed here. At least what she could see in the dark. But Danny always kept the logs freshly treated with a cinnamon color stain and the slate black metal roof in good condition. A flagstone path led up to the red front door, the path lined with hostas and other shade-loving plants. Of course, Danny always had a welcoming light on outside, but that was impossible without the electricity being turned on.

Micha leaned forward to stare out the front window. "Nice place."

"I have very fond memories of staying here with my cousin." Maybe until the end, but then dying was a part of living, too, and she, more than others, knew that.

"I hope this situation doesn't ruin that for you," Micha said.

She'd thought of the same thing. "Guess it depends on what ends up happening here."

Micha turned to look at her. "If I have my way, nothing bad will occur. Layne might be skilled in stalking, but we can track his vehicle and be forewarned if he comes here. Still, it's possible he could figure out we placed a tracker and remove it, so we won't rely only on that and let our guard down where he's concerned."

"Do you think he killed Jamal?" she asked.

Micha worked the muscles in his jaw. "I honestly don't know, but I'm leaning in his direction after hearing about his specialties."

"I wish I had a clue who else could've killed him and is trying to frame me, but I can't think of anyone." She looked past Micha to the cabin, her mind spinning with details. "How do we even begin to find out who it might be?"

"You said Holly was into music and our killer's use of the bocal makes this seem music-related, so we start there and try to locate the killer."

"I haven't found any info on the music connection," Colin said. "But I'll further expand that aspect of my search. See what I find."

"I want to help, too," she said. "Let me know what I can do."

"Let's get you inside, and then we can talk about our next steps." Micha held out his hand, palm up. "I'll need the key to check the place out."

She dug the fishing bobber keychain from her backpack and handed it over.

"I don't like how far away we have to park, but the lot's not cleared any deeper in." Micha looked at Colin. "Turn the vehicle around and keep the engine running."

Colin responded with a serious nod. "I'll back in as close as I can get, but that still leaves a good bit of open space for an attack."

"Just do your best to take a defensive position." Micha bolted into the now spitting rain and up to the cabin. At the door, he looked back at them. He was too far away for her to get any kind of a take on his thoughts, but a sudden memory of Danny flashed before her eyes.

He was standing in front of the door, key in hand, looking over his shoulder at her. His mischievous grin told her that the frequent prankster had one planned, and she should be wary. It didn't take long after opening the door that visit to catch sight of the fake snake. A really good replica, but she'd been looking for something wrong and didn't fall for it.

Did he let it go? No, but he did bide his time. After a few days passed, when she thought it was safe to let her guard down, a frog hopped out from under her covers at bedtime. She screamed like a little girl, and he came running into the room, then doubled over in laughter. That was her last visit with him before the prostate cancer diagnosis. He was far too young for such a disease. Far too young to die. But he had.

Colin moved the vehicle, parking next to Dev, who'd backed his SUV in and sat behind the wheel. Her memory bubble popped with the vehicle's movement, and she lifted an arm over the seat to keep the door in sight. When Micha didn't come out, fear completely erased all thoughts. She started counting in her head to keep memories and fears at bay.

One one hundred.

Two one hundred.

Three one hundred.

Four. Five. Ten. Sixty. One hundred thirty.

The door opened, and she waited, thinking Micha would either wave them inside or head in her direction to escort her inside. He didn't. He set off around the building and disappeared behind it.

"He's checking the perimeter now," Colin said as if he felt she needed an explanation. "We can't be too careful."

"Do you really think anyone knows where we are?"

"No," he said, but there was a *but* in his tone.

Was he thinking like Micha that Layne was into tracking and stalking and might have the skills to hunt her down? Because that was what she'd been thinking for sure.

Micha appeared again on the far side of the cabin and jogged down the path to open her door. "We're clear, but straight inside anyway."

"Got it." She reached for her backpack.

Micha stopped her. "Leave it. Free hands are a good thing. Colin will bring it in after we have you safely inside." He stepped back.

She slid down and flipped up her hood, thankful there was still a lull in the rain and the moisture wasn't soaking her.

Micha walked alongside her, and Colin came behind. She felt the sense of urgency in their footsteps, urging her to move fast. Micha had left the door open, and she went straight inside. Micha joined her, but Colin remained outside and pulled the door closed.

She went to a battery-powered lantern and turned it on, illuminating the large vaulted room that boasted a wood-burning fireplace with rock face climbing up to the high ceiling.

Micha went straight to the fireplace. "I'll get a fire going and then bring a supply of firewood in from the porch."

"You think it's safe to build a fire?" she asked. "The smoke will tell others we're here."

"It could, sure." He grabbed three logs and knelt in front of the firebox. "They would have to have a basic idea of where we were located to begin with for the smoke to be dangerous. And honestly, if they did know our location, our smoke wouldn't make much difference."

"Right." She clutched her arms around her body.

He looked back at her and held her gaze. "I'm sorry, Ava. I don't want you to worry, but I'll always tell you the truth."

"I appreciate that."

"We're fine here for now, and you should try to relax." He gave her an earnest smile. "If or when that changes, I'll let you know."

"But how will you know?"

"Like I said, figuring out who killed Jamal is our best bet. We know who killed him, we know who might be coming for you, then we can see how worthy of an adversary he is."

"Pretty worthy if he killed a guy who specialized in weapons," she said, hating the sound of putting words to her thought.

The door opened, and Micha shot a hand to his sidearm.

Carrying backpacks and tote bags, Colin and Dev stepped into the room, rain running off of their hoods and jackets.

Colin swiped a hand over his face and handed her pack to her. "We'll just grab your suitcase and the groceries and be right back."

The two men departed again.

An overwhelming urge to keep her possessions close hit

her like a punch to the gut. She sat down on the sofa facing the fireplace, put her pack on her knees, and hugged the bag close to her body.

Micha had laid kindling in the firebox and made a tent of wood above it. He retrieved a lighter from a holder on the raised hearth and flicked the flame against the kindling.

"Cheater." She grinned, but her joke felt flat to her.

"Hey." His eyes sparkled with humor. "The first rule of survival is to use what you have at hand, and I have a lighter."

"That's not what you told the group."

"This is a case of do what I say, not what I do." He laughed and then blew on the flame until it was licking greedily against the dry wood, brightening the room with flickers of light.

He nodded at her pack still clutched in her arms. "Old habits?"

"You understand, don't you? Be ready to go at all times."

"I do, but the need to be ready to leave from my foster days were pretty much replaced by Marine readiness." He stood.

"Which is why you had Colin back in?"

He nodded. "You'll find service members or former service members who don't back their vehicles in. But even if it didn't stem from that, common sense says if we have to flee at a moment's notice, pointing our vehicles toward the exits is a wise move."

Hard rain began pelting the roof again as the door opened.

"Got here in the nick of time." Colin set her suitcase down and rain ran down the hard side to puddle on the pine-wood floor.

Dev carried bags of the groceries they'd stopped in the

nearest city to buy straight to the kitchen, the reusable cloth bags splotchy with rain. She set her backpack on the couch and went to help him stow the food. When she was hiding out here before going to survival camp, she'd brought a large cooler that she'd planned to use in lieu of having electricity, so she took bags of ice he'd carried in and dumped them inside the chest.

"This will be good practice for your off-grid living," Dev said.

"Maybe we can even teach you a thing or two yet." Colin laughed.

"Let's get more wood inside before the wind picks up again." Micha led the way to the door, and Colin followed.

Dev started unloading the food bags that held canned soups, breads, and cereals.

The quantity of food soon filled the Formica countertop below the beige cabinets.

She waved a hand over it all. "At least I don't need nearly this much for survival, so I wouldn't have to procure as much food."

"True. We would be hunting all the time or lose weight fast." He laughed.

"Would you ever live off-grid if given the choice?" she asked as Colin and Micha passed her with armloads of wood.

"Not out of choice."

She faced the fireplace. "What about you guys?"

"Give up computers and the internet?" Colin mocked a horrified expression. "No way."

"Not my first choice either." Micha looked at her. "I like teaching it, and I like having the skills to succeed at it if I had to. I would do it though. If someone I loved needed me to."

Was he hinting that if they followed this interest in each

other, he would consider living here with her if they didn't clear her name?

"What about you?" Colin asked. "Now that you've experienced a bit of it, are you wanting to move here full-time?"

"Are you kidding?" She mocked horror. "Not in these conditions. I can leave the city behind, no problem. But I need electricity and running water, and I am certain getting to the outhouse in the rain will get old real fast."

"I spotted rain gear on the hook by the door," Colin said. "I hope it'll fit, and we can share it."

"It should fit you guys. Belonged to my cousin Danny, and he was a big guy."

Micha raised an eyebrow and looked at her. "Then you'll drown in it."

"I'd rather drown in that than a torrential downpour." She laughed. "Can we check that ancestry site now?"

"Let's use my laptop. I can connect it to my phone and use it for WiFi." Colin picked up his bag and took it to the couch where he sat next to her.

"By the way," he said as he got out his computer. "I infiltrated the LARPing Discord group. Buck lied about being in this group. In fact, he and Jamal have known each other for years."

"I wonder why he lied about it," she said.

"Maybe to cover his tracks on the weapons," Colin said. "The group is seriously into weapons and threatening all kinds of actions. Nothing to do with our investigation, but I figure when this is over, if Buck isn't our guy, I'll turn him in from the info I found. He mentions his cache in his backyard, bragging about the quantity of guns. I can bring him to the attention of my cyber contacts at the bureau, and I'm sure they'd be all over him and end up correlating with the ATF contact who Reid has helping."

"Good job," Micha said. "Seriously, I don't think I could

live with myself if we didn't find a way to get those weapons away from him."

"Couldn't agree more." Colin woke up his phone, and his fingers flew over the keyboard. "Login info?"

Micha took out his phone and scrolled down to share it as he stepped behind them, with Dev joining too.

"Okay, I'm in." Colin used his trackpad to move down pages. "No matches."

Ava reached over him and tapped the DNA button. "That's because he never uploaded the DNA report."

Colin nodded. "That's what it looks like."

"I wonder why," she said. "If you go through all the trouble and pay the price for a test, why not finish and see if there's a match?"

Colin clicked the button for account information. "He set this up about the same time he sent the DNA in. Maybe he held off when his mom got sick."

"Maybe," she said. "We need to upload it now. Find out if any family members might have it out for Holly."

Micha nodded. "It's an invasion of his privacy, but then he invaded your life, so payback is only fair."

Ava's phone rang from her backpack, startling her. She snatched the bag up and looked at the screen. "Another number I don't recognize."

"Why don't you give it to me to answer?" Micha asked.

"Thanks, but I can handle it." She pressed the green button to answer. The haunting melody she'd come to know played in the background, and her dinner churned in her stomach.

The same altered male voice sang the words.

In the darkness whispers fall,
I've found you again, now heed my call,
Turn yourself in and don't you bail,
Or in the stillness, nightmares will prevail

"Who is this?" She shouldn't use such a testy voice, but she didn't care. "Quit being such a jerk and identify yourself."

The call ended.

She took deep breaths and looked at Micha. "Sorry I was so rude. I probably made him hang up."

"More likely he never planned to speak to you. He's just trying to play mind games. Don't let him get to you. Especially when he calls because then he'll know he's succeeding."

"You're right." She set her phone on the table. "Next time, if there is one, I'll play it cool."

Micha faced Colin. "If we record the next call, can you remove the distortion on the guy's voice?"

"Probably not." He frowned. "But I can use EQ to try to clean it up. Doesn't always work and it'll still sound off."

"But might be enough to ID the sender?" Micha asked.

"Could be." Colin glanced at Ava. "I'll have to install an app on your phone for you to record calls. Then I'll teach you how to do it, or I can do it for you."

"I'm sure I can handle it."

"You can now, but what about when that music is playing and the song starts?" Colin held her gaze. "You could freak out."

Micha's SAT phone rang in his hand, and Ava jumped.

"Like that," Colin said. "Only worse."

"You have a valid point." She didn't like to admit she couldn't handle a simple task, but whoever was calling her to sing this song was succeeding in freaking her out.

"It's Sierra," Micha said.

"At this time of night?" Ava shook her head. "Wow, they really do work late."

Micha answered on speaker and told Sierra as much.

"I hope I didn't wake you," she said. "Figured I'd get

voicemail, but I have appointments all morning and wanted to share the results for Layne Boyle's DNA report you sent before I go home for the night." Her usual cheery voice came over the speaker loud and clear. "Unfortunately, Layne Boyle isn't a match to the catapult."

"Not surprising," Micha said. "I don't like him for setting the catapult, but I'd hoped he at least touched it at some point and we could link it to him."

"Sorry, he didn't."

"And the blood we found at Buck's place?" Ava asked. "Did he match that?"

"No on that too."

"So back to square one, then." Micha planted his hands on his waist. "We're going to upload his DNA to an ancestry site. See if we can find any family matches."

"Good idea," Sierra said. "But you'll want to be careful not to alert any potential suspects of your search."

"Sounds like you're familiar with these sites," Ava said.

"No real first-hand knowledge. I only know what our DNA expert, Emory, has told us, and that you can either choose to have the matches viewable by others or not."

"You think she might be willing to give me a call and walk me through the pitfalls?" Micha asked.

"I'm sure of it. I'll ask and then have her text you to set up a time."

"Perfect. Thanks, Sierra. We owe you for sure. And a special thanks for working so late to handle this for us."

"No worries. Like I said, I've been in Ava's shoes, and I'll do whatever you need to find your guy."

Micha ended the call and stowed his phone. "As much as I would like to take care of uploading the DNA now, I think it's best if we leave it alone until after we talk to Emory."

"Me too," Ava said.

Colin narrowed his gaze. "I'm sure I can figure it out

without screwing up, but yeah, what would it hurt to be extra careful? If we found a connection right now, we wouldn't contact that person before daybreak anyway."

"Not that I don't trust your skills, Colin." Ava smiled at him. "But I'm thankful to have an expert in this area weigh in so we don't make a mistake and alert the wrong person."

"Exactly." Micha looked at his watch. "Nearly three. I'll take first watch. You all should get some shuteye."

"There are two bedrooms, but it'll be cold in there until the fire heats the place up," she said. "Which, if my memory serves me right, will take several hours."

Dev frowned. "Might be better for all of us to bunk in here."

She didn't like the thought of trying to sleep with Micha watching her, but she liked it better than being cold. "Danny has a bunch of sleeping bags and blow-up beds for when his nieces and nephews came to stay with him."

"Perfect." Micha gave a tight smile. "We could use those. Lead the way, and I'll help you get it all out."

She headed for the large linen closet situated at the end of the hallway between the bedrooms. She pulled open the door, releasing the scent of the cedar-lined walls. Micha reached over her shoulder and grabbed the inflatable beds. She took out four sleeping bags by their restraining cords and spun, thinking he'd gone back down the hall, but he stood behind her.

He smiled at her. "Your cabin and property are pretty sweet."

"It's great. I still can't believe Danny left it to me instead of his siblings or their kids."

"Did you spend a lot of time here?"

"Not sure what a lot is, but more than the others did. When I aged out of foster care and got my life together, I reconnected with my grandparents and Danny's family. We hit it off, and since I grew up without family, I was all for as much family time as I could get. Not his siblings. They were all too busy with their lives and children, so I made a point of coming here as much as I could."

"I hope you're able to enjoy the place when all of this is over." He shifted the beds in his arms, then turned to leave. "I'm looking forward to getting a better look at the exits and river in the daylight."

He'd told her to relax, and she wanted to, but how could she when a comment like that one reminded her of the very real and present danger surrounding her?

16

Nearing ten a.m., Micha followed the narrow path toward the sound of rushing water to scope out a river escape should the need arise. He'd hoped to get that DNA report uploaded before now, but Emory was in court until noon. So he'd moved on to plan B. Checking out escape routes.

In the pouring rain, which meant spiders on the move. Ground dwellers seeking higher ground and warmer places like the cabin to wait out the storm. They came inside after a storm looking for prey as well. Spiders could also hide behind shutters, downspouts, and other protected areas, like the boathouse he would likely step into soon.

He'd become quite the expert on their behavior to avoid them. Now that Ava knew about his phobia, he really wanted to get control of it. He didn't know how. He'd tried everything over the years except therapy. Maybe that's what he needed, but the tough guy—as he thought of himself—running to a therapist because a little spider scared him didn't sit well with him.

Enough. Forget about them and do your job.

As he'd seen on the maps program, the driveway led in two directions, both connecting with local roads. They'd parked the vehicles in such a manner that they could choose the first one and go west. The second one to head east. All depended on the direction where the threat originated. A solid escape if needed, but having a third option was even better.

He wore their only set of rain gear, the camo vinyl helping with the deluge, but not keeping him dry. Despite tying the hood closed, rain oozed inside, soaking the neckline of his shirt. Thankfully, dry clothing waited for him in the cabin, but right now he was wet and cold in the forty-degree temperatures.

He marched down a hill, his feet sloshing in standing water, until the river spread out before him, the swollen body of water angry and fast moving. Ava had said, and satellite photos had confirmed, that this portion of the river was narrow and slow moving, but not this morning. The river had crested the banks, and the current moved at a swift and deadly pace, plunging over rocks and wiping out everything in its path. Water rose on the boat house, reaching a level maybe too precarious to extract the boat.

Could they get it out?

Should he take it out now and risk it potentially filling with water and sinking? Maybe the guys could get it to higher ground and flip it over. Seemed like the best bet, but he had minimal experience with boats. Dev was the water expert in the group.

Micha turned to go back to the cabin to discuss it with him, sure he would want to come out to take a good look. Micha would accompany him but offer the rain gear to him, and Micha would get drenched for sure. It was almost embarrassing that none of them had their rain gear along. Setting bad examples of survival for Ava. But they'd set out to protect her in the city, not on a rural property in record-setting rainfall.

He kept his eye out for any foe, but honestly, he didn't expect anyone. Not only because he doubted anyone could know where they were, but who would come out in this weather when they could wait a few days for the storm to blow over? So the longer the rain poured like this, he hoped, the better off they were. Unless of course, they had to escape. Then the rain became their enemy.

He pushed open the door and found the others sitting on their sleeping bags in front of the fireplace, mugs in hand.

"Man, would I like to trade places with you all." He shoved his hood back. "It's not fit for man nor beast out there."

The others laughed at his reference from *Rudolph the Red-Nosed Reindeer* when Yukon Cornelius said it to Rudolph. At least that's where he'd heard that saying.

He unzipped his jacket and explained what he'd seen at the river. "I hate to ask, Dev, but would you be willing to check it out with me and come up with the best plan for the boat in case we need it?"

Dev frowned. "From what you described, it would be foolhardy to take a small fishing boat onto a flooded river."

Micha had expected this answer. "But less foolhardy than taking a bullet or knife."

"True that."

Micha untied the rain pants. "You can have the rain gear."

"I won't melt." Dev set down his mug on the fireplace hearth. "You can keep it if you want."

"No." Micha stepped free of the pants. "I roped you into this protection detail, and the least I can do is keep you semidry. The cold is another story."

Dev crossed over to him. "Warm up by the fire while I gear up."

Micha stepped across the room and put his hands out to the flames and heat.

Ava smiled up at him, doing as much to warm him as the fire.

"Thank you both for going out there for us," she said. "I don't ever remember Danny saying the river flooded before."

"Might not have," Micha said. "This is turning out to be a freak storm. If the front hadn't stalled over the area, we wouldn't be seeing such big rainfall amounts."

Ave hopped up and looked at him. "I'll get a garbage bag to put over your jacket."

"Thanks," he said wondering how much it would help, but it would probably be better than nothing.

In the kitchen, she opened the sink cabinet and pulled out a big black bag. He could easily imagine her living here. Maybe him, too, enjoying the rural setting with no one around. As a nurse, she could find a job in the nearest town. It might not be exactly what she was used to, but it would remove one obstacle of their being together.

Wouldn't do anything for his reluctance due to his sister's needs, but he'd made some progress on that, right? Before he met Ava, he wouldn't even have considered what it might be like to start a relationship, much less develop to the point that he would think of marriage, but this woman was worth getting a grip on his problems.

She handed him the bag. "I wish I had something better for you."

"No worries." He smiled. "I'll be back here in a flash and can get changed into dry clothes."

"Thank you for yet one more thing I can't repay you for." She squeezed his arm.

Oh, but you have. You just don't know it.

He held her gaze, transmitting what he hoped was his interest, thanks, and caring all in one.

Dev flipped up the jacket hood. "Let's go check it out."

Micha ripped a hole in the bag, tugged it over his head, and punched his arms through. He followed Dev out the door, and they plunged into the deluge. Without a hood, the rain pelted his head and face, running into his eyes. He lifted his hand against the water to see the way.

Dev glanced at him. "You've got it bad, man. I hope for Ava's sake you're still using your brain at full capacity while there's a very real threat on her life."

Micha didn't bother arguing or denying his feelings. He did have it bad, and he obviously wasn't hiding it very well. But..."Don't worry. I've got this."

"So you say, but don't be offended if I'm looking over your shoulder all the time."

Micha did want to take offense, but Ava's safety was the most important thing, so he wouldn't. "Let me know if I'm failing."

"Oh, you know I will." Dev grinned. "What's a bro for if he can't point out your flaws."

Micha tried to sock his buddy in the arm, but he danced away and hurried toward the river. They reached the swollen bank, and the humor rushed away as fast as the water pulsing downstream.

"Whoa." Dev's eyes widened. "Your description didn't do this justice."

Dang. When an expert thought the flooding was worse than expected, Micha knew they were in trouble. "What do you think about getting the boat out?"

Dev faced the boathouse. "It's now or never." He looked at Micha. "But are you sure you want to risk anyone getting in that small boat with the speed of this river?"

"I get that it's a last-ditch thing. But like I said, it would be better than a bullet to the back and sure death if it came down to that."

Dev lifted his hand over his eyes and stood staring. "Okay. Then we get the boat out now. No way you could do it if you were running for your life."

"My thoughts too."

"We need ropes." Dev eyed him. "Safety first and no one goes near that boathouse without a safety line."

"I saw ropes in the shed out back of the cabin on my walk-through this morning."

Dev nodded and widened his stance. "Then one guy secured with a rope will go ahead to the boat house. Anchor himself there. Next guy joins him. Third guy stays on land and ties a rope around a tree, and the other end is fastened to the guy who'll pilot the boat." He pointed at a giant maple. "That tree should do. One guy gets in the boat. The other helps launch it from there, controlling the movement with a tow line."

"This is my responsibility," Micha said. "I'll take the boat."

"Valid point, but I know more about how to pilot a boat than you."

"Even in this situation?"

He eyed Micha. "More so in this situation. So I'll do it, but you and Colin better not let the tow lines get free."

"What about Ava?" Micha asked. "I'm not sure it's wise to leave her in the cabin alone while we do this."

"Better in there than out here." Dev locked gazes. "You want the boat out? It'll take all three of us to get it onto firm ground."

"Then let's get back. You check out the ropes in the shed, and I'll give Ava a quick lesson in shooting a gun so she can defend herself if needed." Micha turned and trudged toward the house.

Giving a person a gun who didn't have any experience with one could be disastrous. But Ava was sharp. She could master firing a gun and hitting a close-up target. At least when she wasn't stressed, but even avid shooters froze in the face of danger. So a novice with a gun was a wildcard.

He didn't know how to prevent that. He didn't think anyone was coming after her at the moment, but it was possible. Anything was possible.

Still, his gut said having this boat as an escape could mean the difference between life and death. Something he had to plan for if they wanted to end this whole ordeal alive.

Inside, Micha soaked in the warmth and tore off the garbage bag. His jacket was drenched. Not a surprise. He took it off and hung it dripping on a wall hook. His shirt was only damp, but his cargo pants were wet clear through. Too bad. He wouldn't change just to get wet again in a little bit. Colin had moved to a chair at the small round dining table, but Ava remained on the sleeping bag near the roaring fire, a book in hand.

She put it down and peered at him. "What's happening?"

"And where's my bro?" Colin's concerned tone touched Micha. Micha and his sister had the same vibe as these two. Not as much joking and teasing, but the concern was there and went both ways.

Micha crossed to the fireplace to absorb the heat and chase out his chill. "We've come up with a plan. Dev is at the shed gathering supplies to carry it out."

Colin got up and came to stand near Micha. "And the plan is?"

Micha shared the details as Dev had laid them out. "It'll take all three of us."

"I can help too if needed," Ava offered.

"You're safer here in the cabin."

Ava sat forward. "But I'll be alone."

Micha bent to raise his pant leg and draw his backup gun. "That's why I'll leave this with you."

Her eyes flashed wide open. "But I don't know the first thing about shooting a gun."

"I'll give you a quick course right now." He sat down beside her.

"But I don't know. I never...I mean...I..."

"Take a deep breath." He took her hand. "I don't think you'll need to use this. In fact, I highly doubt it. We'll only be gone for about an hour and no one knows where we are."

"He's right," Colin said. "It's a very low likelihood that you will have to use the weapon."

Micha appreciated his buddy's support but kept focus on Ava. "Just take the gun. The safety's on, and it can't hurt you. Hold it in your hand. If you can't do it, then you can't. But if you can, it will be an extra level of protection for you."

He held it out and let her be the one to take it from him. She did, turning it in her hands and giving it the evil eye. "I never imagined I would hold a gun."

"You probably never imagined being in this situation either, but you are, and this could save your life," he said bluntly.

Her gaze flashed up to his. "You mean that, don't you?"

"Yes. Even though it's not likely, as I said, if needed there would be no better substitute."

She gave a sharp nod, her eyes filling with resolve. "Okay, then. Teach me and I'll use it if I have to."

"Then here we go. How to fire a handgun in ten minutes or less." He chuckled to lighten the mood, but she didn't even crack a smile. He leaned closer and shared the parts of the weapon, then taught her how to hold it. "Never point it toward another person unless you plan to fire. And absolutely don't point it at your body."

She cupped the gun, and he adjusted her fingers. Then she aimed the gun toward the fireplace, letting her index finger drop.

"Keep your trigger finger along the side of the weapon at all times unless you mean to pull the trigger." He lifted her index finger to rest it outstretched against the weapon's barrel "That will prevent accidental misfires."

She adjusted her finger a fraction. "That's it? I'm holding it right?"

"Yes. But for better accuracy I want you to use a two-handed hold. It will ensure the maximum stability and help you handle the weapon's recoil."

He aided her in placing her other hand. "The only time I would discourage the two-hand hold is if you were needing a free hand. Like to open a door. Or even to try to fend off the attacker."

She looked at the door and lifted her shoulders. "Let's hope if someone walks through the door that I will stop him right there."

Please make that so.

"So that brings up aiming. First you want to align the front and back sights." He pointed at both sights on the weapon. "Point it toward your subject and focus on the front one. The sight will be in focus and the target will be blurry. Do it now. Aim at that lamp near the wall."

She swiveled to point the gun at the lamp. "Got it."

"If this were a person instead of a lamp, you would aim center mass on the body. That will give you the widest target. You'll stop the assailant even if your shot is off by a little. And I want you to think in terms of two shots. Don't just take one. Follow up the first one with a second one right away."

"Okay." She nibbled on her lip, then shook her head hard. "I can't believe this. Not at all. We're calmly sitting here talking about me shooting someone like we might be talking about what's for dinner." Her tone rose with each word.

He couldn't let her lose it now. He rested a hand on her forearm. "Remember. It's to save your life. Otherwise you won't even be shooting." He tipped her chin to make her look at him. "It'll be okay, honey. You can do this. I know you can."

She took a breath. Let it out slowly. "Yes. Yes. I can. You're right. I can."

He smiled at her. "So aim again and take another good breath, then let it out. Lower your finger and pretend to fire, making sure to hold the gun steady."

She inhaled as if this were her last breath, then let it out and glanced at him. "There's so much to remember."

"You can keep practicing like this while we're gone. Just be sure you're not pointing the weapon at the door. One of us might come through, and we don't want you to accidentally take us out."

Her eyes widened. "But how will I know if it's you coming back or the creep who killed Jamal coming after me?"

"Good question. I have my SAT phone but you can't get a signal out here so I can't call you."

"We could honk the SUV's horn," Colin said. "We'll do three short beeps to let you know it's us."

"Great idea," Micha said. Now why hadn't he come up with that? Was he really too close to her to do a good job?

The door opened as if on cue, and Micha spun. Dev

225

entered, colorful ropes slung over his shoulder. "These will do the trick, and we're good to go."

"Today's your lucky day, little bro." Colin grinned at his brother. "Since you'll be in the boat, you can stay in the rain gear, and I'll get a garbage bag." Colin headed for the kitchen cabinet.

Micha turned his attention back to Ava. "I hate to fire that weapon in the cabin, but I need you to at least take a few shots."

"Okay."

Her uncertainty hit Micha in the gut and he didn't want to leave her, but he had no better option. "Let's use that lamp again, but for the poor lamp's sake focus above it. Since you'll actually shoot now. First, flick off the safety."

She found the safety and pushed the lever, then hesitantly lifted the gun. Pointed.

"Once you have your target in sight, let your finger drop to the trigger," he said as calmly as he could.

Her finger dropped.

"Now use the pad of your finger to pull the trigger. There'll be some play in the trigger before you reach the wall, the point when the gun actually fires, and requires you to apply more pressure to make it discharge. Follow through, pulling the trigger all the way back. Then be ready. After you fire the gun you'll feel a backward movement. That's the recoil. Let your body absorb it. Aim and fire when you're ready."

"Okay." She licked her lips. "I think I'm ready."

"One more thing. Only when you're practicing. Check to make sure everyone is out of range of your bullet, then fire when ready."

She glanced around, then aimed again, her concentration sharp.

She pulled the trigger. The sound reverberated around

the room. She held the weapon solidly through the discharge. Then fired again.

"Great job," he said, though he suspected her second shot would prove to be off target for sure.

She lowered the gun, her hands shaking. "I...it was...I never thought I would shoot a gun."

He had no idea how many times she said that, but clearly she was still shocked by the turn of events. "How did it feel?"

She blinked a few times. "Not bad, I guess."

"Good. Then go ahead and put the safety back on and point the gun at the floor. We'll see where your bullets landed."

She followed instructions. Other than the shaky hands, she was keeping her wits about her, and that gave him hope she could pull off a solid shot if needed.

"I'll take a look," Colin said and was already stepping toward the wall.

"You're leaving souvenir holes in the wall," Micha said.

She frowned. "Not sure that's a good thing."

"It's an interior wall, not one of the logs, and we can always patch the holes."

"Found them." Colin pointed at the wall above the lamp about a foot and six inches to the right and the second one about a foot lower and farther right.

"Was that where you were aiming?" Micha asked.

"Generally, but not so far to the right."

"So if this were a person and you aimed center mass. and even if you were off by this much, you would have hit him and stopped him long enough so you could flee the building." He didn't add that she might actually have killed him, as he didn't want her to think in those terms. That could stop her from firing.

"Okay, good."

"Let's take a few more shots, and then we'll be off."

Colin moved out of the way.

She lifted the gun. Looked around. Then fired. A double tap just like he said. She took a breath and fired off two more rounds, then lowered the weapon, clicked on the safety and pointed the gun at the floor.

"Let me look." Colin went back to the wall. He nodded. "Better. All four shots would've hit the guy."

"Then you're ready, except for one thing," Micha said.

She peered at him, her eyebrows drawing close together. "What's that?"

"Changing out the magazine when it's empty." Micha stood. "I'll get an extra one and show you how, then load this one back up and leave you with two full cartridges."

He went to his backpack, feeling her gaze on him. She was still uncertain. He got that, but if she kept her cool, she could take out any assailant who came through that door to threaten her.

The question was—the really big question—if the door was breached, would she panic or keep her cool?

17

Micha bent his head against the wind and rain, tying off ropes with his teammates. The cold river bit at his feet and legs up to his knees. Everything in him screamed to get out of the icy water. Go inside. Dry off. Warm up. But every thought of Ava's safety had him wading deeper to reach the boathouse.

On the submerged dock, he pressed on the door. No movement. He shoved harder. Nothing. Likely water pressure on the other side.

He glanced over his shoulder at Dev. "Help me with this."

Together they applied pressure. Harder and harder. Finally budging it open a fraction. They kept shoving, pushing against the water pressure until it remained open.

The boat that would normally sit on a boat lift floated above the water instead. Made of aluminum, the fishing craft was smaller than Micha expected with a pair of wooden oars lying inside and a tiny motor on the back. Thankfully, the craft looked seaworthy.

They stepped inside the space. The walls had been painted a bright sky blue. The roof held up under the storm, keeping the rain out, and of that Micha was thankful. He slicked the moisture from his face.

Dev lowered his hood and grabbed a lifejacket from the wall to toss to Micha. "Boat looks like a fourteen-footer. Means it'll hold three average-sized people, maybe not guys our size. So if a water evacuation is needed, it won't carry all of us. Two at best. Especially with that dinky trolling motor."

Exactly. And not the thought Micha wanted to have. "You'd be the logical person to go with Ava."

Dev pulled down a second life jacket and shoved an arm into the strap. "Logical, yes, but I know you would never let her go off without you."

Micha put on his life preserver, too. "Do you really think I won't be able to handle the boat?"

"I don't know if *I* can handle it under these conditions, and I've been boating all my life." Dev clipped a buckle on the life vest, then eyed Micha. "But your desire to save the woman you've fallen for gives you motivation I don't have."

Micha still didn't deny the fact he'd fallen for Ava because he had. Lock, stock, and barrel. Or any other way he could say it. He wanted to clear her name and move on with a life that included her. If he could manage it.

"Let's get this boat out of here." Micha buckled his life-jacket, then went to the crank on the wall that was attached to a cable running from the bottom of the door facing the lake to a pulley in the ceiling. He unlocked the crank and started turning. The door groaned up and slid overhead, emitting a painful squealing sound. He continued cranking until the door stood wide open, then locked the crank.

"I'll grab the ropes we ran." Dev sloshed to the river side of the door and fished in two lines, both tied on the other end to the tree by Colin. Dev and Micha had run them along the boathouse first thing.

Dev waded back to Micha. Micha moved to the winch for the boat lift.

"Hold off on that." Dev bent forward to study the boat. "Boat's floating free. My weight might bring it down enough that we'll need to release it, but I don't think so." He handed one of the ropes connected to the tree to Micha and then pulled the other one around his waist and secured it with a complicated knot.

"Using one of your fancy-schmancy boating knots, I see," Micha said, trying to lighten up the mood.

Dev didn't look up but kept tying. "Won't trust my life to just any old knot."

And *boom*, the truth of what they were doing lingered not only in his words, but the dire nature of his tone, and hung in the humid air.

Life and death.

Had been for days. Micha hadn't known such a feeling since his military days, and his tight gut reminded him why he didn't like it. This time was worse. Much worse. It involved the lives of people he cared about. Sure, his fellow Marines' lives were on the line too, but they could protect themselves, and Ava couldn't. Unless she could handle the gun and even then, it was iffy.

Dev catapulted into the boat and settled in the back. "Still floating so I'm good to go after we get a towline fastened."

Micha took the other rope attached to the tree and secured the boat with another knot. Dev inspected the knot and gave a crisp nod of approval. Micha then took the last rope from his shoulder and handed it to Dev to tie to the bow.

"Let's run this plan one more time," Micha said, as he didn't want there to be any miscommunication when Dev's life could be at stake.

"I'll row out of here," Dev said. "Make a sharp turn to the left as soon as the current allows it. If I'm able to do it right away, I'll come up alongside the boathouse, which will hopefully stop the flow of the river long enough for you and Colin to help pull me to shore."

"Then you get out, and together we haul the boat to shore where Colin is babysitting the ropes."

Dev nodded. "That's the plan. Might take a few tries, but yeah. Let's hope it works. Maybe pray too. Couldn't hurt, right?"

"More than that, it could help." Micha closed his eyes. Offered a heartfelt plea for their safety and success. Added one more—to bring this problem to a close and clear Ava's name.

He opened his eyes. Found Dev staring up. Then he suddenly lowered his head and tied off the rope to the bow. "Let's do this. Release the winch, and I'll get out of here."

Micha cast up one more prayer, then released the crank and gave the boat a shove. The cold metal bit into his nearly numb hands, but he kept pushing so Dev didn't have to work as hard.

The boat slipped out, and Dev had to crank the oars to keep it moving ahead. The rear end caught on the boathouse. Dev turned but couldn't keep the front end moving out and free the rear. Nothing for it but for Micha to wade into the frigid water and push it free.

"I got it." He plowed in, stifling a gasp that his body wanted to emit when the water reached his waist.

He grabbed the boat. Shoved hard. It moved forward, but not far enough. Micha went in deeper. To his chest now. His whole body screaming to get out and get dry. He ignored it. Knew he would adjust some. Pushed again and set the boat free.

The rushing current took it, tightening the rope and

jerking on the winch. The rope held. The boat snapped back a fraction, but Dev kept his balance and rowed hard.

Micha plunged toward the side door and out onto the dock, the water only up to his knees. The rain assaulted his face, and the wind whipped into his wet clothing. He didn't remember ever being this cold in his life, but he had to go on. He couldn't let the current take Dev downriver.

Dev rowed hard, his face tight with the exertion. He pointed the boat alongside the boathouse. Micha grabbed the rope and turned, wrapping it around his body and backing up. The current strained his muscles, burning, ripping. He held fast and moved. Inch by inch until the boat was fully protected by the boathouse and the current no longer threatened to take it away.

He let out a breath. Drew another. But his gut clenched. They might have gotten the boat out, and the three of them would get it to shore, but he'd seen firsthand how the current grabbed it like it was a child's toy, not an adult-sized craft. If it turned out to be their only escape, how in the world would he safely pilot the thing with Ava inside?

Would it be the right thing to do for her, or sure death?

A decision he didn't know how to make without God's help. And even then, would he fully trust God if He said go and put her in that boat to set off down an angry surging river?

The guys had been gone for an hour, and Ava was starting to panic. She wanted to pace to let out her anxiety, but she couldn't. She had to keep the gun pointed at the door. To be quiet and listen through the rain pelting the metal roof for any sound hinting at danger. To listen for three sharp beeps signaling her protectors' return. Oh, how she'd come to depend on them and thanked God for the day she enrolled in their class.

But what if they were in trouble? Didn't come back?

Micha left the vehicle keys, but if they didn't return, she wouldn't be able to just leave. She would have to go looking for them. But then, what would she do if she didn't find them? What if they'd been swept downstream?

Her heart started pounding. Her palms sweating. She set the gun on her knees and swiped her sweaty hands over her pant leg.

Please let them be safe.

She took deep breaths. Tried to trust.

The right place for right now.

Yes, remember that.

You might have a gun in your hand. A foe coming for you. But God's bigger than all of that.

The horn sounded. Sharp and clear. Once. Twice. Three times.

She picked the gun back up, just in case, but kept it pointed at the floor. The door flew open. All three men barreled in.

"You made it," she cried out.

"We did. No problems." Micha shed his jacket on the floor and kicked off his shoes. "And we'll tell you all about it, but first we all need to get changed."

She wished the cabin had hot water so they could take a hot shower or bath, but the fire would have to do. "Of course. I'll add a few logs to the fire while you do."

The others had removed their outerwear and shoes too, and the three of them charged past her to the bedroom, stopping to scoop up backpacks and tote bags on the way.

She made sure the safety was on the gun, placed it on the kitchen table, then stirred the fire with the metal poker before adding two large logs. The flames caught, and by the time the guys came back, the fire was roaring and giving off heat that would surely thaw them.

Micha's SAT phone rang from where they'd set it on the table, and he bolted across the room in stocking feet to pick it up. "Micha Nichols."

His expression perked up. "Toby. Good. Good. Mind if I put you on speaker so my team can hear your results?" He paused to listen, then crossed the room and set the phone on a small table near all of them. "Go ahead, Toby."

"I went to the hospice center. The manager was pretty cordial and let me review Ms. Boyle's file. There's no mention in the entire file of an intramuscular injection, much less one given on a day that would still be visible when she died."

"So someone other than the hospice staff injected her with something," Micha clarified.

"Or they didn't record it," Colin said.

Ava leaned closer to the phone. "Having worked at the center, I can tell you it's possible that a drug didn't get recorded, but highly unlikely. All meds are recorded using a scanner much like you see in the hospital. If it doesn't show in her record, there would be an inventory shortage of that drug."

Micha looked at her. "But that could take some time to be discovered, right?"

"Depends on the drug. Narcotics and other controlled substances are inventoried daily."

"I doubt we're looking for such a drug," Toby said. "To kill her, it would require a lethal dose of a narcotic, and she would've died on the spot instead of lingering for days."

"So what are we looking for then?" Micha asked.

"Something that could cause similar symptoms as food poisoning," Toby answered.

"And what might that be?" Ava asked.

"I knew you'd ask me so I looked into it and narrowed it down to one poison." He paused as if wanting the dramatic reveal. "I think we could be dealing with ricin. It's slow acting, will leave a person feeling sick for days, and is often mistaken for food poisoning."

"Ricin!" Ava could hardly believe it, and they seemed equally surprised. "How would anyone even get ahold of that?"

"It's actually quite easy," Toby said. "Ricin's derived from the castor bean. All you have to do is soften the bean. Cook, mash, and filter it. Add some solvents, and you've just made ricin that can be injected or administered in other ways."

Poison. They could really be dealing with poison here. Murder. Plain and simple murder.

"How would someone know how to make this?" Micha asked.

"You can find recipes for it online," Colin said. "I ran across them in my cyber days at the FBI. Especially on the dark web."

She shook her head. "Is there any way to prove that she might've been injected with it at this point?"

"Yes," Toby said. "If the lab still has a sufficient quantity of her blood on file, we can request a tox screen and be sure to add any drug that could be used to poison her with the symptoms she experienced."

"And you'll take care of doing that?" Micha asked.

"I don't have the authority to do that. It will have to come from the ME."

"But you'll request it?"

"I don't know."

"What?" Ava cried out. "How can you even question reporting this?"

"Because I could lose my job." Toby's sharp tone shot out of the phone and filled the room. "I've already put myself in a dicey position. I'm not on this investigation and shouldn't have accessed the file, much less have gone to the hospice center."

Micha gripped the edge of the table so tightly his fingers lost color. "Then you're willing to let a murderer go free for the sake of keeping your job."

Toby hesitated for a long, painful moment. "I don't know."

Micha shot a look at Dev.

"Hey, man, it's Dev." His words didn't carry the anger Ava was feeling but held understanding. "I don't want you to get canned, but I would consider it a personal favor if you could get the ME involved."

"I don't know." Toby sounded like he might be caving.

Dev let out a long, slow breath. "Remember how I got you through that statistics class you couldn't seem to get the hang of but needed to graduate? You almost cheated with three other guys who got caught. You'd have been expelled if I hadn't stopped you and offered to help you figure it out."

"I knew you'd bring that up someday," Toby spit out.

Dev took a step back, as would Ava at Toby's caustic tone. "I wouldn't ask for me, but it's for Ava. She didn't kill Holly Boyle, but she could go away for years if you don't help."

Micha looked at Ava. "If you knew her, you'd know she's a selfless person who cares for the dying and makes their last days better. Doesn't she deserve someone to care for her, too and keep her from going to prison?"

"Okay, fine. I'll tell him, but then it's up to him to decide what to do."

"Will you go to him now and get back to us as soon as you know if the blood is available and he'll run the tests?" Dev asked.

"Yeah," he snapped. "But then we're even, Dev, and you won't bring up the statistics class again."

"You got it."

"And don't come to me for any favors in the future either." Toby ended the call.

"Sorry, bro." Colin rested a hand on his brother's shoulder. "It's rough that it looks like you lost a friend in all of this."

"It's okay." Dev gave a slow, disbelieving shake of his head. "If he gives up our friendship to do the right thing, was he really a friend worth keeping?"

"Only you can answer that," Colin said. "But I'd say no."

Ava tried to smile at him, but she knew it came out sad and pitiful. "Still, it's got to hurt."

Dev shrugged. "No worries. Like I said. Doing the right thing is what we all live for. A guy who has to be coerced into it probably isn't worth hanging out with."

Ava didn't like what had happened. Not at all. But she respected Dev even more for his stance and appreciated his sacrifice for her. She didn't want to dwell on it any longer, though. She looked at Micha. "This is it. Proof I didn't kill Holly."

He tilted his head. "Not exactly proof. Just a supposition. For proof, we really need that tox screen."

"What are the odds that the ME will do it?" Ava asked.

His shoulders tensed. "I don't think they're all that great, and we might have to convince Layne to go the private route of retaining the services of a forensic pathologist to do a private autopsy."

"If he killed his mother, he would surely refuse to do that," Colin said.

"True, but if not, he might agree to it." Micha rocked back and forth on the balls of his feet. "He would have to pay for it, but if he balks at that, we could reimburse him."

She thought it sounded like a good plan, but..."All of which takes time."

Micha nodded. "Time that we don't have to waste while someone is setting their sights on you."

"I was thinking." Colin headed over to the fireplace to hold his hands out.

Dev followed his brother. "Never a good thing."

Colin put a choke hold on him. "Want to say that again?"

Dev laughed. "Okay. I take it back."

Ava tried to cheer up at the antics they likely meant for that purpose, but right now she couldn't find anything to be glad about.

"You always cried *uncle* way too fast." Colin knuckled Dev's head and let go. "Now that the boat is safe and accessible, you really don't need me here, right?"

"It's good to have an extra man, but no," Micha said.

"We can handle this detail with our eyes closed." Dev puffed up his chest and laughed.

Colin rolled his eyes. "My time would be better spent by continuing to look into the music connections and putting in the LARPing group names you found last night. To do that easily, I need my desktop computer and a strong, fast internet connection."

"You need to go to your cabin," Micha said.

"I do, and thankfully our compound isn't too far from here. If we get wind of the suspect finding this location, I can always come back."

"Sounds like a good plan to me," Dev said, backing away. "Even *if* you came up with it."

Colin shook his head.

"I agree," Micha said. "But I don't want you to go until we upload Layne's DNA."

Colin looked at his watch. "I can wait. Emory's calling in fifteen minutes. I'll get logged in and be ready for her. I'll also change Layne's password so he can't easily get back into his account."

"Do it. Then once we get the DNA uploaded, if there's a match you can research it and locate another suspect."

Colin stood looking blankly at Micha for a few moments. "You sound confident that I will."

Micha shifted on his feet. "Not sure if confident is the word, but I know we've exhausted all other leads. If the DNA doesn't pan out, it'll be up to you to ferret out this guy."

Colin swallowed hard. "And if I don't?"

Micha didn't answer at first, but fisted his hands. "Then we'll have to lay a trap to tempt him to show himself, and that's the last thing I want to do."

Ava took a step back. She could read between the lines. They would lay a trap all right.

And the bait? She was the only one who could bring this killer into the open.

Her alone. The bait. Exposed and within her foe's reach, putting her life on the line.

18

Why didn't Micha keep his mouth shut? He'd scared Ava. Big time. That was clear by the way she crossed her arms around her middle, then dropped onto a chair and rocked. Did she think he would use her as bait? If so, he had to change that idea right now.

"If you thought I meant we'd dangle you out there for the suspect to come find," he said, "we would never do that."

She blinked and watched him carefully. Maybe she thought he was lying now to keep her from worrying. "If not with me, how would you get him to show himself?"

He shrugged. "We'd have to figure a way, but I know if we all put our heads together, we could find one if needed. I don't think we'll need it. Colin could still find something on the music connection, and I have a good feeling that this DNA will turn something up."

She arched an eyebrow. "You really think there's family that Holly never told Layne about?"

"I think it's possible, but you knew her and would be a better judge of that," Micha said. "What do you think? Could she have hidden family she didn't want her son to know about?"

"I never considered it before because I had no reason to." She tilted her head. "But if she wouldn't tell him who his father is, yeah, I could see it."

"Did she ever talk about his father with you?"

She shook her head. "I asked. One time. Got a short and to the point answer saying it was a mistake and she didn't want to talk about it. So even though she'd seemed open about pretty much everything else, I left it alone."

"Could mean we're on the right track then. He could have a sibling who knows about him and is looking for him." Micha glanced at his phone. Eleven fifty-five. He faced Colin, who sat behind his laptop. "You ready to do this?"

"After I connect my SAT phone to my computer for an internet connection." He plugged a cord into his laptop on one end and his phone on the other, but his phone dinged. He looked at it. "Text from Toby. The ME will order Holly's tox screen and specifically test for ricin."

"Wonderful!" Ava said.

"That is good news." Micha was glad something finally had gone their way. Maybe this interview would, too. He pulled out a chair next to Colin for Ava. "Go ahead and have a seat so you can see what's going on."

She sat, and he settled in a chair on Colin's other side.

Dev came up behind them to look over his brother's shoulder. "Got my eyes on you, bro."

Colin shrugged. "Used to it. There were always agents looking over my shoulder at the Bureau, waiting for me to produce data or information they needed." He looked back at his brother. "If they didn't rattle me, you sure won't."

Micha's phone rang at noon on the dot. He answered the video call and put it on speaker. Emory, a redhead with black-framed glasses, came on the screen and introduced herself. She had a pleasant smile and sparkling eyes.

"Nice to meet you." Micha introduced everyone. "Thank you for making time for us."

"Of course," she said. "I, too, have experienced a similar problem to yours and will do whatever I can to help. Like processing your DNA. I'm stuck in court all day, but my staff knows to share the results with Sierra when the tests are complete. Now, I have about a fifteen-minute break and then have to get back. So let's get started."

"I have the ancestry site open," Colin said, "and have logged into Layne Boyle's account."

"Perfect. You'll want to find the section to activate the DNA."

"On it." Though Colin looked impatient and like he wanted to move faster, he located the section and followed Emory's basic directions step by step.

Micha didn't blame Colin wanting to move faster. Not only because he'd like to locate helpful information, but because each step had been straightforward so far. Even with his basic computer skills, he could've gotten the data input here without making a mistake.

"Okay," she said. "This is the important part. You can't activate your DNA without letting others see your match. You don't have to let them see your contact information, though, and it's the key part most people miss. See how the message says this will default to publish the information unless you choose not to? Scroll down, and you'll find another explanation and a tiny checkbox for *no*."

"That's terrible," Ava said. "You can hardly see it. They're clearly driving the response that they want."

"Exactly," Emory said. "Which is why I wanted to do this with you. For now, click *no* for your matches to see you. We'll change that when we finish up the activation."

Now Micha was confused. "If we have to let them see the

DNA to determine a match, then why not just do it right away?"

"Good question." Emory pushed up her glasses. "I've found that it's best to finish the activation, then after I've done a final review to be sure this is what I want to do, I toggle the button to *yes*. Record any matches and toggle back to *no* as fast as possible to hide the info again if I don't want it to be public beyond that moment. Your matches will still see the info once, but when it disappears, they might question if there was an issue and it wasn't right. Though it will alert them to a match, it will also put doubt in their mind."

"Which would be preferable to our suspect having a concrete match in front of him to review and question," Micha said.

"Exactly. So choose *no,* then let's go ahead and review the choices you made and finish up."

Colin clicked the review button, and Micha held the phone over the screen so Emory could review the information, too.

"All looks good," she said. "You can see the edit button on the top, and that will let you change the toggle to *yes* when you're ready to record any matches it might return."

Micha turned the phone to face him. "Thanks for walking us through this, Emory."

"No worries. Just call if I can help with the DNA in any way." Her face disappeared from the screen, and the call ended.

"Do it now, Colin," Ava said. "Toggle the switch."

"Not so fast," Micha said. "Do we have what we need to record anything we might find?"

"Not having seen what information might be returned, I assume we can capture it all with screenshots, so yeah." Colin clicked the edit button and a window opened with the box they needed to change to sharing their information.

Colin hovered the cursor over *yes* and looked at Micha, then Ava. "Ready for me to agree?"

"How confident are you that screenshots will work?" Micha asked.

"A hundred percent."

"Then do it," Ava said, feeling breathless. "Click the toggle and let's see if we have a match."

~

Ava held her breath as the computer churned, a wheel on the screen, spinning and spinning. Finally the page populated and listed one match.

"A match!" She leaned closer. "He actually has a match."

"A half-sibling." Colin clicked on the link. "A sister on his father's side."

Ava continued to stare at the screen in disbelief. "So this woman shares the same father as Layne."

"Yes." A wide grin spread over Micha's face. "Her story says she thinks she has a brother, and she very much wants him to email her."

"Then let's do that right now." Colin clicked on the messaging section. "What do you want me to say?"

"Share Layne's first name and that he lives in Portland," Micha said. "Tell her he wants to meet up ASAP and see if she's nearby to meet."

Colin's fingers flew over the keyboard, then he leaned back. "Read it before I hit send."

Ava scanned the message. "Sounds good to me, and it has a strong sense of urgency. Hopefully she's eager to meet her half-brother, and she'll reply quickly."

"Works for me," Micha said. "Hit send."

"Nice work, bro." Dev patted his brother's shoulder. "Now get out of here and see if you can figure out who this woman is."

Micha pushed back his chair and stood. "I assume you'll be taking your laptop."

"You assume right." Colin toggled the button on the screen back to no then closed his computer and patted the top. "Never go anywhere without this baby."

Micha got out his phone. "I'll log into his account on my phone. That way we'll know if the sister responds while you're gone."

"Good plan." Colin put his computer into his backpack and stood. "I'll keep in touch with what I find. Call me if you need me here again, and I'll be back as fast as possible."

"Speaking of fast." Micha looked between the brothers. "I want Dev to drive you so we continue to have two vehicles on site."

Colin cast a sardonic grin at his brother. "Only if I drive to the compound 'cause the guy doesn't know the meaning of *speed limit*."

"Oh, I know it." Dev got up. "I just don't pay attention to it."

They all laughed as Colin shouldered his backpack.

"I can bring back rain gear for everyone," Dev said. "What else do you want me to get?"

Micha tilted his head. "Let us think about it, and I'll text you a list."

"I know one thing I would like." Ava sat up. "I mean, if you guys are okay with it, I'd love to have my bassoon. Playing it soothes my nerves, and they need soothing. I promise not to play late at night."

"I for one am interested in finding out what it sounds like," Micha said. "So I'm good with it."

"Fine by me. If I hate it, I'll tell you." Dev chuckled.

"I'm sure you will." She laughed.

Colin clapped his hands on Dev's shoulders. "Yep, you've got my little brother all figured out. Honesty without a filter. Gets him in trouble all the time. You'd think he would learn, but no."

Dev grinned. "The trouble is worth it."

"I don't think the others around you think that." Colin shoved him toward the door.

They grabbed jackets, Colin picked up his other belongings, and they stepped through the doorway. The room felt oddly smaller without them. Or did Micha seem larger since she was alone with him? They'd only be alone for a short time, but she was acutely aware of him dropping into a chair next to her and his knee brushing hers.

She shifted away.

He raised an eyebrow at her but then went back to his phone without a word.

Good. She wasn't in a mood to discuss why she didn't want to have the feelings for him that she was experiencing. But she also couldn't just sit there next to him. She got up, crossed to the fireplace, and grabbed the poker. She stirred the logs and added one.

"Our wood supply inside is getting low," she said. "I should grab more from the porch."

"I'll do it."

"I might be a self-professed girly girl," she wiggled her fingernails, "but I can haul wood, you know?"

"It's not that. I'm glad to let you do it, but I won't let you go outside when a killer could be stalking you."

"Oh, right. That." Feeling deflated, she returned to the table. "I'm just a bit jumpy. It'll be good to get my bassoon."

He leaned back. "How did you come to play such an unusual instrument?"

"It's a long story," she said.

"We have time." He watched her.

"Okay, but don't say I didn't warn you about how long it is." She grinned. "So I lived in a pretty decent foster home in fifth grade. That's when they started kids on instruments in that school district. Of course, I had no money to buy or even rent one, but I really wanted to play. So the band director said I could choose from one of the school-owned instruments. I chose a saxophone because I liked how it looked."

Fond memories of having something that she didn't have to share with anyone and learning to play it came rushing back, and she couldn't help but smile. "The sounds I produced were so bad my foster parents made me stay after school to practice in the band room."

"Not cool," he said. "But despite that you kept after it."

"I did. Every day." She smiled. "Learning that skill was the one thing I had for myself. Something that when I mastered it no one could take away or steal. Then one day, the band director asked if I would like to learn to play the bassoon. He said it wasn't easy to do, but with my dedication, I could excel at the bassoon and be in a small group, not be like one in a thousand saxophones."

"So you did," he said. "How long did you continue to play?"

"All through high school. Took some time off while I was trying to find myself, but then I saved up money to buy a secondhand one, and now I play in a community band." She smiled. "We have an amazing director. Linda Becker. She was my middle school band director and was the best teacher I ever had. She's retired now and gives a lot of time to the community band and keeps all of us performing at the top of our game. In fact, she was the one who helped me find a bassoon at a reasonable price so I could keep playing."

He smiled at her. "I'm looking forward to a concert tonight."

"I'm not too embarrassed to admit I'm good. I have tons of medals from high school to confirm it. I could've been a music major if I could've gotten a scholarship, but I got one to a solid nursing school instead."

His phone chimed.

"Layne's sister?" Ava asked and couldn't hold back her excitement.

"Yep." He flicked his fingers down the screen. "Her name is Fran Nicks. Lives in Medford. She's willing to meet anywhere as soon as today. She said just name the time and place, and she'd be there."

"Medford would be closer." Ava jumped up. "We could go right now."

"No." Micha sat forward. "Not without Dev."

She could wait that long, right? Yeah, with a little pacing she could handle it. "Okay, then send her a reply. Tell her we'll meet in Medford."

"First I need to find a neutral location where I know you'll be safe."

"Okay, well, do that. Quickly." She shooed him with her hands, hoping he'd search the internet for such a location.

"It will take as long as it takes, Ava. I won't compromise on your safety."

"Fine. Okay. You do what you have to do."

"Starting with a call to Reid to see if he has a suggestion of a meeting place."

"Good. Call him. Then when Dev gets back, we go meet up with Fran in Medford, and maybe we'll learn something useful that gives us the killer's name." She returned to her chair even though she felt as if she might bubble over with excitement for this new lead.

Her phone rang, and she retrieved it from her pocket.

"Another unknown number."

Micha held out his hand. "Let me start the recording."

He took the phone but held it out.

"Here we go." He tapped the answer button on the screen and put it on speaker.

The creepy music started. Then the distorted voice.

In the darkness whispers fall,
 I've found you again, now heed my call,
 Turn yourself in and don't you bail,
 Or in the stillness, nightmares will prevail.

Too bad Ava wasn't handling the recording. Then she would have something other than the creep's threat to focus on. Why couldn't they find out who he was?

Please let Colin be able to unscramble this man's voice so we can figure out his identity.

He finished the song, and she leaned close to the phone. "Can we meet and talk about this?"

Silence.

"Please."

Click. Call ended.

Why had she even spoken? She'd sounded desperate, telling him he was winning.

Why had she done it? Just why?

Now he knew how much his calls were impacting her. Encouraging him to call back again. Great. She would add that to her mounting panic, maybe really lose it when he called back. She needed to let Micha handle the next call, keep her big mouth shut, and remember that she was in the right place for right now, even if it didn't feel at all like that could be true.

19

Fran wasn't hard for Micha to identify. Even though her features weren't similar to Layne's, she glanced anxiously at the restaurant door each time it opened. Fifteen minutes ago, he'd left Ava in the SUV with Dev and came inside to scope out the place Reid had recommended. To check the restrooms. The dining area. Even the kitchen, with the owner's cooperation. He'd claimed he was protecting a celebrity who'd received death threats, and he needed to be sure she was safe.

From his seat at the short counter with attached stools, he could see the entire dining room of the Big Bear Family Restaurant. It was a traditional-looking restaurant except for a few things and was located near the highway. The first wall by the front was filled with stuffed bears for purchase, and the back wall had a large, stuffed black bear. A friendly-looking bear, kind of like the cartoon bear Yogi the Bear.

But those were the only oddities in the room. No obvious threat. Satisfied Ava could join them, he hurried through the downpour to her car door and pulled it open. He leaned inside. "Straight inside and to the back table by the restrooms."

She nodded. "Is that where she's sitting?"

"No. It's a safer location, and we'll ask Fran to join us. Pull your hat down lower. The staff is expecting a celebrity. Let's keep them guessing." He laughed and stepped back.

By the time her feet hit the ground, Dev was by their side. Together they escorted her the short distance inside and rushed past Fran to the table.

"Stay put with Dev." Micha wound through the tables to Fran's location in the front. "Ms. Nicks?"

"Yes?"

"I believe you're here to meet Layne."

"I am."

Now he had to hope she didn't balk. "He won't be coming today, but we're representing him and would like you to join us at our table. We'll help you meet up with him later."

She glanced around.

"The table in the back corner is ours," he said quickly as he thought seeing a woman at the table might help her trust him. "My friends, Devan Graham and Ava Weston, are waiting to talk to you."

She blinked up at Micha. "But I don't understand."

"We'll explain it all right away. If you want to leave once we do, no one will try to stop you." He stepped back to encourage her to move.

"Okay." She got up.

She took measured steps as if thinking about bolting. He followed her around wooden tables with matching chairs to the booth in the back and introduced the others. She took a seat by Dev, and Micha slid in next to Ava.

Micha told her about Layne, the death of his mother, and their role in trying to find out who might've wanted to kill Holly.

"Oh, wow, that's horrible." She clutched her hands

together in a death grip on the tabletop. "And you think I can help you figure that out?"

"We're not sure," Ava said. "But we're looking for anyone with a personal connection to Holly and Layne. How did you know you might have a brother?"

Carrying a pot of coffee, a young waitress with multiple facial piercings and green hair came for their order. Her interruption stalled the conversation just when it was getting good, and Micha wanted to shoo her away, but he also didn't want to alarm Fran. They all ordered coffee, and Dev added a slice of apple pie to his order. They often teased Colin about always being hungry, but Dev came in as a close second.

"BRB with the pie." The waitress poured the coffee and then left. She must've thought everyone understood BRB meant be right back, but that was an awfully big assumption on her part.

"You were just starting to tell us why you thought you had a brother," Ava said before Micha could.

"Oh, right." Fran frowned. "My dad has a problem with alcohol. A big problem, and he really should seek treatment. But he's managed not to totally screw up his life so he doesn't think he needs to go to rehab no matter how much we bug him. Anyway, one night he went on a bender, and I overheard him mumbling about his son and wondering why *she* didn't give him the money."

Now they were getting somewhere. "Did you ask him about it?"

"Sure, but he passed out, and I had to wait until the next morning. He denied having a son and blew it off as the gibberish of a drunk." She bit her lip. "But I could tell he was lying. So I figured, what the heck? Do the DNA test and see if a brother was out there looking too, you know?"

"I can understand that." Ava rested her hand on Fran's for a moment. "His comments must've been a shock."

"Yeah. You got that right." She blinked rapidly as if trying to stem off tears. "He traveled a lot for work, and I figured he might've cheated on my mom. But then I didn't get any matches on my DNA. I'd almost given up when I got your message."

Ava nodded. "And you're probably not happy that Layne wasn't here to meet you. We'll make sure he reaches out to you."

"Good. Good." She cupped her coffee mug, then took a big sip. "You didn't mention Layne's last name?"

"Boyle." Micha watched her carefully to see if any recognition dawned.

"His mother was Holly Boyle? Really." She fell back against the booth and her mouth dropped open. "You're serious?"

Beyond her recognizing the name, he'd touched a nerve. "Is that a name you recognize?"

She slowly nodded. "I have a way older first cousin with that name. I don't know her. Actually, I've never met her. Just saw a picture of her once. My dad said she was into drugs and took off years ago. No one has heard from her at all."

"So she's a cousin on your dad's side then?" Ava asked.

Fran nodded. "We're not real close to that side of the family. Something happened years ago between my dad and his sister. That would be Holly's mom. Not sure what happened exactly, but they had a falling out, and we only see them on holidays when everyone gets together. And of course, Holly had left the family long before I was born and no one talks about her."

The reason was obvious to Micha. Fran's dad had to have fathered Layne. So an uncle had sex with his niece. Consensual or not, no wonder they'd fallen out. He was surprised they didn't report him to the police.

"We'd like to talk to your dad," Micha said before she got over the shock of this, put two and two together, and chose not to cooperate any further. "Can you share his contact information?"

"Yeah. Sure. Norman Nicks. Lives in Medford like me." She got out her phone and scrolled down, then shared his phone number.

"How about an address?" Dev asked.

She provided the Medford address. "But he's not home."

"No?" Micha asked.

"He's been out of town for work for a few weeks."

Out of town. Like in Portland, stalking Ava?

Micha took a swig of coffee to calm his racing mind and present a casual vibe for his next question. "What does he do for a living?"

"He's a conductor."

Micha sat forward. "Like for a train or music?"

She laughed. "Music. Orchestra. He was a full-time symphony conductor when I was growing up. Now he's semiretired and only works as a guest conductor. In fact, he's filling in for the Portland Symphony Orchestra right now."

Portland. Was he really there conducting or just using it as an excuse? Something Micha would verify the moment they got back to the cabin.

"What does your mother think of all of this?" Ava asked.

"Mom died a few years back." Fran turned her coffee cup and stared into it. "I hope she never knew anything about Dad fathering another kid."

Micha hoped the same thing, but could her father have been referring to her mother when she asked why she didn't give the money to Layne? And what money?

"You have any idea what he was talking about when he mentioned giving his son money?" Micha asked.

She shook her head hard, her hair whipping around. "After hearing from Layne, I was going to call Dad and confront him today."

"Could we ask you to hold off on that?" Micha smiled to relax her.

"But why?"

"It could put you and your dad in the thick of things and in danger. I would also ask you not to try to find Layne's contact info and call him for the same reason."

Her eyes flashed wide. "You really think we would be in danger?"

"I do," Micha said, though he wasn't really sure. If her father was the killer and he knew Fran had been in touch with Ava, would he go after his own daughter if he thought Fran possessed information about Ava's whereabouts and refused to share anything she knew?

Could be, and Micha didn't want to see one more woman in the path of a killer.

Ava rode in the back seat of the SUV. Dev drove and Micha rode shotgun, leaving him free to protect her, just in case. Rain still pelted the vehicle, and the sun considered setting for the day, the darkness starting to take over. At this rate they would surely have or had already experienced record rainfall. The roads held water, and at times they hydroplaned. Dev had to slow down as he took a circuitous route to the cabin to be sure no one followed them. But she wasn't driving and didn't have to pay attention to it, and her mind filled with questions. So many questions. Ones that couldn't wait until they got back to the cabin.

"Something surprised me." She leaned forward between the seats. "How could Fran not figure out that her dad fathered Layne with his niece Holly?"

Micha looked back at her. "Seems obvious to us, but her mind wouldn't be as willing to go to an incestuous relationship involving her dad as ours would. It'll likely hit her real soon."

"And when it does, what do you think she'll do?" Ava pressed her hands on her knees. "You warned her not to talk to him about this, but once she figures it out, she's bound to ignore you and confront him. At least, that's what I would do."

"Which is why we have to get to the dad like yesterday," Dev said.

"Colin should have more details for us soon," Micha said. "We'll have to be ready to act fast when he does."

"Yeah," Dev said. "We need to get eyes on Nicks. Which means we need Colin to confirm he is indeed conducting there. If so, Colin can come back to help you, and I can go to Portland. Or we ask Reid to send someone else."

"I don't like being down a guy here. Let me call Reid now to update and warn him in advance that we might need someone else." Micha got out his phone.

Ava sat back to listen to the call. This team worked so well together, and it seemed as if there was nothing they wouldn't do for each other. She'd never known such camaraderie. Sure, she'd been on nursing staffs that cooperated with each other. Been in bands and small instrumental groups that worked as teams. Even went the extra mile at times, but in the end, they didn't have this solid connection. A family connection. Maybe deeper than family as these guys chose to work together.

How well did the significant others of the team members get along? The Maddox brothers were only recently married. No one had mentioned the other guys being in committed relationships. The women connected to the group were also part of a real family by marriage. The wife of whichever of the three remaining men who got married next would be their first non-family female in the group.

If it turned out to be her, could she handle such a role? Embrace it even? The guys were easy to get along with, but her experience told her women could be more complicated.

Micha ended his call. "Reid will provide someone if needed."

Dev pulled into the cabin driveway and slowly navigated the narrow road with water encroaching from both sides. "Flooding is getting worse."

"We need to keep an eye on the levels." Micha leaned forward and peered out the front window. "I hate to say it, but if it gets much worse, we might need to abandon this place."

Dev backed into place, and Micha went to check things out. Ava watched him follow the same procedure as the night they'd arrived. First inside the cabin, then circling the cabin before coming back to the SUV.

Dev turned the engine off and slid out.

Micha opened her door, and she didn't need instructions but knew to go straight inside. She wanted to lower her face to the ground to keep drier, but she couldn't leave everything up to the guys. She had to do her part in watching for her foe. She couldn't imagine what would happen if the guy showed up here.

Would he come in guns blazing, and they would have to flee?

She sure hoped not. Micha shoved open the door. They hadn't been able to leave a fire burning, and they entered the now-frigid cabin.

Dev crossed straight to the fireplace. "I'll get a fire going."

Micha took off his jacket and so did Ava as they went to sit on the sofa. She watched Dev's sure movements, and he had the fire going in a matter of minutes.

Micha glanced at his watch. "It's getting late, and we should have dinner."

"We should've gotten something at the restaurant."

"You're probably right, but I wanted to get back before dark," Micha said. "Easier to see someone lurking around before it's pitch black, and I don't like the exposed distance we have to walk from the vehicle to the cabin."

"Sounds legit. I'll check out our selection of fine cuisine." Dev chuckled and marched into the kitchen to start looking at cans on the countertop.

Micha's phone rang. "It's Colin," he announced before answering. "You have something on Nicks already?"

"Not yet, but got the searches running on him," Colin said. "I'm calling about Holly's will."

"Her will?" Micha shared a look with Dev. "Go ahead."

"I hacked Layne's email. Guy used his mother's date of birth as his password. Surprising for an IT guy not to use a random password. He should know better than most how easy that would be to guess."

"And you found something?" Micha asked, wanting to push him along.

"Yeah. He got an email from his mother's attorney. Said that he'd had a break-in in his office just before Holly died. A bunch of files, including her will, were stolen. He only had a paper copy because she'd changed it so recently and his assistant didn't have time to scan it. He said Holly kept a copy in her safe, and he wanted Layne to go to her house, scan the signed copy, and email it to him."

"Who do you think stole it?" Ava looked at Micha.

"Whoever stands to benefit from the older will remaining in place." Micha frowned. "If they can't find the changed will, then Layne probably inherits everything. He's the most likely person."

Ava took a breath. "Did he reply to the email?"

"Yes," Colin said. "He said he went to her house and didn't find a new will."

"Doesn't mean there really wasn't one there," Micha said. "Layne has a vested interest in stealing the updated will and seems to be the only one who benefits from it going missing."

Dev looked at Ava. "Who told you that you would inherit half the estate? Was it the attorney?"

Ava shook her head. "Holly told me. I asked her to change her will back, but she refused."

"So you never went to a reading of her will after she died?"

"No."

"We need to check out Holly's place," Micha said. "And it's time we confront Layne and put our cards on the table."

"You want to go back to Portland?" Ava asked, trying not to let her worry of him returning there raise her tone.

"I don't mind going, but I don't want to take you back there, and I'm not leaving you here without me." His forehead crinkled in what she'd come to learn was his thinking expression. "Question for me is if interviewing Layne is more important than getting eyes on Nicks."

"Reid could do one," Dev said. "And I could do the other."

"I can head right back to the cabin with you all," Colin said.

"That still leaves us a man down here. Not good when I feel like we're making progress that's going to bring our killer out in the open."

"Is Ryan available?" Ava asked.

Micha shook his head. "Reid said he needed someone to handle the training, and Russ's full-time job won't let him slot into our training schedule. And of course, we can't call him in to go to Portland."

"Okay, so what if we do a video interview with Layne?" Dev asked. "Reid could do it, and we can sit in on it. He could do this first, then locate Nicks."

"Yeah, yeah. We'll be able to see Layne's expressions on video, so that should work. Assuming Reid persuades Layne to talk to us. I'll text Reid." Micha got out his phone and tapped the screen. He'd barely looked up again when his phone chimed, and he swiped a finger over it. "Reid's on board. Will call us once he gets to Layne's place."

"What about Buck?" Dev asked. "We still haven't ruled out his potential involvement in this, and if things really are coming to a head, we should get eyes on him too."

"But who'll do that? With Reid dispatched, only you or Colin could go to Buck's place."

"I'll go," Dev said. "My big bro can come back here and use his laptop to keep digging into Nicks and any other loose ends he's still working on."

"That works for me," Colin said.

Micha gnawed at the inside of his cheek. "Like I said, I don't want to be down a man here, but there's no indication that anyone has located the cabin, putting Ava in immediate danger. So Colin, you go ahead and come back here, and Dev, you'll leave the minute he gets back."

"Which will be when, bro?" Dev asked.

"I'll get keys to another vehicle, and weather permitting, I'll be back in less than thirty minutes." Colin ended the call.

Micha stowed his phone. "Which gives us time to grab a meal."

"How can you eat with all this going on?" Ava got up, wishing Colin had returned with her bassoon by now, as playing it might calm her down. If she could focus on it. "I can't even sit here, much less think about food. I want to do something. Help somehow."

Micha took a deep breath and let it out slowly. "You can help by trying to relax. The cabin is the safest place for you right now, and it's best for you to hunker down here."

He was right. Sure he was, but it didn't make her feel any better to be reminded that each time she left this place it carried a risk.

A risk that could mean her life.

20

Sitting at the table with Micha and Dev, Ava tipped up her glass of water and drained it. They'd just eaten a dinner of canned chicken noodle soup heated in a cast iron pot in the fireplace. Brought her back to her childhood as her foster parents often served inexpensive meals like canned soup, allowing them to pocket some of the assistance money each month.

Not all foster parents were like that. She'd lived with several good families but none who really connected with her. One did introduce her to God, and faith became a constant in her life. God, a father she needed. But otherwise, she'd kept to herself and focused on schooling and learning the bassoon. A really good and constant thing in her life, too, and now it was tainted.

Could she ever play her bassoon again and not think of the bocal in Jamal's neck?

She didn't know but suspected her director, Linda, would find a way to help her continue to play. She was just that kind of person. One who went the extra mile. She'd been a strong role model for Ava in junior high. Keeping her at it through the times she'd found the bassoon too hard to learn and wanted to quit. But Linda had stepped in, even assigning two bassoons to Ava so she didn't have to haul one with her on her three-mile walk home after practice because her foster parents wouldn't pick her up. She could credit Linda for helping to form the woman Ava had become.

As much as she didn't like foster care, she honestly longed for the much simpler time of her youth. But she had to let it go now and think about finding Holly's and Jamal's killer.

She looked at Micha, who was watching her. "Do you think Nicks is really involved in this? Maybe Fran, too?"

"We don't have any evidence for either one." Micha scooped out the last bite of his soup and chewed on the sparse noodles.

"He's a conductor and his music training could make him a suspect," Ava said. "He would for sure know how to write a song and know all about the bocal."

"And it could connect him to Holly," Micha said. "Maybe she performed with him as the guest conductor, and he learned where she lived. He went to see her and asked to see Layne. Then she refused to tell him anything about Layne. Not even his name and especially not where he lived, and Nicks got angry."

"Or he could've read about her in a newspaper story, too." Dev shoved a stack of saltine crackers into his mouth.

"How horrible it would've been for Holly if he conducted an orchestra she played in." Ava shuddered. "I can't even imagine being able to get a note out in a situation like that."

"Colin's researching it." Dev swallowed. "What about the will, though? Would Nicks have stolen it? And why?"

Micha shrugged. "Doesn't make sense that he would even know about it, and what would his motive for murder be? Revenge? I mean if he got angry enough to kill when she wouldn't tell him Layne's name or where he lived, he would likely have killed her on the spot."

Dev brushed cracker crumbs from his fingers over the paper bowl. "Or he could've planned to come back to the house. Break in and look for contact info for his son."

"That sounds possible," Ava said. "Very possible. Or maybe it has to do with that comment his daughter over-heard about her not giving him the money."

"*Him* as in Nicks?" Micha asked.

Ava shook her head. "I was thinking *him* as in Layne."

"Okay, let's go with that." Micha took a drink of his water. "The *she* Nicks referenced could be Holly. The *him* could be Layne and the *money*, her estate. She did give him half her estate, but maybe Nicks believed Layne deserved it all."

Ava thought for a moment. "He would have to somehow know about the will for that to make sense. Maybe he *did* break in to find information on Layne, and he found both wills. He could've looked into me and could've been mad about Holly cutting down his son's inheritance for a nurse."

"But mad enough to kill her?" Dev asked. "And what would that gain? The will wouldn't be changed."

Ava wiped her mouth with a paper napkin. "But if he stole all copies of the new will, everything would go to Layne."

Dev grabbed a few more saltines and held them midair. "Same would be true if she just died and wasn't murdered."

Micha drummed his fingers on the table. "Maybe he thought she had to die before she could change the will again."

That made sense in a sick way to Ava. "I guess if he was willing to kill, then taking Holly out would be the best

265

option to ensure everything went to Layne, but I think he's a long shot at best."

"Agreed." Dev balled up the empty cracker wrapper and fired it toward the trash can. "But we can pencil him in on the suspect list, just in case."

"Yeah," Micha said. "Is there any way we could see Fran involved in this?"

"Not me," Ava said. "She looked legitimately shocked today on all fronts."

"I agree," Dev said.

"Me too, but we don't rule her out just yet," Micha said. "We'll have Colin continue to dig into her, but unless he finds more, we'll focus on the other three."

The sound of a car pulling into the drive cut through the rain.

Micha reached for the lantern and turned it off, then drew his sidearm. Dev lifted his from the holster too. Headlights cut through the dusky afternoon.

"Likely just Colin," Micha said. "But stay put. I'll check it out."

He jumped up and went to the kitchen window. Her heart pounded loudly, sounding like it wanted to thump right out of her chest. A helpless feeling settled over her, and she honestly wished she still had the gun Micha taught her to use.

He glanced out the window. "Yeah, yeah. It's Colin."

Ava let out a long breath, feeling lightheaded with relief. If Colin arriving terrified her this much, what would happen if a real foe came to their door?

Micha had seen Ava's fear when Colin arrived. He felt bad about that, but he couldn't have taken the time to offer comfort when he didn't know who was coming to their door. He had to protect her first. Provide emotional support later.

Which he'd done, but it didn't seem to make much difference. Before Colin had sat down behind his laptop, he tried to assure her that, with him and Micha in place, nothing bad would happen.

She nodded but didn't seem to buy it. Now she sat in front of the fire, her arms wrapped around her body and staring straight ahead. He wanted to try again but decided to leave it alone. Maybe he could engage her in a game of chess to take her mind off it.

He knelt by the coffee table holding the chessboard. He lifted the white knight. Ironic really. He picked this piece when he thought of himself as a knight. But he needed to work on not needing to be a knight in shining armor all the time.

He held up the piece. "Want to play until Reid calls?"

She looked at him. "I guess, though I don't know if I can concentrate."

"Whoa," Colin said.

Micha flashed his gaze to his buddy. "What is it?"

"Nicks isn't filling in as guest conductor at the Portland Symphony. His last gig with them was a year or so ago. There was some sort of incident, and it seems as if they won't have him back."

Ava swiveled to look at him. "Incident involving Holly, maybe?"

"Not sure, but I'll keep digging."

"So where has he been these past weeks?" she asked.

"He could still have been in Portland," Colin said. "Stalking you. Or maybe we were wrong about why Layne didn't upload the DNA. What if Holly told him who his father is? You know, like she wanted to confess it before she died, and now he's working with his dad to keep you from inheriting."

She bit her lip. "So we could have them both after me."

"It's possible." Micha's phone chimed. "It's Reid. He's got Layne pinned down for the interview. Get him on your computer, Colin, so we have a better look at his body language."

Colin connected to Micha's phone while Micha and Ava went to sit close enough to him that they were all in the video frame.

"I'll take lead on this interview," Micha said. "But jump in if either of you have something to ask or say."

"You ready for us?" Micha asked.

"As can be. He's none too thrilled." Reid turned the phone, catching a man sitting on a wide chair.

"Hello, Layne," Ava said.

Layne glared at her. "Stop with the polite social stuff. Just spit out why you sent this bully here and ask whatever it is you want to ask."

Micha didn't like starting out with the guy having an attitude, but it was to be expected. "You have a friend. Jamal Thomason. He's on your LARPing team."

His pale blond eyebrows shot up. "So what?"

"So we found him murdered at his house," Micha stated plainly to get a reaction.

"You what?" He lurched to the edge of his chair, and Reid placed a hand on his shoulder to keep him seated. "But how? Why?"

His surprise seemed legit, but he could simply be a good actor. "He was stabbed in the throat with a part from a musical instrument."

He squinted at the camera. "What instrument?"

"A bassoon," Micha answered, though he wasn't sure if it was a good idea to share this piece of information or not.

"Well, that's a no-brainer then. Ava plays bassoon." He fixed his gaze on her. "Stupid, woman. You strike again. First my mom and now my buddy." He scooted back in the chair. "She's got it out for me, but why?"

"I'll ignore your unfounded accusations," she said. "I have a solid alibi for the time Jamal was murdered."

"And we believe the real killer is setting her up for your mother's murder," Micha said.

Layne tipped his head and studied Micha. "Who would do that?"

"You," Micha said bluntly. "We think it's you."

"Me?" His hand flew to his chest. "No way. I'm not a killer. No. Not a killer." His tone fell off, and he sat silent for a moment. "'Sides, even if I was, I would never kill my mom or Jamal. She was gonna die soon anyway, so why kill her? And Jamal was a good guy. Good friend. He didn't deserve to die any more than my mom did."

Micha had to ignore the last comment about Holly and keep the focus on Jamal. "But you did send Jamal to spy on Ava at our survival camp and had the guy launch a rock from a catapult at her."

"He did what? A catapult?" Layne planted his hands on the arms of the chair.

"He built a catapult that fired a large rock at her," Micha clarified. "It narrowly missed her, or you would already be in police custody facing murder charges."

"Nope. No. Not me." His face paled. "I didn't know anything about a catapult until you mentioned it."

Based on the guy's reaction, Micha was inclined to believe him, but he'd leaned toward believing suspects in the past, too, when they turned out to be guilty, and Micha had learned only to be led by facts. "But you did send Jamal to spy on her."

He eyed Ava. "Well, yeah, but trust me, I don't want you

dead. Death is too easy of a sentence for killing my mom. I want you to rot in prison for the rest of your life."

Ava gasped.

Micha didn't blame her. Not with Layne's vile tone. "But you threatened to kill her."

Layne squeezed the puffy fabric on the chair's arms. "All talk. Just to scare her into confessing to the police." His gaze shifted to Ava. "But did you listen? No. You took off and made it super hard to find you. So when I finally did locate you, I knew I had to keep tabs on you."

"Guess Jamal isn't watching out for her now, though, is he?" Colin said.

"No. I guess not." Layne scrubbed a hand over his face. "Man, he's dead? Really dead? If her alibi stands, who would set her up like that?"

Micha held his gaze. "You mean, other than you?"

"I told you." He slammed his hands down on the chair and dust rose up from the arms. "I didn't do it, and I have no idea why Jamal would've been murdered."

Micha locked gazes with the guy. "See, Layne, here's the thing. Your story rings false to me. You sent Jamal to infiltrate our group, and why would he choose to try to murder Ava without your direction? It's *your* mother who died, not his. He had zero motive to want to murder Ava."

"I don't know." Layne bit his lip. "I just don't know. Maybe he thought he was doing me a favor."

"Come on, Layne." Micha paused for emphasis. "No one commits murder as a favor for a friend. You'll have to come up with something better than that, or the police will throw the book at you."

"Yeah, man," Colin said. "It's not looking good for you. Not at all. You have motive to want your mother dead to inherit her entire estate, and the guy you sent to kill Ava is dead, covering up your connection. And the bassoon piece that killed him was taken from Ava's house, which you had access to. You'd even been in her house. Security footage backs that up."

"But I..." He shoved a hand into his hair and stared ahead. "They can contact the detective I turned the video over to. He can vouch for me."

"In what way?" Micha asked. "If they believed your story about Ava, then you wouldn't have to keep threatening her to confess, right?"

"The detective wasn't real cooperative," he mumbled.

"Which is why you still needed Ava to confess," Micha said.

"Yeah, but..."

"What about an alibi for yesterday between the hours of eleven a.m. and four p.m.?" Micha asked.

He sat forward, an earnest look on his face. "I'm in IT and work from home, so I was here. Alone. Working."

"Which you can't prove, right?" Reid asked. "I didn't see any security cameras when we arrived, so you don't have that to prove your whereabouts."

He gnawed on his lower lip again. "But I didn't do it. I tell you, I'm innocent and have to find a way to prove it."

Micha hated to admit it, but he liked seeing the guy squirm. "Looks like you're beginning to see how Ava feels. She's innocent of killing your mother, too, and has to prove it. But she also has you breathing down her back to do so."

"You mean like you're doing with me right now?" He raised a defiant chin.

Micha wanted to fire an equally defiant glare back at him, but he took a breath to cool down so he didn't escalate things. "Not just us. I told the detective all about you, and he'll soon be in contact to question you, if he hasn't already."

"Thanks for nothing, man." He pointed his chin at Micha.

Time to change things up. "Maybe I could help convince him of your innocence, but only if you cooperate with me."

Layne arched an eyebrow. "In what way?"

Seemed like Micha had him on the fence and just needed to close the deal to get him to talk honestly. "Tell me about any evidence on Ava that you turned over to the police."

"What evidence?" he asked. "I only have the video that I told her about. The one that shows her feeding poison to my mom."

"It was cookie dough, not poison," Micha said. "If you knew your mother well, you would know she loved cookie dough, and Ava was just trying to get her to eat when she'd stopped doing so." Micha fought off his anger on Ava's behalf. "You should be thanking her for making your mother's last days better instead of blaming her for her death."

"Thank her?" He gaped at Micha. "Hah, like I'd do that. Not when she coerced my mom into signing over half of her estate to her. It should've been mine."

"Is that what this is about?" Micha asked. "The money? If you would've talked to Ava about it you would have learned she doesn't even want the money and would hand it over to you."

Layne stilled. "Yeah, probably if I take back my story about her poisoning Mom, but I want her to go to prison for that more than the money."

"How many times do I have to say I didn't kill your mother?" Ava stabbed her finger at the screen as if poking Layne in the chest. "I loved her."

Micha wished Colin weren't with them so he could take her hand. "Don't you think having a tox screen run would be the first thing to do before you accuse someone of poisoning your mom?"

"Tox screens and all of that stuff is up to the police."

"Then since they didn't run one, you have to know that they didn't believe your mother was poisoned," Micha said.

"So what? Now that they have the video, I'm sure they do."

"And if they don't?" Reid stepped closer to Layne. "If you wanted to know the truth, you would make sure it happened. As the next of kin you could even have the tests run."

"I know what happened, and it's up to her to prove it didn't." Layne crossed his arms. "So why would I pay for some stupid tests?"

"Because I'm asking you to request them." Micha eyed the guy.

"I don't know." He frowned and leaned back.

Micha curled his hands into fists to keep from yelling at the guy. "Do you want to cooperate here or do you want me to make sure the detective suspects you of killing Jamal?"

"Fine." He released the chair arms and sat up. "How do I arrange it?"

Micha wanted to gloat, but it was a small victory when so much more needed to happen to prove Ava's innocence. "Give me your phone number, and I'll be in touch with instructions."

He rattled it off.

Micha entered the number into his phone. "If there's anything else you need to tell me about your quest to pin your mother's murder on Ava, now would be the time."

"I might've given Jamal a note to put in her backpack. A song."

"Did you write the song?" Ava asked.

"Me? Nah. I'm sure my mother told you I don't have

those skills. I took a song she composed and put words to it. Just trying to scare you and put some pressure on you to turn yourself in."

"And you called her repeatedly to play the song?" Micha asked so they could hopefully bring him up on charges for stalking her.

"What? No. No." He shook his head hard. "Never did that."

"You do know all of this could fall under stalking?" Colin asked. "And you're looking at prison time."

"Well, I didn't do it." Out came that pointed chin again. "Besides, anything I did, I did for my mom. My motives are pure."

Micha leaned closer to the screen. "But misdirected, and regardless of your motives, a jury would find you guilty if Ava decides to bring charges."

Layne sagged in the chair. "I don't know what to think anymore."

"And this is all you did?" Micha asked. "Everything?"

"Yeah."

"So who else might've wanted your mother dead?" Colin asked.

"No one. I mean, she was the best."

Ava scoffed. "Not like you told her that or spent much time with her."

Layne's eyes narrowed. "I didn't really know that then, but now that she's gone I can see it. Huge regrets in not treating her better. Being there more for her. Especially at the end. If I could change it..." He choked on his words.

Too bad he didn't figure that out sooner. Micha almost felt bad for him. Almost. But again, he could just be lying to draw them off track. "Even though she wrote the song that you had Jamal give to Ava, there could be a musical connection here with the bassoon bocal."

"If you say so."

"Did your mother make any enemies in her concert world?" Micha asked.

Layne shrugged. "Like I said, I didn't spend much time with her, and I don't know what went on in her professional life."

"You never went to hear her play?" Ava asked.

"No. I..." He shoved a hand in his hair. "Besides, these artsy people aren't really the typical killer type, are they?"

"Anyone is capable of committing murder with a strong enough motive," Micha said. "What about someone in your family?"

"There's no one besides me and Mom. At least, not that I know of. I never knew who my dad was. I think he was a one-night stand, but Mom would never admit it. She got really mad whenever I brought him up."

"And you never tried to find out who he is?" Micha asked, knowing they could catch him in a lie and use it for more ammo to get him to cooperate.

"I did a DNA test before on one of those ancestry sites to see if I could find a match. Then she got sick. When I learned she was terminal, I figured if it hurt her so much just to talk about him, I'd hold off. I could always go looking for him after she was gone."

At least he'd done one nice thing for his mother before she died. "Do you know a man named Norman Nicks?"

"No. At least, not that I know of. Could've met him at work, I suppose. I meet all kinds of people. Why? What's he done?"

"Nothing you need to concern yourself with," Micha said, but it ruled out Layne working with his dad to try to kill her. "I'm done with this guy. Anyone else have anything?"

No one spoke, so Micha met Layne's gaze. "I will expect

three things that you'll comply with, or I will make sure the detective wants to bring you up on charges."

"What?" His whiny voice grated through the computer.

But again Micha ignored his attitude for the greater good. "The first is that you cooperate with whatever we need in this investigation when we need it. No delays. When I say jump, your only question should be how high."

"Okay." Layne blinked at him as if innocent of all charges. "And the second thing?"

Micha glared at the man. "You stay away from Ava. No notes. No calls. No threats."

"I can do that."

"Then third, when this is all over, and we've found the person who murdered your mother—if she was indeed murdered—you will apologize to Ava and never give her a moment's trouble again. Even if she doesn't return the other half of your inheritance to you."

"But I—"

"No buts. You follow my terms, or I work with the police to bring charges against you."

"Fine."

Reid moved closer to the guy. "You do know we have the manpower and ability to keep tabs on you and will know your every move, right?"

He shrugged. "I didn't, but okay."

"So wait for my call on the blood test and stay away from Ava."

"Just so you know," Reid said. "Former FBI doesn't mean I don't still have contacts in the agency to help bring those charges. So heed Micha's warning because I'd be only too happy to help send you to prison for terrorizing a woman. That's the lowest of the low."

Micha couldn't have said it any better and let it lie at that.

"Hang on, Micha," Reid said. "I need to talk to you in private."

The camera moved down the hallway and out the door.

"You want me to keep eyes on this guy or go look for that will?" Reid asked.

"What do you recommend?" Micha asked.

"I go to Holly's place." Reid's tone held unwavering confidence. "Despite what that guy just told us, the will speaks to a very strong motive to commit murder, and it would be good to confirm that it is indeed missing."

21

Time for all of them to get some shut-eye, but Micha wouldn't sleep. They'd heard back from Reid confirming that the will was indeed missing, giving Layne motive to commit murder. So Reid returned to Layne's house, but his car was gone, though Colin's tracker showed zero movement.

The only explanations that fit? Layne had found the tracker or they had technical difficulties. The device could have malfunctioned or the battery could've died. Neither should've happened, but they could. And once they'd told him they were watching him, he certainly could've gone looking and found the tracker on his vehicle frame.

Either way, Layne was in the wind, and Micha was rethinking the interview with him. If the guy wasn't guilty, why take off? He could be a really good liar, and Micha had bought into it. Micha moved him back to the top of his suspect list and would be on the lookout for him all night.

Thankfully, Dev had eyes on Buck, so he wouldn't be threatening Ava tonight. He'd hunkered down for the night in his little shack, and Dev would keep watch.

"Wait, what in the world?" Colin rubbed his face and blinked at his computer screen.

"What is it?" Micha asked, not liking his teammate's tone. "You find something?"

"Yeah, something I can't believe didn't come up before now." Colin looked up at them. "Holly Boyle isn't really Holly Boyle. She changed her name when she turned eighteen. She was born Harmony Wiggins, daughter of Wade and Georgia Wiggins."

"A surprise but not shocking," Micha said. "Makes sense if she didn't want her family to find her that she would want to change her name."

"Yeah, I could see that happening," Ava said.

"No wonder none of them ever did locate her or Layne, if they even tried to," Micha said. "Can you do a deep dive into her family, Colin?"

"I'll get it running right now." His fingers flew over his keyboard.

"Then both of you should turn in," Micha said.

"Gonna be hard after that surprise." Ava blinked. "Not that it likely matters, right? If she had nothing to do with her family, they sure wouldn't be involved in this."

"Not likely."

"Okay, search running and queued up on the server back at my cabin." Colin closed his laptop. "It'll run while we sleep, and hopefully we'll wake up to some helpful information."

"I'm tired enough to sleep, that's for sure, but still not sure I can," Ava said. "Mind if I use the bed by the fire again?"

Mind? Yeah. Every sense in Micha's body was attuned to her movements, and her sleeping in the same room where he could watch her didn't help. But he also liked knowing she was nearby, and he had eyes on her to be sure she was okay.

"Be my guest." He smiled.

"I won't have a problem dropping off." Colin stretched "I know you plan to keep watch all night, but wake me if you change your mind, and I'll take a shift."

Ava looked up at Micha. "You won't sleep because we can't track Layne, right?"

"Right," Micha said. "But don't worry. It's very unlikely he knows where we are."

She nodded, but her eyes were dark with worry as she slid fully dressed, boots and all, into the sleeping bag. Micha stoked the fire and went to sit at the table facing the door, his sidearm resting on his knee.

Hours passed. Slowly ticking with the old battery-powered wall clock in the shape of a big mouth bass with the hands in its belly area. The only other sound was the rain beating against the roof and an occasional hoot of an owl to keep Micha awake.

Well, that and maybe also watching Ava as she slept. Despite her concern about dropping off, she did, after tossing and turning for an hour or so. He enjoyed seeing her relaxed. Peaceful and not afraid. Would they still be together when this was all over, and he could see her at peace all the time?

He wanted that. A lot. More than he'd known.

He yawned and slapped his cheeks to stay awake. He would make coffee if it wouldn't wake Ava and Colin. But only a few hours until daylight when he could brew it extra strong in the old percolator they used in the fireplace. He could also relax a notch because they could visually see if a threat lurked outside their door. Right now the night was pitch black, and anything he might be able to see was obscured by rain.

A gunshot rang out from outside the cabin, splitting the quiet. Then a second one.

Colin came to his knees from the mattress, reaching for his sidearm.

Micha dove for the lantern, switching it off and plunging the room into darkness. "Stay down, Ava!"

Terrified eyes peered up at him in the firelight. "That's gunfire, right?"

"Right."

Two more loud reports.

Boom. Boom.

One after the other.

"Doesn't sound like he's firing at us, but it's coming from a short distance away." Colin stayed low and eased up on the living area window.

"Stay down and follow me, Ava," Micha commanded as he crawled behind the refrigerator, his sidearm in hand, to the safest place in the room. Sure, the log walls would keep bullets out, leaving the windows and door as the most penetrable surfaces, but slugs could get through the chinking between logs, too.

She scrambled behind him and tried to sit up.

He rested his free hand on her shoulder. "Stay down. Less of a target that way."

Colin reached the small window by the door. Pulled back the curtain.

"One man," Colin shouted. "Handgun. Passing our vehicles now, on his way toward us. I can't make him out in this rain."

"One guy means he's outgunned. Two to one." Micha held his hand out to tell Ava to stay put and moved to the kitchen window. The man, gun outstretched, marched their way. Purpose in his step, but too far away in the low visibility to identify him. "He fits Layne's build, but seems awful confident in his shooting abilities."

"There was plenty of time for him to get here after Reid left his place," Colin said. "Nothing in his background suggests he's a shooter, though."

"It could be Buck, who we all know loves his guns, except Dev has eyes on him."

"I have no clue how anyone could've found us. It's next to impossible."

In the dim light from the fireplace, Micha locked gazes with his buddy. "You weren't followed here from the compound, were you?"

Colin's shoulders rose. "I'm offended you even need to ask that, and before you suggest it, there's no way anyone got into the compound to put a tracker on our vehicles without an alarm going off."

The guy aimed and started firing at the cabin. He emptied one clip and popped another one in with the confidence of an experienced shooter.

"No matter who it is, he's coming for us," Micha said, hitting the floor and crawling toward the refrigerator again. "And he seems to know what he's doing."

Colin glanced back. "He's acting as if he thinks we won't return fire."

"Then he doesn't know us." Micha gritted his teeth as he reviewed the situation and formed a plan. "Still, I'd rather not take a life if we can avoid it."

"He might not give us a choice."

Exactly what Micha was afraid of. "The log walls give us more protection than most buildings, but the place isn't bulletproof by any means."

"You two could leave via a bedroom window," Colin said. "Get in the SUV and drive out of here while I pin him down."

Micha shook his head. "And leave you behind and under fire? No way."

"I'll be fine."

"All three of us go or none of us goes." Micha left no chance in his tone that Colin could think this was optional.

"Agreed," Ava said.

"Fine. Be that way." Colin backed away from the window. "I can't be responsible for Ava staying here and getting hurt, so we all go."

Micha nodded. "Before we do, we return fire from three different points in here. The last position being as close to the front window as possible. That should keep him guessing as to our plan and make him think we're moving closer to him and plan to shoot it out. The moment I take that last shot we head to the back bedroom. Circle the building. Lay down cover for each other if needed. Get Ava to the vehicle and take off."

"Solid plan," Colin said.

"Then let's take those last shots. Colin, you from your location. Me from mine. Then you escort Ava to the back bedroom, and I take my last shot." Micha helped her up and met her gaze. "Ready?"

"As I can be." She clutched his hand. "Be careful."

He nodded and shoved his phone deep into a cargo pocket and zipped it closed. "We'll freeze out there in the cold rain without jackets, so I'll grab them, then we take our shots."

He bolted across the room to grab them from the hook by the door, dropping Colin's on the floor next to him and handing Ava hers behind the fridge. He slipped into his and zipped it. "Take your shot, Colin."

His gun exploded in the quiet of the cabin. Ava jerked, but he held fast and waited a beat to make it appear as if he was moving, then fired. "Ava, to the back now!"

283

Colin and Ava bolted from the room, and Micha moved to the window. Saw their shooter coming closer. Fired, aiming close but not hitting him. The shooter stopped walking and returned fire.

Micha fled down the short hall to the bedroom.

He pushed Ava toward the window and raised it. He plunged into the driving rain and reached back to help her through the opening. Colin followed, sliding the window closed.

Micha led the way, easing along the cabin's side wall. Ava came behind him, Colin taking up the rear. They moved in sync. Blinking hard, he batted rain out of his eyes to see clearly. At the corner, he held up his hand to take a look. He glanced around the corner of the building, then back out of view. Glanced again and took a longer look. "Clear. Straight to the vehicle."

He went ahead and wanted to take Ava's hand, but he needed to keep both his hands free for his weapon. They charged through the rain. Reached the SUV.

"What? No." He stared at the front grill. Bullets had pierced the engine. Likely damaging it beyond control. The first shots they'd heard. Even if the SUV started, they couldn't risk the vehicle breaking down and leaving them as sitting ducks.

He pushed Ava toward the other vehicle. Same thing. His mind raced. His gut clenched, and he wanted to hurl. But he had to stay in control. Stay in charge.

A gunshot rang out from inside the cabin.

Time to go to plan C.

"The boat," Colin said, obviously agreeing. "I'll get the two of you launched, then head into the woods, take cover, and call for backup."

"Why can't we come with you?" Ava asked.

"Alone, I can disappear in the woods. Three people, not so easily. The odds are great he would take one of us out."

"The boat's our best chance." Micha grabbed Ava's arm and dragged her toward the river.

"But Colin," she protested. "He could shoot Colin."

"Don't worry about me," Colin said. "If he sees you two take off in the boat, he might not even come looking for me."

"We have to move. Now!" Micha held fast to Ava's arm and stepped as fast as he could in the mucky, wet soil sucking at his feet. Go too slow and the shooter could reach them. Too fast and Ava could fall, making certain the shooter had more time to catch up to them.

They reached the boat. Without a word, he and Colin took opposite sides and flipped it over. They recovered the oars and placed them inside and fixed the motor to the back.

"Get in," Micha directed Ava. "On the bottom."

She climbed in and quickly lowered herself down.

Colin and Micha slid the boat on sodden soil to the water. Micha climbed in before the river's roaring current took the boat with Ava alone inside.

"See you soon, bud," Micha said.

"Of course." Colin pushed off.

The current caught the boat and swung them around in time for Micha to see Colin race for the trees.

A gunshot rang out, and Colin dropped.

Had he been hit? Just taking cover?

Just in case he could move, Micha had to buy time for him to get away.

"Here! We're over here," he shouted as loudly as he could to be heard over the noisy rain. "It's us you want."

The gunman turned. Micha didn't remain seated to see if he took the bait or not. He dropped to the floor of the boat, laying on top of Ava and letting the roiling current carry them away.

$$\sim$$

The boat caught. Spun. Rose. Fell. Water spilling over the side, soaking Ava. She couldn't breathe. Not only from the terror of the rushing water. From the cold. The shooter after them. Colin possibly shot. Micha's heavy weight on top of her. He was protecting her. She got that. She would ask him to ease off, but while he was protecting her, he wasn't sitting up and making himself a target for the shooter, whoever he was.

But how could she not be terrified? She'd peeked over the top after Colin launched the boat and had seen him go down. Was he okay? Shot? Dead? All because she didn't do the right thing and turn herself in to the police when she should have instead of invading the lives of these fine men?

Tears came to her eyes, and she couldn't stop them. She sobbed. Hard.

"Hey, hey," Micha said. "Don't, honey. We'll be okay."

"Even if I believed that, what about Colin?"

"He'll be fine, too." Micha raised up on both hands, removed his weight, freeing her to take a hearty breath. "Turn over. Look at me."

She did as asked, her back instantly soaking up the rain in the bottom of the boat.

He gently moved wet strands of hair from her face. "Let's pray for Colin and leave him in God's hands. There's nothing else we can do for him right now. We have to move on and try to save our own lives."

"Okay." She led them in prayer, her voice breaking and her tears ramping up.

"Let me." Micha took over for her, his prayer surprisingly eloquent in such a difficult time.

"Now," he said. "I need you to trust God. Leave Colin in His hands and get control of your emotions."

She didn't know if she could do that. But she had to, right? She wasn't the only one in danger here, and if she didn't help, Micha could die. She sucked in cleansing breaths and willed herself to stop crying. She forced herself to remember the days in foster care when life seemed the bleakest, and remember how God brought her through those times. She had to believe no matter what happened today, He would bring her through this, too.

The right place for right now. Remember that too.

"That's it," Micha said. "Deep, even breaths."

He took slow ones, mimicking the pattern she should follow.

She did and finally had a chance to realize how calm he'd remained in all of the terror. *Amazing.*

She had to be of assistance, not a liability. "What can I do?"

"We've traveled out of the shooter's range by now," he said. "I'll sit up and take control of this boat to try to get us to shore. I need you to stay put but listen and act on any directive I give the moment I give it. Okay?"

"Yes. Of course. I'm in control now, and you can count on me."

"That's my girl." He kissed her forehead. "Okay, here we go."

He climbed to the seat and braced his feet on the sides of the boat, then glanced around. The wind buffeted his body, threatening to heave him overboard, but he remained seated.

She understood them not wanting to outright shoot this man after them, but if they had, Colin would surely be alive, and they wouldn't be fighting for their lives on a rushing river. But taking a life, even the life of someone threatening you, was a big deal. Maybe not in television or movies, but in real life it stuck with you forever, and she didn't wish that on either Colin or Micha.

"I see something ahead," he shouted. "A light. Going to try for it." He leaned forward for the oars.

"Wait," she shouted to be heard over the churning water and heavy rain. "I can hand them to you."

"Do it now!"

She reached the one on the right and passed it up to him, holding firm until she was sure he had a good hold on the ancient wooden oar. He put the metal oarlock in the holder on the side of the boat and left it inside resting on the seats, keeping a hand on it.

Please don't let it be washed overboard.

He held out his free hand. "Give me the other one."

She rolled and grabbed it to carefully maneuver it out from between the seats. She raised it up and the wind caught hold of the wood, fighting to take it from her hands. She tightened her grip, straining to hold on until the gust died down.

She fought hard, her arm muscles straining as if they were being pulled from her body. She got her arms down and hugged the oar to her chest until the wind eased up.

"Good work," Micha yelled. "Hand it up now."

She lifted what felt like a hundred pounds in her stressed muscles when they were probably pretty light under normal conditions.

Micha grabbed hold, inserted it into the holder and then took the other one. "Here we go."

He leaned back and dropped the oars into the water.

Please, please let him hold on and succeed in taking us out of danger.

288

~

Micha's muscles labored beyond anything he'd ever experienced, the water fighting his effort to direct the boat to the shore. Dev had given him a quick lesson on how to drag one side and row with the other. He followed the instructions, but Dev had been right. This was a foolhardy move.

No matter his attempts, the current continued to win. The boat plummeted down the river, winding around a curve. Logs floated by. He shoved them out of the way with the paddle. Barely keeping from missing a large one. If it had struck the boat, they could've capsized.

He had to work harder. Do better.

He shifted into the turning position again. Pressing his legs against the boat until he thought they would collapse from the strain.

He leaned forward to lower his body from a wind gust and caught sight of Ava looking up at him. She needed him. He was all that stood between her and death.

No way he could let her die. But he needed help.

Where are you, God? I can't do this alone. I need help. Lots of help.

The wind died down some. He sat up. Felt God's presence. Not physically, but in his heart. Knew that whatever happened, it was God's will. Didn't mean he didn't need to keep trying. Working hard. Just meant God was in control of what happened, and God had equipped Micha with the tools He wanted him to have.

The boat surged up. Shot ahead. Around a bend. The shore the closest it had been.

Now was the time.

He dropped the right oar. Let it drag. Rowed with the left. They made some progress. Inches really. But he kept hold. The inches grew to feet, the boat now moving toward the shoreline, a light in the distance.

He pinned his focus to the light and kept working. Hard. Harder. His muscles begging for release. The cold zapping them. Fatigue zapping them.

A worship song came to mind. Lauren Daigle's song *Hold On To Me* played in his brain.

He let the words wash over him like the icy water. Let them strengthen him.

He kept holding on to God. On to the oars. The boat moved in the right direction. The shore just feet away now.

Yes, he could do this. He held fast. Kept them moving and piloted the boat to shore, pointed at a fallen tree that he hoped would stop them and hold.

The boat struck the tree. Their downriver descent stopped like a car ramming into another one. He was catapulted forward. Had to brace his hands to keep from smothering Ava.

He landed and wanted to hug her, but no time. "We made it. This is over."

"Praise God!" she shouted.

"But now we need to see if Colin's okay." He pushed up. Drew his gun.

"You think the shooter could've followed us?" she cried out.

"Not on the water, but you can never be too careful." He climbed from the boat, hoping he was right. He reached a hand to help Ava up, but kept his gaze on the area.

Ahead he spotted a small shack and, farther inland, a streetlight burning down on what was likely a road or maybe a parking area, the light beckoning him. He wanted to race for it, but first off, his muscles wouldn't let him run, and second, running would be foolish. Care was what they needed to take.

He helped Ava over the side of the boat, then tucked her behind him and started toward the road.

They reached the shack. Mounted above the door, a wooden fish declared Wally's Fishing Shack. Right. A fishing shack made sense so close to the river and could give them shelter while he called Russ for backup.

He moved toward the door.

A figure materialized out by the road. His arm raised. A gun in his hand. Their shooter?

Micha couldn't stand there to determine the person's ID. He jerked on the shack door handle.

Unlocked. Good.

He shoved Ava inside just as a gun report cut through the air. He grabbed her in his arms. Dove for the floor. Taking the fall on his shoulder and keeping his back to the front wall to protect her.

"How?" she cried out. "How could he have found us?"

"He must've followed the road downstream." Micha rolled toward the back corner, swiping at thick cobwebs. "Lay down. Make yourself a harder target to hit."

"And you?"

"Can't sit here and wait for him to pin me down." He held her gaze in the darkness. "I'm going after him."

22

"No matter what happens, stay put and use the gun if needed." Micha had given Ava his backup, and now he gave her a hug and drew his weapon.

He crept to the door. Stepped out. Crouched down. Waited for the shooter to materialize in the dark again. Gun raised.

Nothing. No one.

Micha couldn't linger out in the open. Gun still in shooting position, he bolted for the trees.

A shot rang out. The bullet sliced through his upper arm. The pain pierced his body, and he took a tumble on the slight incline. He rolled and rolled, the arm screaming in agony on each turn. So what? He now knew the shooter's location. If Micha moved fast but quietly, he could circle around and take him from behind.

He bent low. Kept moving. In and out of trees. Blood trickled warm on his arm.

Please let it just be a scratch. I have to save her. Please.

The song lyrics for *Hold On To Me* came back again.

He would do more than hold on. He would let go. Trust.

I can't do this alone anymore. I have reached the end. I need You.

Micha released his need to control everything. Moved confidently ahead, doing his best but relying on God on the way. He felt like David going after Goliath. Micha might be facing a giant, but he had God on his side.

He skirted through the woods. Coming parallel to the shooter. Micha spotted him but was too far away to make out his face. The guy stood. Feet planted. Arms out. Gun in hand. A solid shooting position that, if he hadn't been coming for them, Micha could admire. The shooter knew what he was doing and felt confident doing it.

Didn't matter. None of it. Not who he was or how confident he was. Micha had to take him down, no matter what.

He eased slowly ahead. Ducking when needed. Belly crawling at times. His military training all coming back.

Once a Marine, always a Marine.

On and on he moved. Passing behind the shooter. Turning toward him after he'd left enough room. He disturbed a bird. It took flight.

The shooter spun. Fired.

"Stupid bird," the shooter mumbled. "Too bad I didn't wing you."

Micha gave the shooter time to settle down, then started his forward movement again. Slow. One foot in front of the other. Treading on the wet ground littered with pine needles. Thankfully wet from the rain instead of crunchy to give him away.

He came close to the shooter.

Ten feet. Five. Three.

"Drop your weapon," Micha called out.

The shooter spun. Held fast to his gun. Steadied his arm.

He's going to fire.

Micha launched himself. Flew through the air and

barreled into him. Took him down. Losing his own weapon in the process but freeing his hands. He grabbed the shooter's hand. Wrestled for control of the guy's gun. It went off. The bullet went wide.

Micha slammed his elbow into the guy's wrist. The gun loosened, but he held on.

"You heard him!" Ava's voice came from above. "I have my gun trained on you, now drop yours."

She'd caught the shooter off guard, and Micha wrestled his gun free. He pressed it into the guy's chest and sat back. "Don't move or I shoot."

The guy relaxed, his arms dropping to the wet ground.

Micha took a good look at his face. Not Layne. Not Buck. Not even Norman Nicks. Even if he didn't fit the description of these three guys, this guy was older. Micha would put him in his sixties.

He risked a quick glance at Ava. "You were supposed to stay put."

"I couldn't. Not when I might be able to help."

"Well, you did. Thank you." He hated to admit that he was saved by a girly girl and would like to think he could've taken the guy without help, but he would never know.

She came closer and looked down on the shooter. "Who are you?"

He sneered at her. "Wouldn't you like to know?"

"I would."

"Too bad."

Micha didn't want to waste time arguing but got to his feet. "You can put the safety on your gun, Ava, and we'll head back to the fishing shack to call Russ."

Micha nudged the shooter with his foot to his side. "Get up and don't give me a reason to use this."

The older guy pushed to his feet, surprisingly agile for his age.

Micha pressed the gun into the guy's back. "March to the shed."

He strode ahead, dragging his feet, but Micha prodded him to keep going. His head swiveled as he walked. Likely looking for a way to escape.

"Forget about running," Micha said. "Do it and you're a dead man."

They moved over sodden soil, Ava coming behind them. Through the rain. The sound of rushing water covering any other noise.

They reached the door and stepped over the threshold.

Micha glanced at Ava, who closed the door behind her. "No electricity. Get my phone from my lower pocket on my right side. Use the flashlight app to look around. See if there's a lantern or candles. Something to help us see."

She kept her chin up and glared at the man as she skirted him to reach Micha. He pushed out his leg to give her better access to the pocket just above his knee. She unzipped it with a trembling hand.

Everything in him screamed to punish this man for scaring her like this. He could hardly wait until this was over and he could hold her. Comfort her.

She got out the phone and turned on the light and shone it on the wood walls. One held cabinets with a countertop littered with fishing gear. Various poles hung on another wall. Paddles on another.

"There." She shone the light on a stool near the door revealing what looked like a battery-powered lantern. She rushed over to it and more light soon flooded the space.

"Good work," Micha said. "Now find something I can use to restrain this guy."

She picked up the lantern and moved over to the counter. She set it down and pulled out drawers to search inside. "Nothing."

"What's that in the corner?" he asked. "An anchor with rope?"

She took the lantern to shine it on the space, revealing the rusty anchor and thick rope as he hoped.

"Back away, Ava, and I'll secure him."

She left the lantern and crossed the room.

Micha poked the guy in the back. "Over there now and have a seat. Back to the anchor."

He complied without a word.

"I need you to hold the gun on him, Ava, while I tie him up," Micha said. "Just remember everything I taught you except not to point it at someone. Point it straight at the creep and shoot if needed."

"Be glad to." She got his backup gun from her jacket pocket and moved up next to him. She held the gun with the confidence of someone who'd been shooting for a life-time, not someone who just had a ten-minute lesson.

Her expression in the shadowy light was determined and rigid. The guy must've thought so too. He didn't struggle while Micha secured his wrists with one end of the rope and wrapped the end connected to the anchor around his ankles.

Satisfied he wasn't going anywhere, Micha stood and tried to take the gun from Ava's hands as she no longer needed it. She held tight, her focus locked on the shooter.

He had to gently pry it free. "You're safe now." He wanted to take her into his arms but wouldn't do so in front of this creep. "I'll get Russ on the phone after I check on Colin."

Micha retrieved his phone from the counter, and, keeping his eyes on the shooter, he dialed.

Colin answered on the third ring. "Dude, you two okay?"

"Fine," Micha said and opted not to tell him about his arm that seemed to have stopped bleeding but stung like crazy. "Put in quite a ways downstream. And you?"

"I'm good thanks to you drawing the guy's attention."

"Glad to hear it. You can tell me all about it later, but now I gotta get Russ out here to arrest the shooter."

"He's there?" Colin's voice rose.

"Trailed us on the road. Was waiting when I managed to break free of the current."

"I called Russ, and he's here with me. Give me your GPS, and I can send him your way."

"I'll text it to you." Micha ended the call, located their GPS positioning on the phone, then sent it to Colin.

"Colin's fine, and Russ is on his way." Micha stowed his phone and crossed over to their suspect.

He searched the man for ID.

"Don't touch me," the guy said.

"You can stop me anytime. Just give me your name."

He clamped his lips closed.

Micha located a wallet. Opened it. Took out his driver's license and shook his head. "Well, well, well. You're not going to believe who this guy is."

Ava wanted to know the shooter's identity but at Micha's surprise she wasn't quite sure she did. Still, she had to know. "Who is he?"

"Wade Wiggins."

"Holly's father?" Ava blinked at the man. "But why? What have I done to you?"

He sneered at her. "Tried to get your grubby hands on my grandson's money."

She took a step closer to him. "Not that I got my grubby hands, as you say, on anything, but you mean his mother's money."

"Nope. It's mostly mine. I gave it to Holly."

297

Ava didn't know how to react to that.

"Why?" Micha asked.

"None of your business."

"Okay," Micha said. "I wasn't that interested in what's got to be a lame story anyway."

What? Not interested?

"Not lame at all." Wiggins glared at Micha. "Holly didn't provide for the kid like I would've hoped. Doing her music instead of getting a regular job. So he's had to struggle in life. Turns out my other daughter can't have babies. He's the only grandkid I'll ever have, and I wanted to help him along in life. So I gave Holly a hundred grand to give to him when he turned twenty-one. She didn't do it. She just kept it."

"You were trying to buy him off, then?" Micha shook his head. "You should've felt bad *before* you kicked her out and left her as a single parent."

"Oh, don't go getting on your high horse with me." Wiggins sneered. "You only know her story, but she seduced my brother-in-law. What was a guy supposed to do when she came on to him like that?"

"I doubt that's really what happened," Ava said. "But even if it did, he was the adult and should have walked away."

"No matter. What's done is done. It wasn't the kid's fault, so I tried to help him out. But Holly wouldn't have anything to do with it. She said she would have to tell him about why I threw her out, and she wouldn't do that. She wouldn't let him know he should never have been conceived. But she would be glad to take my money and keep it for herself because she said I always lived for money, and she wanted to make me pay."

"So you talked to her?" Ava asked.

"When I found out she was dying, I went to see her at the care place." He shifted his focus to Ava. "She told me she was giving half the money to you. Gloated even. I told myself not to get mad. Not even when she spit in my face and refused to arrange a meeting with my grandson, but the room turned red with rage. I wanted to choke her. I didn't. I managed to get ahold of my senses and realized the police would hunt me down for murder."

"Right. You stopped because of the police, not because you were going to murder your daughter."

He raised his chin. "She threw my help in my face. I humbled myself to come to her, and she treated me like dirt."

"Kind of like you treated her then?" Ava shook her head. "So that's when you poisoned her with the ricin?"

"Not then, but yeah. She was dying, and my grandson had to come first now. The cancer was God's way of punishing her for luring my brother-in-law into sin. So in a way I was doing the Lord's work. I went home and learned how to make it that very day."

"The Lord's work. Hardly." Ava knew one thing for sure. The best thing Holly ever did was get as far away from this man as soon as possible and never reveal Layne's identity to him to ruin his life, too.

"Our God does not work that way, but you won't get that so I'm not going to bother explaining." She glared at him. "Then you went back to the center and injected her leg."

"In the middle of the night a few days later. I got in her face to tell her it was me and why she had to go early. Too bad she was high on painkillers and didn't know what I did."

"And then you stole her revised will from her house so Layne would get everything," Micha said.

"Indeed."

"And this's the only time you talked to Holly in all these years?" Micha asked.

"Actually no, I saw she was playing a concert before that

299

and followed her home. She wouldn't tell me anything about my grandson then either, so I bugged her place to see what I could learn. When she died, not only did I discover Layne's identity when he came looking for his mother's will, but I heard him say in a phone call that he believed Ava killed Holly, and he was trying to get you to confess. Thought I'd help that along a bit to keep the cops away from me." He cackled like a madman, or at least what Ava thought a madman might sound like.

"What exactly does that mean?" she clarified. "I'm really unclear as to what you did."

"Figured that would fool you." A cocky smile found his lips. "I bought off his friend. That Jamal guy he had tracking you. At first, he was more than glad to take a shot at you with his little catapult. But then he got cold feet and was going to rat me out to save himself."

Jamal. This creep partnered with Jamal? Ava could hardly get her mind around it. "So you killed him with my bocal that you stole from my house to keep him from talking."

"Prove it." His grin widened, and she wanted to rush him and wipe the smugness from his expression.

Sirens sounded nearby. He sobered up and clamped his mouth closed.

Good, that took care of his arrogant attitude. She just had to keep remembering he would be going to prison, likely for the rest of his life, and she could live with that.

"That will be Sheriff Maddox come to haul you off," Micha said.

But Ava wasn't done with Wiggins. "You were the one who kept calling me to play the song Layne put together, too."

"I was." He smirked. "Didn't like that, did you?"

She didn't bother to answer.

He frowned. "I want my grandson to have his money, but between you and me, he didn't have the guts to follow through on any of this. So I took over, and he didn't have a clue."

"How did you find me, anyway?" she asked. "I was so careful, and no one else has located me."

He lifted his chin, that haughty expression back. "I stopped in to search your place one day, and the deed for your little cabin here came in your mail."

What? I was so careful. "But my mail was supposed to be held by the post office."

"Guess they screwed up because there it was sitting in your mailbox like it had come just for me." He lifted his shoulders. "Guess when you live right things go your way."

"Not going your way right now, are they?" Ava said, her mind trying to grasp that a simple postal error had caused her so much pain. Could have cost her life. Micha's and Colin's too.

The siren wound down and stopped. Micha went to the door and opened it. Strobing blue lights filtered into the little room, and he soon greeted Russ.

Russ stepped into the shack and took hold of Micha's arm to draw him closer and stare at it. "Bloody. You're wounded. Need me to call an ambulance?"

"Wounded?" Ava raced across the room. "Let me see."

"It's really nothing," Micha said. "You can look at it later."

"Then let me get this guy out of here, and you can give me a statement, so she can look at it." Russ pushed deeper into the room.

She tried to take a look now, but he turned away. Not before she caught sight of the blood she'd missed seeing in the low light. Had he been shot? Nothing she could do now, so she turned her attention to Russ, the third

Maddox brother. He seemed to be a force to be reckoned with.

He was a larger-than-life guy who had a scowl on his face. He looked more like Ryan than Reid and was more muscular than either of his brothers.

Micha introduced them.

"Sorry for what you've gone through, but you can tell me all about it after I get this guy in my deputy's custody." He freed Wiggins's ankles and glanced up at Micha. "Interesting restraint."

"You gotta use what you have." Micha laughed.

Russ replaced the wrist restraints with handcuffs, then lifted Wiggins to his feet and marched him toward the door. Russ looked back. "Hang tight."

He shoved Wiggins out the door.

Micha closed it behind him. "Too bad the shack owner doesn't have a woodstove in here to warm it up."

She gave him a bold look. "I can think of one way for us to warm up."

He shuffled back a step. "Why, Ms. Weston, are you flirting with me?"

"I believe I am. Is it working?"

"Oh, yeah." He hurried across the room to her, swatting a spider web out of his way before sweeping her into his arms and kissing her.

His lips were cool, but the warmth of his body stemmed the cold air seeping through the building cracks. She reveled in his touch. The heat of his body. The strength in his arms telling her that everything was all right. Would be all right with him at her side.

She drew him closer. Clutching the back of his head. Snaking fingers into his soft hair. Clinging and letting the kiss go on and on. The back of her mind trying to break through and get her to admit she really should end the kiss and look at his injured arm.

Just one more second. Or two. Maybe three.

She finally pulled back and looked up at him and took a vigorous breath or two. "Now I need to make sure your arm is okay enough to wait for care until we get back to civilization. If you're a good boy and let me take a thorough look at it, then we can resume where we just left off."

He started to take off his jacket. "You'll be hard-pressed to find a better-behaved boy in all the land."

She laughed and loved that the terrible stress of the past week was over. She could resume her life. But where? Micha lived in Shadow Lake. She lived in Portland.

A no-brainer. She could move to the cabin, turn on the utilities and get a job in the nearby city. Then she would be close enough to properly get to know this man.

Not like she didn't know him now. Days of being under extreme stress showed her the kind of man he was.

The forever kind, and one she wasn't about to let go.

23

Four weeks later

Ava held Micha's hand and walked by his side along the sidewalk to Reid's big lodge. He looked handsome in a deep green polo shirt and leather jacket along with crisply pressed khaki cargo pants, the crease he'd said was a holdover from his Marine days. She loved his neat appearance as long as he didn't expect her to iron her clothes, too. If he wanted to do hers, too, more power to him, but he wouldn't likely be slaving over an ironing board.

He glanced at her, then away. He'd been acting odd all morning, not telling her why they were coming to see Reid. Ava didn't know what was causing Micha's discomfort. Now that the forced intimacy of them being thrown together to keep her alive was over and they were simply dating, maybe he was having second thoughts about a relationship with her.

She didn't get the sense of that. Especially when they kissed. Maybe he'd learned something about the investigation, and he'd brought her to Reid's place to discuss it.

Thankfully, in addition to Wiggins' confession to them, the ME had run Holly's blood tests and located ricin. The police also found the supplies at Wiggins' place to make the ricin, along with a box of syringes, and forensics found his DNA in Ava's music room and on her bocal. All charges had been dropped against her, but authorities hadn't located Holly's will and were required to use her original one, where everything went to Layne.

Ava didn't mind. Holly's attorney started the process to dispute it as he knew her wishes. As her attorney, he believed it was his duty to enforce them. Ava didn't care about the outcome, as she didn't want the money anyway. If she received half, she would give it to charity.

Buck's AK-47 wasn't registered properly, and he was behind bars not only for owning an illegal machine gun but for buying the other weapons from Squib without proper applications. Since his disregard of the law was so egregious, the ATF was trying to make an example of him and seek the maximum prison sentence. Layne had been arrested for his part in stalking her and was in jail along with his grandfather, both awaiting trial without bail in the same county facility. A perfect time for them to get to know each other, but not in ideal circumstances.

Maybe this visit was about the DA changing his mind about bringing charges.

Micha rang the doorbell, then turned to kiss her on the wide wraparound porch. "Remember, I only want what's good for you."

"Okay, Micha." She stepped back but held his hands. "What's going on here?"

The door opened before he could answer. Reid stood there along with his daughter and their cute little dog, Bandit, who was white with a black mask. Ava had already met the team and their families, so she knew Jessie had just turned nine and was a sweet but mischievous little girl. Today, her soft, blond hair was pulled back in a ponytail that bounced as she danced with excitement. She wore a denim skirt and jacket with black leggings and bright pink shoes.

Reid wore khaki tactical pants and a polo shirt like most of the guys on the team seemed to favor, even when not wearing their logo-embroidered company shirts. "Come in."

Jessie grabbed Ava's hand and dragged her inside. "I'm so glad you're finally here."

This did not seem like a meeting to talk about the investigation. She glanced back at Micha, and he cast her a sheepish look.

Okay, so what or who was awaiting her?

Jessie led Ava into the large family room decorated with balloons and streamers. People popped out from behind the furniture yelling, "Surprise!" and "Happy Birthday!"

"But," Ava looked at Micha, "I didn't tell you it was my birthday."

"I know, but I saw your date of birth on your driver's license on the police report."

She didn't know what to say. No one had ever thrown her a birthday party. Not her mom. Not a foster family. The closest she ever came was when one family made cupcakes for her. She lived with them for three years, and each year she had a single candle on one after dinner. Still, at least they remembered.

The guests came forward, starting with Barbie. Mother to the Maddox brothers, she wore one of her usual long, flowing dresses, and her shoulder-length hair streamed down her back with a braided band around her forehead. She looked as if she'd stepped straight from the sixties, and her personality fit the love era, too. Ava marveled that an easygoing woman like Barbie had raised such strict rule-following sons.

"You and Poppy did all of this, didn't you?" Ava asked, mentioning Reid's housekeeper.

"Jessie, too. She said you need to have all your birthdays rolled up into one big party with everyone who cares for you." Barbie waved a hand over the group that included the entire Shadow Lake Survival team and their significant others. Ryan was holding his adorable baby boy, and Russ's young and rambunctious son darted through people.

Ava caught sight of Micha's sister in her wheelchair by the back wall. Her daughter, seven-year-old Charlotte, timidly stood beside her. Micha had told Ava Charlotte had once been outgoing, but since her mom's accident and her dad walking out on them, she barely talked with anyone but her mom and Micha.

She looked like she was ready for a party, though. She wore a pink dress with a knit top and tutu bottom made of tulle. Her shoes were white, high-top sneakers, and a sparkly barrette held back her shoulder-length hair, dark like her mother's and Micha's. Very fashion-forward.

"Well, thank you, Barbie." Ava hugged the woman who held her tight.

"You are part of my family now, and your birthday will never be forgotten as long as I have a say in the matter." She squeezed hard and then let Ava go.

Micha joined them, and Barbie smiled at him. "I hope you realize what a gem you found in Ava."

"I do."

"Then maybe you should put a ring on it and say the real I do." Barbie giggled and walked into the crowd.

"We should go say hello to your sister," Ava said before Micha had to tell her that he wasn't ready for any *I dos*. "She looks a bit overwhelmed by everyone."

Micha curved his long fingers around Ava's hand, and together they crossed the room. Ava squatted by the chair. "Thank you for coming. I know it's hard to attend a party when you don't know many people."

Tristin waved a hand, the muscles in her slender face tightening. "It's not that. I...it's just..."

Micha was immediately moving closer, concern etched in his expression. "What's wrong?"

"Nothing's wrong. I don't want to take away from Ava's first party ever, but I'm about to burst with needing to tell you something."

"Go ahead." Ava smiled. "Now I'm about bursting with the need to know."

"Have I mentioned she's one of the good ones?" Tristin asked Micha.

"Only about a hundred times, like everyone else." He grinned. "Now what do you have to tell me?"

"Not tell as much as show." She moved her feet to the floor and leaned down to flip up the footrests on her wheelchair. She locked the chair, then planted her hands on the armrests and stood.

"What?" Micha gaped at her. "Wow. Oh wow. You can stand."

She grinned. "Just barely and not for long, but the doc says if I keep following my PT drill sergeant's instructions and do the work, I should regain full function."

Ava knew her drill sergeant was Micha. He worked out with Tristin every day, never missing a session except during the week he'd protected Ava.

Micha swept his sister into his arms and swung her around like a rag doll.

Charlotte grinned up at the pair. Ava's heart burst with joy, and tears found her eyes. She didn't know if she was happier for Tristin, Charlotte, or Micha, as all three of them needed this good news.

Thank You! Oh, thank You!

Ava kept smiling at the trio. "This is the best birthday

ever. I mean *ever*! A party, sure, but you standing, Tristin. That's the best thing I've seen in eons."

Micha lowered his sister back into her chair. "How long have you been keeping this from me?"

"I first got some feeling back when you were off on your camping trip. Then a few PT sessions while you were protecting Ava confirmed I could stand on my own."

Micha kissed Charlotte's cheek. "I'll bet you're so happy for your mom."

She nodded, and her freckled face split wide in a smile. Micha grabbed her up and spun her, too. She squealed with joy before he set her down and kissed the top of her head. "Now you and I need to make sure she works hard so she can progress."

"Oh, great," Tristin said. "Bad enough you crack the whip, now you'll have my daughter doing the same thing."

"Don't worry, Mommy," Charlotte said, an impish look on her face. "I won't use a whip."

They all exploded with laughter, including the child who'd been so quiet.

Barbie joined the group. "I think it's time for all of us to have some cake to celebrate the good news."

Jessie charged up to Charlotte. They were a few years apart in age and could become good friends if Charlotte opened up again. "I like your dress, Charlotte. I already asked Dad if I can have one like it."

Charlotte smoothed her hands over the tulle. "Thanks. Your denim is cool too."

"But yours is better for a party." She glanced over her shoulder. "Don't tell my dad, but he's not the best at shopping for my clothes. But now that he married Megan maybe I can ask her to take over. Want to sit with me for cake?"

"Sure." Charlotte looked at her mom. "Is it okay, or do you need me?"

"Go. Have some fun with Jessie." Tristin shooed her daughter away.

"We can go get Ella, too. She's my new sister. She's been kinda sick and we can't tire her out so be careful, okay?"

"Okay."

Charlotte raced off with Jessie to the corner where little Ella stood with her mother Megan. She'd recently married Reid and was a bit shy about fitting in, but Ava had spent some time with her and she was so warm and caring that Ava knew she would be accepted without a problem.

Jessie held out her hand and Ella accepted it. Jessie pulled the younger girl who had a gaunt face, but bright eyes behind her to the refreshment table, where Barbie had started to put candles in the large sheet cake.

Tristin sighed in contentment. "Seeing her coming alive again is even better news for me. I hope as I continue to improve, she won't always be thinking she needs to stay by my side, worried if I need her help."

Jessie scampered back to them and skidded to a stop by Ava, her rubber-soled shoes squealing on the hardwood. "C'mon, Ava. We're gonna light the candles, and you haveta blow them out."

Ava squeezed the child's hand and went over to join the girls and Barbie, where a plethora of candles were burning on the cake.

"It's overkill," Barbie said. "But I thought since this was your first party ever, you should be able to blow out the right number of candles."

"Thirty-two of them. I counted. That's like a lot!"

People close by laughed, but Jessie looked confused.

"It is indeed a lot," Ava said.

Jessie peered up at Ava. "Since this is your first party, and you don't know how to blow out candles, and you have *so* many of them, I can help you."

"Jess," Reid said. "Let Ava do this herself."

Ava hugged Jessie to her side. "I'm glad for the help."

"Yippee!"

"Charlotte and Ella, do you want to help too?"

They both gave timid nods.

Ava went to them and put her arm around Charlotte's shoulders, then moved Ella in front of her and rested her other arm around Jessie. The four of them bent over the cake.

"On the count of three, you all blow and everyone else sing," Barbie announced. "One. Two. Three."

Ava's heart was so full of love and joy that she blew with everything she was made of, and so did the girls. The song blessed her more than anyone could know. But God knew her heart. He was listening and hearing her thankfulness in the prayer she offered up.

The candles whispered out, smoke rising into the room. The guests clapped, and Ava could feel the affection in their eager, smiling faces.

"I can never thank you all enough for coming to my first ever birthday party," she said in the sudden silence. "It's just like I imagined it would be. Well, except there are a few more candles on my cake." She laughed to keep her tears at bay.

They joined in, and the room filled with laughter, soothing every bit of her unease over being the center of attention.

Barbie handed Ava a slice of rich chocolate cake with fluffy white frosting then gave cake to the girls. Ava took a large bite and basked in her guests' caring as one by one they came to get cake and wish her well.

She'd felt God's love over the years, but never human love like this. How much she'd missed out on for so long, but thankfully she had God all those years. And now she was blessed beyond belief that this room was full of amazing people who took time out of their lives to wish her well.

Barbie circled an arm around Ava's shoulders. "I hope this party is everything you hoped for."

"That and so much more, and I can't thank you enough for making a little girl's dreams come true. I feel like I finally have a family."

"And one who will be here for when you need us." She nodded at Micha, who was hanging back but watching them. "And I suspect this guy wants to make that more permanent."

"You think so?"

"Oh, honey. He's hooked. Everyone can see that."

He smiled at her, and she crooked her finger. He was the person she needed to thank. Whether he hung decorations, baked a cake, or not, he set the ball in motion, and without that there would be no party.

She cut off a large bite of her cake and looked up at him. "Open wide."

She shoved the bite into his mouth. He moaned. "So good. Poppy's cake, I assume."

"Well, you know it's not something I made." Barbie laughed and crossed the room to her husband, her laughter trailing after her.

"Thank you for my party," Ava said.

He hesitated before speaking. "I hope it's okay."

"More than okay. It's everything I dreamed of as a child."

A broad smile lit his face, and she could hardly keep from throwing herself into his arms.

"I wanted to surprise you," he said. "I waited for you to tell me it was your birthday."

"But I didn't," she said as she'd gotten used to that as a

kid. If no one knew, there was no way they could disappoint her.

"No, you didn't." He worked the muscles in his jaw. "And I didn't want to do something wrong, so I asked you about parties when you were little. I knew when you told me no one ever threw you a party so you don't celebrate the day that I had to do something. I figured you deserved to be celebrated, and everyone here agreed with me."

"I will never forget it." She let the warmth in the room envelope her and the caring beaming from this man topped it all off. "And it's even more special that Tristin can stand now."

"Yeah, man, wow." His smile widened. "A great surprise. I'm so relieved. God heard our prayers. Doesn't mean I still won't need to help her and Charlotte, but not nearly as much once she's walking again."

She squeezed his arm. "You're the best brother."

"I'm getting there. Relaxing my protective instincts. Not hovering over her so much. Sure, I worry at times, but I'm trying to remember to let God take over, not me."

"Well, I'm glad you took over my birthday." She smiled at him. "Your grand gesture is greatly appreciated."

"I need to—privacy. We need privacy. C'mon." He set down her cake, grabbed her hand, and led her out onto the porch, swatting away cobwebs running from the large swing to the ceiling before he took both of her hands and faced her. "You deserve grand gestures and so much more. I love you, Ava. I know it's quick, but when you know, you know."

"I get it." She stroked the side of his face. "I love you too."

He reached up for her hand. "You better stop that if you don't want a PDA to be the highlight of your birthday party."

"I'm fine with that." She raised her arms up to his neck and stood on tiptoes to kiss him.

Her turn to take charge and let him know how much she

loved him. Kissing him hard. Pulling him tight against her. Deepening the kiss. Reveling in thoughts of kissing him for the rest of her life. Forever. With her foster care background, the word forever didn't exist.

She leaned back. "You realize what you've done, don't you?"

He watched her, his gaze probing. "Something other than throwing a party?"

She nodded. "Three times now, you've battled through cobwebs for me. Twice when we were running from Wiggins and just now. Facing spiders for me. That's got to mean something, right?"

He frowned for a second, looking warily at the web. "I didn't even notice. But, yeah, it probably means a whole lot. Guess there are more important things in my life now than my fear of spiders."

"With my aversion to dirt and grime and your dislike of spiders, we are the most unlikely pair to have met in a wilderness survival group." She traced the side of his face under a bright beam of sun shining on him.

"But we did, and I hope we'll discover we're even more compatible and build a lifelong relationship."

She liked the sound of that. A promise of a future proposal, if they continued to enjoy being together after they discovered more about each other.

She smiled up at him. "I promise you this. I will do my very best to protect you from spiders to infinity and beyond."

He laughed. "I'd return the favor, protecting you from dirt, but I'm pretty sure you don't want me to promise to bathe you." He winked. "But I won't ask you to go camping or into the wilderness with me unless you want to go."

She laughed, then let her mind think only of a future.

"Do you remember when I realized I was in the right place for right now?"

"Yeah, it's a great way to look at things." He circled his arms around her waist and leaned back.

She had to ignore his touch to go on. "Instead of just applying it to being in a bad situation like I was in, I should apply it to the good times, too, right?"

"Yeah, sure." His fingers tickled the side of her neck.

She could barely go on without kissing him again but had to.

"Then Micha Nichols," she touched his cheek, "I want you to know I'm in the right place for right now. But the moment we say 'I do,' *for now* will become *for as long as we live*, and it will always be the right place as long as I am with you."

~

Thank you so much for reading *Shadow of Hope*. If you've enjoyed the book, I would be grateful if you would post a review on the bookseller's site. Just a few words is all it takes or even leave a rating.

You'll be happy to hear that there will be more books in this series. Read on for details.

SHADOW LAKE SURVIVAL SERIES
When survival takes a dangerous turn and lives are on the line.

~

The men of Shadow Lake Survival impart survival skills and

keep those in danger safe from harm. Even if it means risking their lives.

Book 1 – Shadow of Deceit
Book 2 – Shadow of Night
Book 3 – Shadow of Truth
Book 4 – Shadow of Hope
Book 5 – Shadow of Doubt – July 8, 2024
Book 6 – Shadow of Fear – November 4, 2024

For More Details Visit -

https://www.susansleeman.com/shadow-lake-survival-series/

Shadow of Doubt - BOOK 5

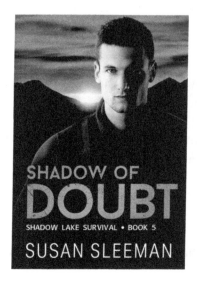

A cyber-stalker and a murder threaten her life...
When IT specialist, Brooklyn Hurst's cyber stalker grows bolder and the police refuse to do anything about it, she has to take drastic measures. Like fleeing the only home she's known to a place so off the map that the stalker would never think to look. When she discovers, Colin Graham, a former FBI agent and now Shadow Lake Survival cyber expert, is looking for a live-in caregiver for his mother, she applies for the position and is hired via an online interview. She quietly packs up everything she can fit into her car and disappears in the middle of the night, ensuring that her stalker doesn't follow her.

Will the danger draw the couple closer together or push them apart?
She fits in perfectly with Colin and his mother, but he'd never met a more jumpy and fearful woman in his life and is sure something is wrong. As they grow closer, he gains her trust, and she shares about her stalker. As if talking about her stalker conjures him up, he makes his appearance in Shadow Lake. Had Colin betrayed her? Done something stupid to bring danger to her doorstep again? Should she run again or could she trust Colin? Colin knows running isn't the answer and promises to keep her safe. But can he do so while also protecting his heart from pain again?

PRE-ORDER SHADOW OF DOUBT NOW!

STEELE GUARDIAN SERIES
Intrigue. Suspense. Family.

A kidnapped baby. A jewelry heist. Amnesia. Abduction. Smuggled antiquities. And in every book, God's amazing power and love.

Book 1 – Tough as Steele
Book 2 – Nerves of Steele
Book 3 – Forged in Steele
Book 4 – Made of Steele
Book 5 – Solid as Steele
Book 6 – Edge of Steele

For More Details Visit -
www.susansleeman.com/books/steele-guardians

NIGHTHAWK SECURITY SERIES
Protecting others when unspeakable danger lurks.

A woman being stalked. A mother and child being hunted. And more. All in danger. Needing protection from the men of Nighthawk Security.

Book 1 – Night Fall
Book 2 – Night Vision
Book 3 – Night Hawk
Book 4 – Night Moves
Book 5 – Night Watch
Book 6 – Night Prey

For More Details Visit -
www.susansleeman.com/books/nighthawk-security/

THE TRUTH SEEKERS
People are rarely who they seem

A twin who didn't know she had a sister. A mother whose child isn't her own. A woman whose parents lied to her. All needing help from The Truth Seekers forensic team.

Book 1 - Dead Ringer
Book 2 - Dead Silence
Book 3 - Dead End
Book 4 - Dead Heat
Book 5 - Dead Center
Book 6 - Dead Even

For More Details Visit -
www.susansleeman.com/books/truth-seekers/

The COLD HARBOR SERIES

Meet Blackwell Tactical- former military and law enforcement heroes who will give everything to protect innocents... even their own lives.

Prequel - Cold Silence
Book 1 - Cold Terror
Book 2 - Cold Truth
Book 3 - Cold Fury
Book 4 - Cold Case
Book 5 - Cold Fear
Book 6 - Cold Pursuit
Book 7 - Cold Dawn

For More Details Visit -
www.susansleeman.com/books/cold-harbor/

ABOUT SUSAN

SUSAN SLEEMAN is a bestselling and award-winning author of more than 50 inspirational/Christian and clean read romantic suspense books. In addition to writing, Susan also hosts the website, TheSuspenseZone.com.

Susan currently lives in Oregon, but has had the pleasure of living in nine states. Her husband is a retired church music director and they have two beautiful daughters, two very special sons-in-law, and three amazing grandsons.

For more information visit:
www.susansleeman.com

Made in United States
Orlando, FL
30 August 2024

50969846R00183